Breathless

Transform your time-starved days into

A LIFE WELL LIVED

GARY R. COLLINS

Tyndale House Publishers, Inc.
WHEATON, ILLINOIS

Library of Congress Cataloging-in-Publication Data

Collins, Gary R.
  Breathless : transform your time-starved days into a life well lived / Gary R. Collins.
    p. cm.
  Includes bibliographical references and index.
  ISBN 0-8423-0196-8 (sc : alk. paper)
  1. Time management—Religious aspects—Christianity. I. Title.
BV4598.5.C65 1998
248.4—dc21   98-24159

Printed in the United States of America

03 02 01 00 99 98
8   7   6   5   4   3   2   1

To Ann and Edmund Chan—
Two lives well lived in Singapore

THE GREATEST THING
YOU CAN LEAVE BEHIND
IS THE EXAMPLE OF
A LIFE WELL LIVED.

STEVE FARRAR

CONTENTS

"You wouldn't be able to go to Hong Kong with me in a
couple of weeks, would you?"

"Are you serious?" I asked.

Gary and I were having a late dinner near O'Hare airport
when he was struck by the notion of having me travel with
him on one of his many overseas speaking engagements.

"Julie isn't able to join me on this trip," he continued,
"but maybe you could come along and do some speaking
with me."

A few days later Gary and I were on a jet headed to Asia.
It remains one of the great adventures of my life—not the
trip, but my relationship with Gary.

When Tyndale House asked me to write a foreword to this
book about a life well lived, I didn't have to think twice. Gary
is more than a traveling companion. He's more than a friend.
He's my confidant and mentor.

Gary has shown me a life well lived. Not because he lives
his life perfectly. But precisely because he doesn't. When he
invited me into his life several years ago, he opened up all
the chambers of his heart, mind, and soul. He has shared
with me his victories and his defeats, his passions and his
problems, his dreams and his disappointments. And he has
listened to mine.

I once confessed to Gary that I was having trouble consistently reading and meditating on the Bible. "I get so busy," I admitted.

"Me too," he replied. We commiserated for a while, and with a little probing, I got Gary to reveal what was working for him. He then made a promise to walk with me through the Scriptures.

"How can you promise to do this with me when you are already so overscheduled?" I asked.

"We'll help each other," he said, "as iron sharpens iron."

Each day we read the same passage, and when I confess to falling behind, he never makes me feel guilty. "No problem," he says. "Just skip ahead to catch up."

Gary's spiritual passion—even in the whirlwind of a busy life—is authentic. He has no time for self-righteous talk and religious clichés. He walks his talk. Dozens of examples shoot through my mind. On the dark streets of Denver, I once saw him help a frantic stranger who couldn't pay a cab fare. I've seen him transform the countenance of a frazzled coffee-shop server by showing respect and expressing a sincere interest in the person. And I've watched him cope with personal crises and disappointments in ways that always honor God.

Another life lesson I've learned from watching Gary is the value of serious soul searching. I've never known another person who is more deliberate and diligent in taking stock of his character. He continually reads his inner compass, making sure he is on track, not veering from the purposes he believes God has given him. Gary once asked me, along with several other people who know him well, to complete a twelve-page assessment that would help him refine his gifts and goals. That's typical of Gary—always open to evaluation, always wanting to improve.

More than anything else, Gary wants to live a life that honors God. So do I. That's why I've eagerly anticipated this book. I've wanted to know how Gary, who gets so much done, allows his soul to catch up in the midst of running at a breathless pace. This book is not about "three easy steps to live a great life." It's a book written by a pilgrim who invites you on a journey to explore how you can have a meaningful and purposeful life. He doesn't pretend to have all the answers, but he is willing to share many of the questions and point you to other people who can help you find a path that will allow you to discover the unique gifts and purpose God has for you.

I encourage you to study this book with an open heart. Expect it to touch you and shape you. Give yourself to the task of looking at your breathless life and allowing God to redirect you to the goals and activities that really matter.

When I get to be Gary's age, I hope I have all the energy and vision that he has. I want to finish strong, as he is. I too want to leave a legacy that honors God and helps people grow. I want a life that is well lived.

Gary's well-lived life has touched mine. Through this book, I think it will touch yours, too.

LES PARROTT III, PH.D.
Center for Relationship Development
Seattle Pacific University

PART ONE
Breathless:
Life in a Whirlwind

CHAPTER 1

Rushing
Getting Control of
Our Time-Starved Lives

IT HAD BEEN "one of those days" for counselor Michele Ritterman, too short to get everything done and too long for fighting her losing race against the clock.

After seeing the last of her clients, the frenzied therapist hurried home and began throwing dinner together while her eight-year-old son—who had spent the day in his own pint-sized version of the rat race—played a fast fingered game of Nintendo in the living room. "When will dinner be ready?" he yelled impatiently above the ongoing staccato of the game's tinny bleeps and electronic music.

"Thirty-five seconds," Ritterman replied, glancing at the flashing numbers on the microwave.

"That's too long," complained the impatient boy, never suspecting what would come next.

The frazzled mother exploded. "That's it!" she screamed. Yanking the microwave plug from the wall, she picked up the bulky oven in her arms, staggered to the back door, dumped the whole thing—macaroni-and-cheese dinner and all—into the garbage can, then stormed back into the house.

"I looked at my son, now standing in the kitchen staring wide-eyed at his suddenly crazed mother," Ritterman wrote later. "The next time you ask, it will be two hours!" she announced. "We are going to eat like normal people from now on! We are going to have a life around here again." Then, calmly, she began the process of cutting up a large pile of vegetables and steaming them slowly with rice.

"At that moment, I was in a rage against time," wrote Ritterman. "It took me a little longer to realize that all of us—my husband, my children, myself—had allowed the outside pressures of school and work to invade our home and completely absorb what used to be savored as family time."[1]

Dr. Cynthia Shelby-Lane had a different time problem. Behind a locked door of the emergency-ward rest room of Sinai Hospital in Detroit, the doctor sought to withdraw. It was past midnight, and she had been soaring on adrenaline for hours, dealing with gun wounds and bloodied bodies pulled from twisted wreckage at accident sites. Desperately craving a few minutes of solitude, the doctor had slid away from the hustle and hurts for a little space to think and unwind. But the staff knew about her refuge, and someone slid an EKG scan under the rest room door. "What are you doing?" Shelby-Lane sputtered with exasperation. "You know this is my quiet time."[2]

"Her cry defines an era," suggested a writer in *U.S. News and World Report*, where this story first appeared. Many of us claim to be worn down and "extraordinarily stressed out," even though we have more leisure time, spend more time and money on recreation, and enjoy more time-saving and efficient technology than adults did a generation or two ago. Like Michele Ritterman and Cynthia Shelby-Lane, millions of us live hectic, time-starved lives. We may not trash the microwave or seek solitude behind the locked doors of public rest rooms, but in our own ways we struggle to control the demands for our time as we run breathlessly through life.

Almost everybody agrees: we're all too busy. We tear into our days, trying to do more than is humanly possible during any twenty-four-hour period, then we beat ourselves up when we don't get everything done. We like to complain about how busy we are, but often these complaints sound less like protests and more like pride. To be busy has become a badge of honor in our society, where busyness is equated with being important. Suggestions that we slow down often aren't taken too seriously. So we drive feverishly through life, pushing hard on the accelerator while we protest about the speed.

Maybe there was a time when hectic lifestyles were limited to overachieving career climbers in corporate offices, but that isn't true today. Pressure-packed teenagers run from school to work to social events—too often using drugs to help them cope or suicide to open the door for escape. Stay-at-home mothers rush to pick up kids, hurry to soccer practice between church meetings, race to after-school activities, struggle to make dinner while also getting the kitchen remodeled. And in all of society, some of the busiest and most overbooked people are officially "retired."

Several years ago a friend presented me with a cartoon he had drawn of me on a treadmill. I look like a Hindu god with multiple hands—holding a book, typing on a keyboard, carrying a suitcase, grabbing a phone, hanging on to keep balance while I continue running. The caricature even includes

5

a Christmas tree because my artist friend knew that putting up the holiday decorations, and taking them down in January, is added pressure that I begrudgingly permit to invade my life every year.

For too many of us with treadmill lifestyles, the pressures never seem to go away. We feel deluged and driven by never-ending demands, deadlines, and distractions. The increasingly frenetic tempo of change makes our previous experiences seem irrelevant, forces us to dismiss the wisdom of the ages, and fractures our sense of continuity with the past. We are left with fast-paced present moments, filled with "'entertainment' that numbs us into stupor, timesaving devices that keep speeding us up and daily routines that leave us breathless."[3] Is it surprising that many people with time-starved lives have slid into cranky exhaustion?

A few years ago we believed that VCRs, microwave ovens, cellular phones, fax machines, and a host of similar electronic devices would save time and make our lives simpler. Now we realize that "labor-saving devices" shorten our tasks so we can squeeze more into our already overburdened schedules. As a result, our bodies are drained, our spiritual lives are neglected, our work is less efficient, our friendships are superficial, and our lives are engulfed with feelings of fatigue, frustration, and futility. Technology that promised to increase efficiency has robbed us of our privacy and filled our lives with incessant information and interruptions. Cellular phones and beepers, answering machines and voice mail, E-mail and faxes, call waiting and call forwarding—all have invaded our lives and led us to expect that we have the right to interrupt others and that they, in turn, will interrupt us even in the privacy of our homes.

CONTROLLING OUR TIME-STARVED LIVES

How do we cope with all of this technology, change, stress, speed, interruption, and time pressure? As I have plowed through stacks of books and articles about our breathless lifestyles, four solutions have appeared repeatedly: multitasking, escaping, downshifting, and managing time. Let's evaluate each of them.

Multitasking

While I type these words, my relatively unsophisticated computer can remember what I wrote last week—or last year. This machine keeps track of everything that I have told it to do. It can play music; give me a word from the built-in thesaurus whenever I ask for one; get me quickly to the dictionary; log me on to the Internet, where I can check the accuracy of a quotation or find a new citation; help me locate a Bible reference; come up with the latest news or weather forecast; tell me the time and date; play a video version of Martin Luther King's "I have a dream" speech; and check the spelling of every word in this paragraph. This is multitasking—doing and keeping track of a variety of tasks at the same time. Computers do it well. People find it a little more difficult.

Of course, people were multitasking long before the invention of computers. Mothers have done it for centuries: cooking dinner, talking with neighbors (now most often by phone), handling the kids, and doing the laundry all at the same time. Chances are you were multitasking the last time you drove a car. You handled the steering wheel, watched the traffic, listened to the radio, and maybe sipped coffee. As you drove, perhaps you talked on your portable phone, conversed with the person sitting next to you, and/or kept an eye on the kids in the backseat.

But multitasking takes a toll. Because of the limitations of our brains, we are restricted in how much we can do at one time. If we try to do too many things simultaneously, we are likely to get distracted, to make more mistakes, to wear ourselves out, to lessen in our productivity, and to see break-downs in communication with our families and co-workers. Multitaskers risk pushing themselves to the point of exhaustion while they try to keep on top of everything that crowds into their multifaceted lives.

Escaping

Pressed by the demands of their busy and time-starved lives, many people give up for a while and escape from the demands by withdrawing into worlds of fantasy. They retreat to their sitcoms, soaps, sports channels, and conversations with strangers on the Internet. In what has been called a "techno-logically hallucinogenic culture" of VCRs, computer games, virtual-reality headsets, and multichannel television, we use "entertainment" to identify with fantasy figures who don't have to live by the rules we encounter, don't face the stresses that we face, and aren't pressured by the demands that scream for our attention and threaten to overwhelm our lives.

Of all the ways to cope with our breathless schedules, escaping to electronic worlds of fantasy can be the most addictive and the most dangerous. Escaping lulls us into lethargy, rips us away from reality, feeds our fascination with freakish behavior (revealed without hesitation or shame by the guests on daytime talk shows), and gives simplistic solutions for complex personal problems. With the flick of a switch we can

withdraw from the hectic pace and submit ourselves to the
mercy of a small group of movie and media professionals
whose creations reflect new and often destructive attitudes
about sex, sexism, crime, business, politics, social issues, and
lifestyles.[4] Someplace I read that the average American now
watches more than forty hours of television a week and that the
average household keeps a set turned on for more than seven
hours every day. Add to this the millions of videotapes that are
viewed every week and the addictive appeal of computers and
the Internet, and we have some indication of the extent to
which escape—even more than shopping—has become our
major modern pastime and diversion from breathless living.

Sooner or later, however, most of us have to come back to
reality. As the pace quickens, we look for other ways to cope.

Downshifting

Elaine St. James was a businesswoman with a five-pound
black leather planning and appointment book "the size of
Nebraska," according to her description, when she and her
husband decided to scale down their lives. They sold their
house in favor of a low-maintenance condominium and
"decluttered" their lives by throwing away the things they
didn't need. Along the way, she started making notes about
what she was doing and turned these into best-selling books
with titles that include *Inner Simplicity, Simplify Your Life,*
and *Living the Simple Life: A Guide to Scaling Down and
Enjoying More.*[5] If you want to get control of your time and
busyness, say the proponents of "voluntary simplicity," you
should start by ridding your life of the stuff that our consumer-
based economy encourages us to keep accumulating.

Several years ago I heard something similar in a series of

sermons based on the New Testament book of Philippians.
We live in a world marked by upward mobility, Bill Hybels
reminded his congregation. A lot of us live to promote ourselves, to advance our own careers, to push our personal agendas, and to arrive at the top of the heap with enough money,
power, and material possessions to feed our desires for self-
indulgence. In sharp contrast, the biblical writer tells us, "Do
nothing out of selfish ambition or vain conceit, but in humility
consider others better than yourselves. Each of you should
look not only to your own interests, but also to the interests
of others."[6] This is followed by perhaps the most revealing
description of Jesus in the whole Bible. He "being in very
nature God . . . made himself nothing, taking the very nature of
a servant."[7] His life was marked by downward mobility. Jesus'
life involved no self-promotion, career building, or striving for
money, power, possessions, or fame. Jesus came to serve, not
to be served. He came to give, not to get. With two status-
seeking, upwardly mobile disciples, he proclaimed that the
way to be great is not to lord it over others or to have authority
and prominence; true greatness comes to those who serve.[8]

Amy Saltzman had no lofty theological ideas like this
when she wrote her best-selling book *Downshifting*.[9] Saltzman, a baby boomer, was a successful magazine editor who
found herself trapped in a lifestyle of so much busyness that
even her leisure time had a hurried quality. In her job cover-
ing career issues for *U.S. News and World Report*, Saltzman
had seen too many exhausted career climbers whose outwardly successful lives lacked substance. These were people
whose breathless striving to reach the top was leading only
to more work, less time to do what they wanted to do, and a
faster pace on life's treadmill. These were self-drivers, creat-

ing their own rushes of adrenaline, galloping through life with no time to stop and enjoy their achievements. Many who seemed to be adapting and thriving on the fast track were beginning to show signs that they were the least emotionally stable people of all, even though on the surface they seemed to be gliding smoothly through life.[10] Before it became faddish, Saltzman argued that we need to change our images of success, slow the pace, and capture more balanced lives through downshifting. In exchange for a less hectic pace of life and greater control over their time and schedules, downshifters decide to live with less money, fewer possessions, simpler lifestyles, and a realization that there may never be success for them in terms of fame, riches, and influence.

These are admirable goals, but they are difficult to put into practice. On a Halloween night recently, a friend scrambled to keep up as his kids raced from house to house, filling their bulging bags with more and more candy. "Slow down," my friend urged, but his children kept going at their breakneck speed. "We've got to keep rushing," one of them explained as he dashed by, because "the faster you go, the more you get." Early in life these young people had learned a lesson that infects our minds and makes downshifting hard: We live in a society that is propelled by the premise that faster is better.

Some prominent people have succeeded in bucking this mentality. When presidential adviser William Galston's ten-year-old son wrote a letter complaining that "baseball's not fun when there's no one to applaud you," Galston quit his influential White House job to spend more time at home and at his son's baseball games. Jeffrey Stiefler resigned as well, leaving his prestigious position as president of American Express to "work a less intense pace and spend more time with my family." Newspaper columnist Anna Quindlen, once rumored to be the first woman in line for the top editor's job at the *New York Times,* made a similar decision to be at home with her elementary-school-age children and to write novels.[11]

Probably I should admire those high-profile people who have the courage and the financial resources to quit their fast-paced jobs, shed clutter from their lives, and spend time with their families. When my life gets hectic, I sometimes think about quitting. But for me quitting my job isn't feasible, abandoning my responsibilities isn't always possible, and down-shifting isn't easy, although I keep trying. Swept along by a flurry of daily commitments, we all know in our hearts that something needs to change. For many that doesn't involve downshifting; it means managing our time and getting better control of our schedules.

Time Management

Some time ago I bought a big easy chair that could be pushed to a prone position and turned into a vibrator intended to relax tired muscles. But the chair never got much use, and eventually we gave it away. I'm hesitant to admit this, especially in print, but at least until recently I haven't had much room in my schedule for sitting in easy chairs. When people have commented on my boundless energy and ability to get things done, I have been invigorated and motivated to keep going, crowding more and more into my time-pressured life. Like many other men (and increasing numbers of women), I have allowed work to become an addiction. And like an alcoholic in denial, I have tried to convince myself that I'm really not a workaholic— despite disturbing evidence to the contrary.

This may not describe you, but a lot of us love to work.

Our vocations are exciting, motivating, challenging, and exhilarating. Tell us how we can cram more into our event-filled workdays, and we rush off enthusiastically, ready to accept new challenges, but with little thought to downsizing or slowing the pace. We're the kind of people who might be reached by a flyer like the one that came in my mail after I started to write this chapter. Advertising "America's #1 Seminar," the mailer promised that for $155 and a day of my time, I could manage my priorities and have "maximized productivity." The advertisement boldly proclaimed that by attending the seminar, I could learn innovative ways to "juggle many jobs without dropping the ball," beat the urge to procrastinate, and learn how to get more done in less time by "working smarter not harder."[12]

Maximizing productivity is the essence of time management—the most popular way to get control of our breathless lifestyles. Stephen R. Covey, who is the undisputed current leader in this field, suggests that we have gone through several "generations" of time management.[13]

The first was based on a *go-with-the-flow mentality* that recognized the existence of schedules and outside pressures and encouraged people to cope by making notes and keeping to-do lists. Book authors and seminar leaders taught people to organize their tasks and responsibilities, develop better filing systems, protect themselves from interruptions, and learn to delegate. Above all there was emphasis on making lists and writing reminders about the things to be done.

A second generation of time management focused on *planning and preparation.* We learned about efficiency, planning ahead, scheduling future activities, setting goals, concentrating on doing the most important things first, and keeping close track of deadlines and commitments. This approach has relied on tools—the right planner, calendar, computer program, or notebook—to help us track responsibilities, organize tasks, and keep aware of what needs to get done.

More recently, we have come into a third generation, which moves beyond the techniques and focuses instead on *values and priorities*. There is less emphasis on control and more on discovering and organizing our lives around goals, beliefs, and other things that really matter. Even this leaves people frustrated, however. We may have decided on our priorities, but many among us still sense a gap between all of the things that demand our time versus what we really consider to be important and worth doing. We can be very grateful that we live in an era and in communities where we can afford the luxury of pondering issues like priorities and values. Throughout history and in many countries today, I wonder how many people long just to find a job or to have life's basic necessities. These people would never have the luxury of pondering what is important or of thinking about "a gap between our priorities and all of the things that demand our time."

In an effort to deal with this gap, Covey now admits that many people have become turned off by time-management programs that make them feel scheduled and restricted. They are beginning to realize that time management is really a misnomer. We don't need to manage time—that's impossible. Instead we need *life* management. This fourth generation of management argues that we have put too much emphasis on worrying about efficiency, managing time, controlling our lives, planning schedules, making lists, limiting interruptions, struggling to do what is urgent, or managing things and people. All of these activities show how we have become ruled by the *clock* that represents our commitments, appointments, and efforts to plan our days and manage our time. Instead, we should be guided by a *compass* that represents our principles, direction, visions, and conclusions about how we really want to live our lives.[14]

WHERE ARE WE?

All of this sounds very inspiring, but how do we make it work in practice? Have we reached the stage in history where we cannot live fulfilling, productive, God-honoring lives without incessant interruptions and a never-ending struggle to balance, juggle, manage, and cope with the pressures of our multitasking lives? Must we always feel deluged with things to do and not enough time to get everything done?

When I first thought about writing a book to answer questions like these, I didn't want to tell my friends. I thought they would laugh at the thought of a high-energy, hyperactive guy like me writing a book about life management and balanced lifestyles. Before abandoning the project, however, I talked with a friend who suggested that my lifelong struggles with busyness uniquely qualify me to write about these issues. I have tried most of the time-management methods. I've read many of the self-help books and filled out the questionnaires that often are included. I have tried to evaluate my life to see where I have been consumed by the itch for more, and, even as I have worked on this book, my wife, Julie, and I have been in the midst of some downshifting. I have applied most of the oft-repeated techniques for controlling my life and managing stress, and while I rarely watch television, there have been many times when I have looked for other ways to escape the treadmill lifestyle.

Where am I now?

I'm in transition, making good progress. I still carry a calendar, make lists, keep abreast of schedules, and try to limit interruptions. I have learned to say no to opportunities that it might be nice to accept, and I am accepting the obvious conclusion that God doesn't expect me to do everything. I still have a long way to go, but even Julie agrees that my life pace is more balanced and less hectic than it once was.

Most of the methods suggested by this chapter are only stopgap procedures. Since most of the time-management guidelines and methods depend on our own willpower or abilities to stick with some program, most tend to be abandoned when the time pressures mount or when we want the excitement of adding something new to our schedules.

Maybe you are like me, skeptical of time-management programs promising to help us with our schedules. Maybe you are dubious about simplistic plans intended to make our lives less cluttered or about pop psychology recipes for taking charge of our out-of-control lives. In some ways and for some people, each of these can be helpful, but for runners on treadmills, there isn't much time or energy to master time-management tools. When the treadmills race, we can't concentrate on anything else, and there isn't much opportunity or motivation to slow down or to focus on God.

But nobody can run forever. Sooner or later our bodies, our families, or our increasing inefficiencies tell us that supermen and superwomen do not exist in real life. Eventually we have to face the question of how we can have useful, productive, fulfilling, God-centered lives in the midst of all the change and chaos of this present age.

This is what the following pages of this book are all

about. We will consider what it means to live a life that is under control and not fueled by our concerns about time. We will look at some traits that any of us can develop for breaking the breathless pace and having more balanced lifestyles. Along the way we will see clear examples of people whose lives are productive and fulfilling without being breathless.

There is hope. The scurry and stresses of our generation can fall into perspective without draining the fun and challenges from life. It isn't easy, but we can control the hectic pace of our breathless racing and exchange the treadmill existence for lives that are genuinely well lived.

TAKING A STEP TOWARD
Catching Your Breath

As you reflect on this chapter, take some time to answer these questions. You may want to do that in a journal, with a friend, or in a group. Allow the questions to help you focus on how you will begin to slow down.

1. In what areas of your life do you feel as if you are on a treadmill?
2. In what area would you most like to gain control?
3. Are you a multitasker? What are the benefits and disadvantages for you in multitasking?
4. In what ways do you try to escape life's pressure? Are these healthy or unhealthy escapes? What can you do to curb unhealthy escape?

5. Do you need to downshift or downscale? In what areas? Whose help will you enlist in doing this?
6. What has been your most successful method of managing time? In what ways have time-management methods been unsuccessful for you?
7. What is your goal in trying to manage your life? What do you hope to gain?

CHAPTER 2

Defining Moments
Ten Traits of a
Life Well Lived

O N THE DAY of her birth in the town of
Skopje, nobody could have predicted that Agnes Gonxha
Bojaxhiu someday would have international fame and be
listed consistently among the world's most admired people.
In a culture dominated by men and superpowers, who would
have thought that a little girl in a remote part of Europe
would someday meet with presidents and kings? In a world
enamored with youth, riches, pleasure, and success, would
anyone have expected that millions would look with awe on a
frail old woman who owned almost nothing, who had no interest in self-comfort or self-promotion, and who was content to
spend her life working in one of the largest, poorest, and
most polluted cities in Asia?

Mother Teresa didn't claim to be doing anything extraordinary, but she was respected around the world for her life of
simplicity and service, her message of love and caring, her

devotion to Christ, and her impact in an era that has few female heroes or respected Christian role models. When she decided to be a missionary nun, she had no inkling of what was ahead. She had always had a pioneering spirit, and she knew from the start that she wanted to go to India. But she expected to be a teacher, and that is how she began her service in Calcutta. Then one day she experienced what might be called a defining moment.

Never in good health and weakened by a heavy workload and food rationing, the nun succumbed to tuberculosis and was unable to continue her teaching. Her superiors urged her to enter a Darjeeling retreat center where she could find rest and recovery in the foothills of the Himalayas. Soon she was on a train, traveling through the countryside, and it was there that she received a call. "The message was quite clear," Mother Teresa reported later. "I was to give up all and follow Jesus into the slums—to serve Him in the poorest of the poor. I knew it was His will and that I had to follow Him. There was no doubt that it was to be His work. I was to leave the convent and work with the poor, living among them. It was an order."[1] More than two years passed before the church gave her permission to leave the convent and begin her now-famous work, but the experience on that Indian train was a turning point that set the direction for the rest of her life.

"WHO CAN ARGUE WITH A LIFE SO WELL LIVED?"

Unlike Mother Teresa, I have never experienced a clarion call about what God wanted me to do. I have never seen a vision, talked with angels, or had an ecstatic religious encounter that has redirected the course of my life. But I have had occasional defining-moment events that have triggered new thinking, solidified ideas that had been floating in my mind, given a clearer view of the future, or sent me in unexpected directions. Indirectly, Mother Teresa was involved in one of those events.

The story of her speech to a prayer breakfast has been told often. Addressing a group of religious leaders in Washington, D.C., Mother Teresa spoke about her work and boldly criticized the prevalence of abortions in America. Her largely pro-life audience responded with enthusiasm. They applauded her speech with vigor and then waited politely as the pro-choice president of the United States took his place at the podium to give a response. Wisely and graciously, President Clinton didn't challenge the antiabortion views of the famous guest speaker. Instead he began his remarks by observing that nobody can argue with "a life so well lived."

I heard about this at a time when I was struggling with questions about how I should live the rest of my life. President Clinton's words stuck in my mind like superglue. They continually nudged my thinking, stimulated the direction of my reading, and led to a lot of consideration about what it means for anyone to have a well-lived life. I had reached a turning-point age and knew that I wanted to be productive and useful for the rest of my life. When I looked at my breathless, adrenaline-addicted lifestyle, however, I knew that this was not what God intended. I began to realize that the ultimate answer to a fast-paced life was not in the *time*-management books that I had been reading, useful and practical as they can be. The answer was to be found in *life* management. I reached a conclusion that now seems so obvious: *If we have lives that are well lived and pleasing to God, our schedules will start to take care of themselves.*

FIRST THINGS FIRST

"If you were to pause and think seriously about the 'first things' in your life—the three or four things that matter most—what would they be? Are these things receiving the care, emphasis, and time you really want to give them?" With these words, Stephen Covey, Roger Merrill, and Rebecca Merrill begin their widely acclaimed book about life management.[2] On the first page, these authors challenge the notion that if we control our time and learn to "work harder, smarter, and faster," we then will be able to live more peaceful, fulfilling, and meaningful lives.

I agree that, for most people, there is a gap between what is deeply important to them and how they spend their time. Many of us live with an urgency addiction, driven by the "high" of pushing to do the things that are crying to get done. Rarely do we find time to think about issues that are of lasting significance but that aren't crying for immediate attention. Most of us don't want better time management or the security and identity that comes from being frantically busy. Instead, we want balance in our lives, interdependence with others, and the peace and power that come from "principle-centered living."

Jesus Christ isn't mentioned much, if at all, by Covey and his coauthors, and their references to spirituality are not drawn specifically from biblical teaching. But the authors stress values and reach conclusions that most Christians would applaud. It does seem true that when we live by the compass instead of by the clock, we will order our schedules and our lifestyles in ways that reduce breathless running and replace the hurry with rich relationships, inner peace, balance, and the confidence that we are doing what matters most.[3] The keys to such life quality are in the choices we make every day. We must learn to pause with some frequency, to consult our inner compasses, and to put first things first in our lives.[4]

This conclusion looks good on the page of a book, but it's harder to print it into our brains and make it work in our lives. In the midst of hectic daily schedules, pressure from our peers, and excessive demands on our time, it's not always easy to pause to consult our inner compass. Even in times of urgency and nonstop demands, however, we still can make wise choices that flow naturally out of the experiences, values, and beliefs that are at the core of our lives.

Something like this was on my mind a few months ago when I entered a crowded theater in the center of Cieszyn, a Polish city within walking distance of the Czech border. The place was jammed with young people. They filled every seat on the main floor, crowded into the back of the room, overflowed the balconies, and spilled into the hallways.

I was not naïve enough to think that they had come to hear me give my invited talk about drugs. Most of them didn't even know that I was on the program. But posters all over the city told them that Tomasz Żółtko would be there. He is a deeply committed Christian who, at the time, happened to be the number one pop singer in the country. When he stepped onto the stage, the audience exploded with enthusiastic applause. He sang one song then introduced me.

When I got up to speak, I thought of the times many years ago when our church youth group would go to local rescue missions and preach to men who really wanted a warm meal but who knew they had to endure a religious service first as the price of their dinner. Were those Polish kids thinking of me and my talk in the same way? I pushed the thought from my mind and pressed on with the aid of my translator. All of the people in that audience had grown up under Communism, and their country was struggling to live as a democracy. Things were not perfect—everybody knew that—and there was widespread complaining. The listeners were polite and attentive, but I was aware that Tomasz was waiting in the wings, so I communicated only one basic message: *life does not depend so much on our circumstances as on our choices.*

That is true when young people in Poland or elsewhere are thinking about drug use, illegal behavior, or illicit sex. It applies as well when we meet the pressures of living in our own homes and communities; when we face the routines of doing our jobs, raising our kids, paying our bills; and when we face decisions about what to do with Christ's claims for our lives. And this message gets to the core of our efforts to have lives that are well lived.

Throughout history, men and women—young people too—have made choices that set the courses for their lives. Mother Teresa, by choosing to say yes to the call she heard on the train fifty years ago, began a ministry that has had worldwide impact. Many people have made choices that are self-centered and that lead to great destruction; but others have chosen to love and learn, and in the process they leave the legacy of a life well lived. The people whose lives we admire are not perfect—we're all sinners—but they have made choices that set the direction of their relationships, careers, lifestyles, ministries, and values. Flowing from this core has been an ability to live above the pressures and a freedom from the barrenness of a busy life.

WAKE-UP CALLS

Sometimes when I stay in hotels, I call the front desk and ask for a wake-up call. The next morning the phone rings, and I can choose either to get up or to ignore the call and go back to sleep.

Have you ever noticed that we also get wake-up calls in life? Usually these are reminders—occasionally dramatic reminders—that we need to take an action, make a choice, or change some life direction. Such a warning came to a friend recently when his hectic pace was interrupted by an unexpected illness that looked life-threatening until the doctors found a more accurate diagnosis and decided it was less serious.

This scare may have been a divinely ordained wake-up call, urging my friend to slow down if he is to avoid a real collapse later. Like the morning calls in hotel rooms, these life wake-ups can stimulate us to take action, or they can be turned off while we go back to whatever we were doing when the call came.

Life's wake-up calls jolt us from our breathless routines and call for our attention. An opportunity or appointment is missed because some paper got buried on a cluttered desk. A spouse announces unexpectedly that the marriage is over. An illness stops us in our tracks. Wake-up calls like these are hard to ignore when they first shatter our worlds. We can pick ourselves up and go back to our old lifestyles as usual. But we also can turn those attention-arresting events into defining moments—turning points that lead us to new ways of thinking or to life-changing decisions that set a different direction for the course of our lives.

Wake-up calls and defining moments both call us to choose and to act. The fact that you have chosen to read this book and have read this far suggests that you are concerned about your breathless lifestyle. Could this book be a wake-up call prompting you to change? Could God use the words on this page to create a defining moment in your life, a call for movement away from the urgency addiction that may tyrannize your life and toward the more healthy experience of a life well lived? Think about this before you read further.

THE MODEL OF A LIFE WELL LIVED

If you had to choose a person who best models a life that is well lived, whom would you choose? Would it be an older friend, a fellow church member, a family member?

I would like us to think about Jesus as that model. Certainly, he lived on earth during a different era. People in his time and culture did not have to cope with electricity, modern technology, E-mail, sensory bombardment from television, or information overload on the Internet. Jesus never owned a watch, and I doubt that he carried an appointment papyrus, ready to jot down the location of his next breakfast meeting or power lunch. But maybe we need to see Jesus in a new light. Could he be a model—the best model—for technology-triggered, time-pressed moderns like us?

The Gospels show that Jesus was jostled by crowds, goaded by critics, pressed by needs, hassled by his detractors, misunderstood by his followers, and hounded by self-righteous intellectuals always looking for opportunities to trip him up. His pressures were not identical to ours, but they were persistent, demanding, and draining. In the midst of all this, however, he never seemed to be overwhelmed, time-pressured, or breathless. He handled the busyness without buckling under or burning out because he had a per-

TEN TRAITS OF A LIFE WELL LIVED

The well-lived life is marked by:

1. **Spiritual passion:** Loving God with all your heart, soul, and mind
2. **Compassionate caregiving:** Loving your neighbors and others
3. **Character:** Developing values and guiding principles
4. **Balance:** Keeping equilibrium and perspective
5. **Vision:** Living a focused, purpose-driven life
6. **Teamwork:** Working with others to share and grow together
7. **Adaptability:** Dealing with new trends and continual change
8. **Soul Care:** Keeping control of your lifestyle and private worlds
9. **Growth:** Continually learning, sharpening your mind, and moving forward
10. **Hope:** Living in the present with awareness of the future

spective that allowed him to live a balanced life in the midst of all the demands. If we look at Jesus in the midst of bustling crowds or incessant demands, we see a person whose way of living can be a practical and relevant guide to help us control our spinning lives in a new century.

Traits for Living Well

What was Jesus like as a person? What traits characterized his well-lived life, enabling him to be calm, productive, and unhurried, even in the midst of pressing demands?[5] How can his characteristics, first seen centuries ago, have any relevance to adrenaline-fueled people like us?

The list on page 27 suggests ten traits that Christ demonstrated during his years on earth. Two of the traits—spiritual passion and compassionate caregiving—are fairly obvious to us from Jesus' teachings. The other eight traits were never mentioned in these terms in Scripture, but we can infer them from Jesus' life, from how he lived in peace and productivity despite the frequent whirlwind of people and pressures that surrounded him.

In the chapters that follow, we will consider these ten traits that Jesus modeled, looking at each from a contemporary, life-management perspective. Each of these traits must form the core of any life that is well lived and that leaves a legacy. Developing these traits is the only way to get ultimate control of our own breathless, time-pressured lives.

TAKING A STEP TOWARD
A Life Well Lived

As you reflect on this chapter, take some time to answer these questions. You may want to do that in a journal, with a friend, or in a group. Allow the questions to help you focus on how you will live a more balanced life.

1. Who has lived a life that you would say is "well lived"? What can you learn from that person?
2. What experiences have been defining moments for you? How have you changed because of these experiences?
3. What experiences have been wake-up calls for you? How have you changed because of these experiences?
4. Which of the ten traits listed at the end of this chapter do you most want to develop? Why?

PART TWO

*Breaking the Pace:
Living Less
Pressured Lives*

CHAPTER 3

Spiritual Passion
Getting beyond the Religious Talk

T HE MAN in our church was enthusiastic. He had made a New Year's resolution to read the Bible for the first time, starting in January with Genesis 1 and continuing until he finished the last chapter of Revelation. I admire his determination, but I wonder what he will think as he makes his way through books like Leviticus and Deuteronomy. These are not the most interesting books of the Bible, with their seemingly endless details about the laws that God gave to his people centuries ago. The books teach us about God's holiness and give insights into what God is like, but they can be tedious to read and they don't appear to have much relevance for our technology-propelled generation.

In Jesus' day, however, devoted Jews memorized the Law along with interpretations that had been added over the centuries. One day some of these religious leaders asked Jesus to cite the greatest commandment in all of the Law. The question was probably meant to be a test question, but Jesus responded without hesitation: "Love the Lord your God with all your heart and with all your soul and with all your mind," he answered. "This is the first and greatest commandment."[1]

These words were taken from the *Shema,* the basic creed of Judaism. They were words that every Jewish child would have committed to memory, words with which Jewish services still begin. They were words directing believers to the lofty goal of giving God our total love, love that permeates our emotions, directs our actions, characterizes our thoughts, and dominates our lives.

My bookshelves have several dozen books about time management, finding balance, and similar issues. Most don't mention God, and I don't know of any suggesting that the "first and greatest commandment" of Jesus has relevance for modern people who struggle to keep from drowning in the torrential demands at their homes, offices, and workplaces. True, people are currently interested in spirituality, but the best-selling books about angels, soul care, or enlightenment don't say that loving the Lord with all our hearts, souls, and minds can help control our breathless lifestyles. The first and great commandment seems like ancient "God talk" that is difficult to apply in practical ways today.

A Placid, Unflappable Jesus?

When psychiatrist M. Scott Peck first read about Jesus in the Gospels, he was "thunderstruck." Peck did not have a religious background, so he had expected the biblical writers to give public-relations accounts of Jesus, written in glowing terms and with exaggerated embellishments. "I had assumed that [the Gospel writers] would have created the kind of

Jesus three quarters of Christians still seem to be trying to create," the famous psychiatrist wrote. He had expected to see Jesus "portrayed with a sweet, unending smile on His face, patting little children on the head, just strolling the earth with this unflappable, unshakable equanimity."[2] Instead, Peck found a Jesus who was very real—a man who was sometimes sad, lonely, and frustrated with the inability of his followers to get the point of what he was saying.

The Jesus in the Gospels was not the lifeless, dispassionate figure that appears in ancient icons and paintings. Jesus was honest, sometimes to the point of being tactless. He hated sin and never waffled about his impeccable standards, but he preferred to spend time with sinners whom he could challenge and who were willing to change rather than with pious and rigid religious leaders. In *The Jesus I Never Knew*, Philip Yancey concludes that Jesus was "brilliant, untamed, tender, creative, slippery, irreducible, paradoxically humble."[3] He was a Jesus who stands up to scrutiny, but also a Jesus who surely would understand the pressures of modern living. If he walked the streets of New York, Buenos Aires, Paris, or Djakarta today, his advice to time-starved people would be similar to his advice to those crafty first-century religious leaders with the legalistic minds: *If you want to get on top of a breathless lifestyle, find time to know God better and learn to love him with all of your being.*

WHO'S GOT TIME FOR LOVING GOD?

When Darrell Bock first went to seminary twenty years ago, he had a goal and great expectations. He wanted to learn about God, to love God, to know God. But Bock's real passion was to serve. He was determined to do everything he could for the kingdom, to make an impact, to be part of a generation that would change the world. He had learned to manage his spiritual life in goal-driven, task-oriented terms, doing whatever he could to mature spiritually. His prayers were like strategy sessions during which he would inform God about the tasks that needed to be done, ask for divine blessing, and often add a recommendation or two about how the task might best be accomplished.

Today, Bock realizes that the action-centered faith of his student days came from a baby-boomer mentality and accomplishment-oriented culture. He was driven by a sincere but feeble attempt at living life on his own terms with a little bit of God thrown in.[4] This type of faith is still too common among committed believers. It is a faith that reinforces our driven lifestyles but leaves us feeling empty, disappointed, and still breathless.

In contrast, the Bible urges us to aim for something different; to make it our ambition to lead a quiet life so that outsiders look to us with respect.[5] God himself urges us to be still so we can know him and experience his strength, power, help, compassion, and calming influence.[6] Times alone with God can be rejuvenating and can keep our busy lives in perspective.

But who has time to be alone with God? According to the late priest-psychologist Henri Nouwen, bringing solitude into our lives may be the most difficult discipline for modern people like us.[7] We pack our days and our lives so full that we leave no room for retreat, for listening, for being still, for learning to love God with our whole being. We want to make every minute count, so it's easy to feel that time with God is wasted. Eventually, time for solitude or for building an intimate relationship with God gets pushed further and further down on our priority lists. Sometimes it is squeezed out altogether, even in people who are busy scurrying about determined to do the Lord's work. In our hyperactivity we fail to realize that ministry is never really fruitful unless it grows out of consistent, reflective, intimate times alone with God.

Martha learned about that. Probably you know her story. When Jesus came to visit Martha's home, she was distracted by all the activities of preparing a meal and offering Jesus hospitality. But apparently the pot on the stove was not the only thing simmering in that ancient kitchen. Martha was so annoyed by her sister's unwillingness to help her that she complained to Jesus about it. "Lord, don't you care that my sister has left me to do the work by myself? Tell her to help me!"[8]

I relate to Martha. I like to be doing things. Sometimes, like Martha, I am "worried and upset about many things," but it's easier for me to keep pushing than to be like her sister, Mary, who sat quietly at Jesus' feet, listening to what he said. To be honest, I wish Jesus had given Martha a little applause for her busy service. Instead he gently came down on the side of Mary and stated that her quiet way was the better way.

Generations of spiritually attuned writers have agreed. It is in quietness that we learn "to fine-tune our receptivity to God's presence, his will and his word," wrote Australian church leader Rowland Croucher. When we discipline ourselves to pull away, even for brief periods, we find balance for the spiritual life "between being and doing, between contemplation and action, between words and silence."[9]

Do Croucher's words strike a chord with you? Have you found that when you have been able to retreat into quietness and time for reflection, your ability to love the Lord with your whole heart and soul and mind has deepened?

Philosopher Blaise Pascal wrote that the sole cause of human unhappiness is that we don't know how to stay quietly in our rooms. While Pascal's statement is an oversimplification, it does point out that we are often uncomfortable with the idea of taking time for peaceful reflection that might force us to face our burdens and stressful circumstances. We "prefer the hunt to the capture. That is why men are so fond of the hustle and bustle; that is why prison is such a fearful punishment; that is why the pleasures of solitude are so incomprehensible."[10]

HIGH-PERFORMANCE SOLITUDE

Without mentioning Pascal or anything religious, psychological researchers recently agreed that quiet reflection and solitude can bring special benefits, especially to those of us who face incessant demands for our attention, energies, and skills.[11] It doesn't matter what we do with the time, according to the researchers. Walking, jogging, meditation, systematic relaxation, or sitting in a hot tub can all be helpful if they give opportunity for solitude. These times alone replenish our psychological energy and physical well-being, as measured by reduced stress hormones, improved immune functioning, lower blood pressure, and other physiological changes.

Times alone also allow us to contemplate who we are and where we are going. Solitude fosters creativity, letting us think about new ideas without the censorship and evaluation that comes from expressing our thoughts in public. Everyone needs time alone, say the researchers, even though we differ in the amount of solitude that we need and prefer. Even so, a lot of breathless-type people ignore their tired bodies or the urgings of their frustrated families and conclude that, despite the potential benefits, they don't need any time for personal reflection. So they keep going.

Busy people might be more convinced and interested if they could rush their solitude, rejuvenation, or times with God. Performance-driven people like their busy lives to be organized, controlled, and maximally productive. They would prefer to pull out their calendars and schedule a block of time where there could be a highly productive period of solitude. The goals would be for getting recharged and for loving God with their hearts, souls, and minds—before moving on to the next action-packed appointment. Of course, that isn't how it works. Rushed, goal-directed solitude doesn't accomplish much.

I once heard a widely admired Christian leader talk about this. He had been rushing for weeks, responding to incessant demands, driven by his determination to make things happen. One day he realized that he had been giving so much that there was no more to give. He didn't collapse physically, psychologically, or morally. But he realized that he had been running, Martha-like, with all kinds of projects, activities, and preparations. To use his illustration, the batteries in his life had run down. Unlike so many of us who try to "run on empty" or without any battery power, this leader knew that he had to stop and recharge. And he knew that, like charging the battery of a car, recharging his life would take more than a few minutes. It might take weeks rather than hours. But he knew that without taking time to recharge, his effectiveness would collapse and his hectic church-related activity could come to nothing.

If we pace ourselves, we won't need long periods away, as this Christian leader did. We will find that shorter but consistent times of solitude will slow us down, calm our minds, rejuvenate our bodies, and give us opportunity to be with God. Time alone will help us see our lives and values more clearly so we can discern where to make needed adjustments to our priorities and lifestyles. *Finding time for solitude may be the most important practical step to free us from the control of our action-packed schedules and to give us lives that are well lived.*

BRINGING LIFE BACK INTO FOCUS

I don't know if Solomon had much time for solitude, but we do know that his life was successful. He had wisdom, wealth, and women, but at the end he despaired and wrote that "everything is meaningless."[12] Solomon described the great projects he had undertaken, the things he owned, the houses he had built, the wealth he had amassed, the pleasures he had experienced, the delight he had taken in working hard, and the status he had attained.[13] Surely Solomon was addicted to his own adrenaline and driven by a curiosity to see how much people like him could accomplish during the "few days of their lives" on earth.

What did Solomon gain from this experiment and from his labor, his drive for money, his push to get ahead? This is his conclusion: "Frustration, affliction and anger."[14] Isn't that a surprising answer from one of the most powerful men of all time? Solomon says that he takes nothing from his labor, that

he can carry nothing in his hand.[15] There can be fun and
excitement in a hyperactive life journey, but in the end Solomon concluded, "Much dreaming and many words are meaningless. Therefore stand in awe of God."[16]

Think about this for a minute. The adrenaline rush does
fire us up, and there's nothing wrong with working diligently
and knowing that you have studied, worked hard, and done
your best. But all of this is futile, and life doesn't count for
much if we fail to step aside periodically and stand in awe of
God.

What Awes You?

The things that "awe" us are a good indication of what we
value in life. Some time ago, the male members of a small
group I was part of decided to go skiing for a day. They were
all younger and more experienced skiers than I am, so they
seemed a little surprised when I accepted their invitation to
join the group. Soon they went off to the slopes, charging down
the hills with breakneck speed, while I joined the beginners to
practice the basics. In our midst was a little boy who could not
have been five years old. He had mastered the art of skiing
very well. I watched him weave back and forth on our little
hill, sometimes go down the slope backward, and leave the rest
of us in a pint-sized cloud of snow dust. I stood in awe of his
abilities and expressed this to one of my friends who had come
to see how I was getting along on the bunny hill.

"You're right. This kid's skills are awesome, especially for
one so young," my friend remarked. Sensing that I felt a bit
eclipsed by this young boy's abilities, my friend said, "But
just remember, Gary, that you've done some pretty awesome
things too. We all have."

My friend's comments suggest that sometimes we stand in awe of the accomplishments of others and dwell on our apparent inadequacies; but in the process we forget about the good things that God has allowed into our own lives. Some people stand in awe of themselves, caught in an ego trip of unrestrained individualism that leaves them pushing perpetually to keep ahead of everyone else and striving to retain their own assumed positions of superiority. Equally sad are the people who stand in awe of nothing. Their lives tend to be empty, often cynical, and without purpose.

Standing in awe of God frees us from all of this, writes Wayne Schmidt, pastor of a growing church in Michigan. "If there is nothing at the center, there is no anchoring point. Everything is adrift." But if we take time away to stand in awe of God, we are freed from "frantically seeking to meet all the expectations of others, from self-reliance, from climbing the corporate ladder." During our adult lives, the work we do will change. Technology will demand that we develop new skills. Our lives will include new challenges, joys, and disappointments. But, Schmidt writes, "The most important qualities of life—a life of integrity, a strong work ethic, treating people with dignity—arise out of the changeless core that is constantly re-energized in the presence of God."[17] In that divine presence, we can focus most clearly on the things that last.

THINGS THAT LAST

I am awed when I ponder the life of Jesus. He didn't have any interest in success, money, possessions, prestige, accomplishments, or being accepted and liked—all of the things that dominate so many modern lives and contribute to our pressures. Jesus knew that these things are temporary. They don't last. His values were elsewhere.

At the time of his baptism, Jesus heard a voice from heaven affirming that the Father was well pleased with the Son. As I read through the Gospels, it appears that this desire to please the Father and do his will was the major motivation that kept Jesus going. If we can define passion as an urgent drive to do or be something, then this was Jesus' passion: to honor, obey, and please his Father. Hearing the Father's "well done" was what really mattered.

I too want to please and obey the Father and be like his Son. In theory, this is a wonderful goal, but in practice it is a lot harder. My sometimes exhilarating, sometimes exhausting pace of life gets in the way. Even my times of solitude can drift into daydreaming or mental problem solving that takes my attention far from the Father. It is then that I look to another description of Jesus (found in Mark chapter one).[18] It was a very busy day for Jesus. He had gone to the synagogue and done some teaching, dealt with a severely agitated man at the synagogue door, healed the mother-in-law of one of his disciples, and then met the needs of a whole town of people who gathered at the house where he was staying. He must have been bone tired when he got to bed.

In the morning, however, he got up before dawn, left the house, and went to a solitary place, where he prayed until he was interrupted. The interruptions didn't come from his critics or from people disinterested in his ministry. The interruptions were from his friends, who came with the message that "everyone is looking for you!"

How might you have felt in a similar situation—wanting a little peace and quiet but interrupted by friends with big to-do lists? Jesus must have surprised his followers by calmly announcing that he was not going to return to the crowds who were trying to get his attention. He was planning to go elsewhere instead, to be with a different group.

In the midst of the pressures and demands on his time, how could Jesus confidently know where to go and how to spend his day? Apparently his time alone with his Father, in a solitary place, had reminded him again of why he was on earth. He knew his life purpose (we'll say more about this later), but he also set his immediate priorities based on that quiet time of prayer and reflection in the presence of God. Neither the demands of pressing crowds nor the urgings of his friends could distract him. Because of his passionate desire to please, obey, and spend time with the Father, he knew the divine guidance that enabled him to make calm decisions in the midst of pressure.

I wonder what his day might have been like if he had never taken that time for prayer and reflection?

WHAT'S LOVE GOT TO DO WITH ALL OF THIS?

You might agree that times of solitude are good for busy people. Perhaps you can also agree that we clarify our priorities and slow our lives when we stand in awe of God. But that first and greatest commandment of Jesus isn't about slowing down or taking time for solitude; it's about loving God.

That's not easy. I know how to love my kids. I can see them, touch them, hear their voices, and know their personalities. I can love my wife with acts of kindness, with words, and with physical intimacy. But it's not easy to love somebody whom we don't see with our eyes, touch with our hands, or hear with our ears. And even if we agree that this kind of love is possible, what can that have to do with taming our breathless lifestyles?

Everybody knows that love is a feeling, but of course it involves a lot more. Like all emotions, feelings of love wax and wane, so if people who love each other are to keep their love alive, they need to put their love into action. They need to spend time with each other, to keep learning about one another, and to do things that express appreciation and care. The same is true of loving God. If our love is to grow, we need to spend time with him, keep learning about him, express our praise to him, and do what pleases him. If you love me, Jesus said, you will keep my commandments and obey me.[19]

BACK TO THE COMPASS

How does this and all that we've said thus far impact our lives and help us with our schedules? Earlier we mentioned the writings of Stephen Covey, whose books have made a great impact on time-pressured people. Covey and his coauthors write that we should be less concerned about the hands on our clocks and more willing to be guided by the "true north principles" of the compass.

True north on a compass is not a matter of speculation or individual judgment, dependent on the results of a vote. True north is a reality that is independent of any personal opinions. When we plan our schedules and lifestyles according to the compass, Covey argues, we don't build on subjective personal opinions about how to live. Instead, we live according to basic, universally accepted principles like thrift, the value of saving for the future, trust, integrity, moderation, self-discipline, fidelity, responsibility, compassion, or the importance of honoring commitments. "Bottom line, the power to create quality of life is not in any planner. It is not in any technique or tool. . . . The power to create quality of life is within us—in our ability to develop and use our own inner compass so that we can act with integrity at the moment of choice."[20]

I have a friend who would disagree with part of Covey's assessment. My friend has been passing through some moments of choice and growing times in his life. Actively involved in a host of useful and admirable activities, he has impressed me and others with his ability to keep everything in life moving smoothly. "But it hasn't been working very well," he stated over lunch recently. "I've been going from place to place, servicing the different activities on the perimeter of my life but ignoring the core, where there are issues that need to be dealt with and painful wounds that need to be healed." With help from a competent Christian counselor, my friend is growing and refining the core values of his life. He is building a more principle-centered lifestyle in place of building so much of his life around the demands of a busy schedule.

My friend understands that his life principles are based on something more than a subjective inner compass. Reliable "true north" principles that get rooted *within* us as part of an inner compass must come from *outside* of us. These principles for living come from the God of the universe, the God who created us, revealed himself in the Bible, showed us his standards by giving that Old Testament Law, and sent his Son, Jesus, into the world so we could see what God is like. My friend is an unusually dedicated Christian who is devoted to loving God with his heart, soul, and mind. The more he spends time with God, knows him, loves him, and seeks to be obedient, the more my friend becomes aware of and able to embrace those core, God-given principles that will set his life compass, guide his schedule, and determine how he will live.

SOMETHING MORE TO DO?

Does all of this sound like something more to do? Busy people don't need more items on their to-do lists, more entries in their date books, more demands for their time.

We can tell people that they need to love God with their hearts, souls, and minds, and most will agree, especially in our society where a majority of the population still claims to believe in God. We can describe the benefits of solitude, of spending time alone with God, of being still, or of taking time to recharge one's batteries, and many people will enthusiastically endorse the idea.

But when we suggest that we should find time on our schedules for this recharging, personal reflection time of solitude, many people will express resistance. *It's a great idea,* we think. *It's just that there's no way to fit it in.*

Maybe we *have* to fit it in. When I was a graduate student, I made a life-changing decision. It wasn't radical, and I didn't think much about it at the time, but in the midst of my hectic schedule I decided to take Sundays off. I worked long and hard during the rest of the week, but on Sundays I went to church, lingered over lunch, had a nap, did some casual reading, and spent time with friends (when I could find any who weren't studying). This was a conscious decision to schedule a once-a-week break for physical and spiritual rejuvenation, taken at a time when I had a lot of daily pres-

45

sures and insecurities about my ability to complete a degree
program. For most of my adult life I have kept this resolve.
I can't prove it, but I think I work more efficiently and get
more done during the week when I live according to that
biblical principle of resting for one day in seven.

In the midst of some very busy demands in his life, Martin
Luther reportedly stated that he would have to spend more
time in prayer because he had so much to do. That's not my
style, and it doesn't describe anybody I know. But the principle of regular, preferably daily, times away must be a part of
our lifestyles if we are to avoid the barrenness of a busy life.
For me to do this, I have to put it on the schedule and stick
with the plan. And sometimes all of us need a little help.

Keeping Accountable
Several months before starting this book, I was discussing
some of these issues with a young college professor who has
one of the busiest schedules of anybody I know. His days
are spent rushing to and from classes, committee meetings,
speaking engagements, counseling sessions, student appointments, writing times, and meetings with a stream of off-
campus visitors. When he complained that there was no time
to read the Bible or even to squeeze in a few minutes for
reflection now and then, I suggested an experiment. I gave
him a little devotional book that will get him through the
whole New Testament text in one year and includes some
Old Testament and devotional readings. Then I suggested
that we agree to hold each other accountable for reading
through this book at the same pace, a portion a day, even
though we may be miles away from each other. It's working.

A plan like this is easy to put in place. You need only a

few ingredients: a conviction that time alone with God is valuable, a desire to make it work, a friend who can hold you accountable, a willingness to put this one extra thing on the schedule, and a recognition that it is best to start slowly, without taking huge blocks of time.

Three centuries ago, a young Frenchman named Nicholas Herman decided to become a lay brother among the barefooted Carmelites in Paris. He was a humble man who worked in the kitchen of the monastery and wrote letters that became the basis of a book that Christians still read. In *The Practice of the Presence of God,* the monk whom we know as Brother Lawrence described how he could think about God and communicate with him even in the midst of the pots and pans and people in the kitchen. Like many of us, he didn't have long periods of time alone or the luxury of a quiet place to pull away for solitude and loving God. He concluded that "prayers . . . however short, are nevertheless very acceptable to God," and he developed a mindset of loving God in the midst of his daily life.

For us, loving God in the midst of our daily struggles may mean getting up a few minutes earlier, riding in the car with the radio turned off, putting time with God into our appointment books, pausing to consider God while we change a diaper or, like Brother Lawrence, looking for opportunities to quiet ourselves within even while we do routine parts of our work. This is practical spirituality that builds beyond any God talk.

What you believe will set the tone for the life you live. If you understand the value of solitude and believe that it is important to spend time loving and knowing God, the tone of your life will reflect this. There is no better way to start getting control of our time-pressured lives.

If you still aren't convinced, try it anyway. You might be surprised at the results.

TAKING A STEP TOWARD
Developing Spiritual Passion

As you reflect on this chapter, take some time to answer these questions. You may want to do that in a journal, with a friend, or in a group. Allow the questions to help you focus on the next step God is calling you to take in living a life of spiritual passion.

1. In what ways have you found time for loving God?
2. What are your obstacles to loving God with your whole being? What can you do to reduce those obstacles?
3. How can you build in times of solitude for getting to know God better?
4. What awes you? How can you put yourself in a position to allow God to awe you?
5. Whom will you ask to keep you accountable for spending more time with God in an attempt to learn to love him more?

CHAPTER 4

Compassionate
Caregiving
Reaching Out to
Touch Someone

F JESUS came to live in this time-pressured
world today, I wonder what his life would be like? Would he
have a fax machine, E-mail, cellular phone, and pager? I
wonder if he would have the time to put on blue jeans and relax by walking around a mall on Saturday? How would he respond if he met neighbors who were having marital problems
or struggling to deal with a teenager on drugs? What would
he think if he walked beside you or me wherever we went,
watched our lifestyles, and rode along as we drove in our
cars? What would he say or do about violence in our streets
and homes, famine in our world, sleaze in our movies, greed
in our lifestyles, unfaithfulness in our marriages, or corruption in our corporations and governments? I wonder what he
would think of our busyness in the church?

We can only guess in answering these questions, but of one
thing we can be certain: based on his lifestyle when he walked

on earth, Jesus would be not only aware of human need but also deeply compassionate in response. He was sensitive to the children, concerned for the poor, committed to healing the sick, deeply touched by the grieving, and willing to relate to sinners so they could find forgiveness. We see this repeatedly as we read the Gospels, and we see it in Mark 1, a chapter of the Bible that illustrates the ten traits of a life well lived.

One day when Jesus was worshiping and teaching in the synagogue, an emotionally distressed, demon-possessed man cried out, probably disrupting the meeting. Jesus rebuked the demons and undoubtedly brought relief to the man, who might have suffered for years.[1] When he found Simon's mother-in-law sick and in bed, Jesus took her hand, helped her up, and brought complete physical restoration.[2] At the end of the day, when Jesus might have preferred a relaxing evening with his friends, he was available to help the whole town, who had gathered at the door, bringing their needs and their needy relatives.[3] Jesus had boundaries; he did not let demanding people completely dominate his life.[4] Nevertheless, when a leper approached and begged for healing, Jesus was "filled with compassion." He reached out and touched the man—despite his communicable disease—and the man was cured.[5] These kinds of compassionate acts dominated Jesus' entire life.

Servant Caring

One of the most thought-provoking events in Jesus' life had nothing to do with people in need, but he used the occasion to make a startling statement about caring. Two disciples came to Jesus and boldly asked to be prominent in his kingdom. These men were greedy for prestige and position. At the urging of their mother, they asked to be seated, one at

the left of Jesus and the other at his right. It isn't surprising
that the other disciples were indignant when they heard
about this attempted grab for status, but all must have been
amazed at how Jesus dealt with the issue.

Nonbelievers like to "lord it over" other people, Jesus
said. They like to throw around their authority, but that's not
the way it should be with his followers. "Instead, whoever
wants to become great among you must be your servant, and
whoever wants to be first must be your slave." Jesus pointed
to his own life as a model. He had abandoned his right to
power and position and had taken a servant role.[6] His life
was marked by sensitivity to others and by caring.

I struggle with these kinds of issues more than I care to
admit. Sometimes I have trouble with the idea of servanthood.
Nobody notices what I do until I don't do it! says a bumper
sticker that gets to the heart of this issue. Servanthood implies
that we do what we are expected to do, even if nobody notices—
except when we let down.

For over twenty years I have had a goal—to be used by
God, in some way, to make the church a more caring institu-
tion around the world. This desire has been a driving force
in my life, a motivation behind a lot of what I do. It is the
underlying theme for an organization of Christian counselors
that I lead, a major motivation for the travel and speaking
that forms so much of my life, a force at the core of the books
I write—including this one.

But it is so easy to get distracted by things far removed
from caring or servanthood. Concerns about success, about
being accepted, about not disappointing people, about how I
compare with others in my field—all can get in the way and
sidetrack me from serving and caring. I have too much con-

cern about book contracts, deadlines, or sales and not enough about the impact of my books, about making contact with nonbelieving neighbors, or about giving help to people in need. I write books about caring, counseling, and helping other people, but sometimes I'm so busy writing and giving seminars on caring that I have no time to care.

Do you ever feel the same way? Do you find that even though you want to be a caring person, you are often distracted by busyness and your own concerns? Maybe you have a pressure-packed job and incessant demands for your time, energy, and attention. Maybe you have a house full of growing children who need your attention and involvement. Maybe you have commitments—good commitments—that keep you from being the servant you feel God wants you to be.

Jesus talked about being a servant when he answered those two disciples who wanted to be great in the kingdom. In what theologian William Barclay called "one of the most revealing passages in the New Testament," Jesus stated that the way to be great in God's kingdom is to be a servant.[7] He gave a similar message when he told the disciples to love their neighbors as themselves and when he issued a new commandment that we love one another and in this way let the world see that we are his disciples.[8]

OBSTACLES TO CARING

Why doesn't my life, and maybe yours, show more active caring? What obstacles to caring get in the way?

Too Busy to Care?

We already know the most obvious obstacle to servanthood: we're busy and we don't have spare time for caregiving, especially when the needs of others arise suddenly. At times we can plan ahead by calling or visiting with a person who is lonely, preparing a meal, taking somebody to the doctor or to an airport, helping with a move, or giving counsel. We can fit these into our date books.

But crises are different. People don't have heart attacks, job layoffs, accidents, tornadoes, family deaths, or car break-downs on schedule. Sometimes when people need help, we can feel as if our busy lives have been invaded and inconvenienced. It is easy to feel that servanthood is demanding, disruptive, and even annoying—especially today, when everybody is so busy.

At times I ask God not only to make me more caring but also to give me more opportunities to be a servant and to learn servanthood. If you pray in the same way, be prepared for surprises. God might answer in unexpected ways. Sometimes he provides opportunities for us to serve, and at the busiest times in our lives. At other times he may teach us about caring by giving us an unexpected demonstration of what caring is really like.

Our family had that experience after I had finished the previous chapter and before I began to write this chapter about caring. We experienced an unanticipated flood that inundated part of our home and destroyed a lot of our possessions. Julie and I struggled to deal with the damage, but our efforts were in vain until the following Saturday morning, when seventeen people from our church came to help us clean up. They brought everything: brooms, mops, tools, coffee, donuts, lunch—including paper plates with plastic knives and forks. And they brought their strong arms and a cheerful willingness to tear up soggy carpet, carry away

waterlogged furniture, sort through drenched and dripping
books, and mop the muddy floors. Every one of those people
had a busy lifestyle. They came on a holiday weekend when
most had other plans. They showed me, as I had never seen
before, what caring and servanthood really are like.

We who live with breathless lifestyles sometimes need
dramatic reminders that caring is a way of life that doesn't
always fit our timetables. Servanthood isn't learned at time-
management seminars, and it can't be scheduled; it flows from
the inside out. Genuine servant-caring comes as God moves us
or uses other people to prompt us. Often he works through his
Holy Spirit within us, creating the love, inner peace, patience,
gentleness, kindness, and other spiritual fruits that form the
basis of selfless serving.[9] This is caring that is far removed
from our concerns about career success, prominence, getting
other things done, or keeping focused on our preplanned
time-management programs. It is servanthood that radiates
from within, even when we feel too busy or too weary to care.
It shines from lives that are well lived.

It Hurts Too Much

I first met Peter Kucmic in his native Yugoslavia, when the
future seemed bright, the dark shadow of Communism was
lifting, and people were optimistic. Peter was a pastor, a
seminary president, a Christian leader in Eastern Europe,
and a man filled with hope for his beautiful but oppressed
part of the world. When we met again, not long ago, Peter
talked about the deep divisions, appalling devastation, and
indescribable cruelty that has ripped apart the old Yugoslavia. We talked about the people of Bosnia, Serbia, and Croa-
tia. I heard about murder, rape, terror, hunger, family

violence, and homes in ruins. But we also talked about courageous and loving people who encourage and care for each other, regardless of ethnic differences; who share meager possessions and risk their lives to protect neighbors and strangers in times of danger. I was told about relief efforts and refugee camps, often arising from compassionate churches with few resources but an eagerness to give.

Why does all of this seem so far away? Why do we so casually ignore the stories and news reports about political chaos in other parts of the world? Why am I not moved by stories about violence in the streets of our cities, by physical and sexual abuse in homes across the country, or by hunger and instability throughout Africa? Passively, we read magazines and watch television that "trivializes the important and elevates the trivial." But in our affluent society, why do we seem so unconcerned that hemorrhoids get more attention than famine in Ethiopia or that soft drink companies get more airtime than global warming?[10]

Probably there are two answers, and they go to the core of why we don't care more: it hurts too much to get involved, and we feel so helpless. It is draining and heart-wrenching to let ourselves get involved emotionally with the pain in this world. And when we do see the sad pictures of suffering little kids with incredible needs, we feel woefully inadequate, overwhelmed by the futility of one person trying to make a difference half a world—or even half a mile—away.

Centuries ago, God gave a message to people far removed from modern Bosnia, Rwanda, or strife-torn Northern Ireland. "Stop doing wrong, learn to do right!" we read in Isaiah 1:16-17. "Seek justice, encourage the oppressed. Defend the cause of the fatherless, plead the case of the widow."

These are not easy words to apply today. None of us can go to all of the needy places in the world to give help. We don't have the time, and most of us don't have the interest to keep abreast of all the hot spots in the world. We haven't got unlimited resources to pour dollars into all the appeal envelopes that come to our mailboxes. We can pray—and maybe you do—but it is hard to know what to pray for or how to intercede for strangers whose struggles and stresses we have never experienced or can't really comprehend. And even when we decide to get involved, we again encounter the persistent pressure of our busy lifestyles.

In the midst of the busyness it is helpful to remember that the God of the universe does not expect any of us to care for every need in this world. As we have seen, even Jesus set priorities. When he heard about needs, he focused on some and turned away from others.[11] Remember, too, that caring can't be done alone. We need help, from God and from the community of fellow believers. Only then can we make the greatest impact.

It is not too simplistic to ask God what he wants you to do. Maybe you will be led to familiarize yourself with one or two of the needy places in the world so you can pray more knowledgeably. Perhaps you will choose to support relief organizations or urban ministries that are on the scene of pain and need. Maybe you'll be involved in more personal ways—volunteering at a local food pantry, preparing meals for the homeless, or going abroad for a time of service. Expect God to give you direction and the strength to deal with the pain. Expect, as well, that true caring may be costly.

When Greed Gets in the Way

For three years, Hal Lancaster has been writing a column on career management for *The Wall Street Journal.* "Is there a soul out there drawing breath and a paycheck who doesn't struggle with time management?" Lancaster asked in a recent column. He concluded that "cookie-cutter time-management systems just don't work because everyone is different" and because our chaotic lives are filled with too many distractions, unpredictable events, interruptions, and changes of plans.[12] The column captured my interest, but it failed to mention that some of our busyness and lack of time for caring comes because we are too concerned about money.

Recently I heard about a college student whose goal was to make a lot of money. "What's wrong with greed?" he asked his ethics professor, who apparently had challenged the modern drive to get more for ourselves. If we tell students like this about the joys of caring, about the efforts of Peter Kucmic in Europe, or about the sacrifices of Dietrich Bonhoeffer, we aren't likely to convince them. If we say that we live in a world where there ought to be sharing because some have much and others have so little, people like that student probably won't be moved.

Raised on television and exposed to a never-ending stream of carefully crafted commercials, the young student likely has one message deeply implanted in his brain. It is a message presented creatively and persuasively, telling him to indulge every whim, meet every need, buy every product, expect happiness in every purchase. "Over and over people hear that their needs for love, security and variety can be met with products," therapist Mary Pipher writes in her perceptive critique of our culture.[13] Viewers, including the very young, may reject the appeal of a particular ad, but over time they buy the message that products and purchases fill emotional voids and bring fulfillment.

Maybe the professor understood this when he answered the question about greed by taking an approach that might have touched the young man's focus on himself. "My answer to the student was that I have never met or known of a greedy person who was truly happy," the professor said. "Greed, by its very nature, is always seeking more. There is never enough. The greedy person is never satisfied, never fulfilled, never happy."[14]

Many of the people in my generation raised a cadre of baby boomers by feeding them a diet of materialism, hedonism, status-seeking, and self-gratification. Now we are all coming to realize that greed and me-first selfism never produce lasting happiness. No longer do we believe that affluence is an American birthright; that we will get what we dream about if we work hard or have enough faith and possibility thinking. We are beginning to see the distrust, insensitivity, cynicism, and ultimate unhappiness that come from lives of conspicuous consumption, self-gratification, and unrestrained individualism.

"We are not the sum of our possessions," George Bush said in his inaugural address. "We cannot hope only to leave our children a bigger car, a bigger bank account. We must hope to give them a sense of what it means to be a loyal friend; a loving parent; a citizen who leaves his home, his neighborhood, and his town better than he found it." Caring people leave their world in better shape than they found it. They don't get so busy making money and building careers that they lack the time or inclination to show compassion. They are people whose lives are genuinely well lived.

The Cost of Caring

In the summer of 1939, Hitler was on the move. Austria and Czechoslovakia already had been "assimilated" into the Führer's military machine, Poland was on the brink of collapse, and the world was beginning to comprehend the horror and magnitude of Hitler's imperialistic intentions.

As Nazi forces moved across Europe, they moved within Germany against the resistant underground Christian church that was led by Dietrich Bonhoeffer, among others. Seminary students were arrested, Christians had their passports seized, and Bonhoeffer himself was forbidden to write or publish.

In the United States, a group of seminary professors urged Bonhoeffer to come to America so that "his life might well be saved for the work of the church after the war." The church leaders in Germany endorsed the plan, and in June of 1939, the German theologian was standing on the deck of a ship heading for New York.

But Bonhoeffer was tormented by the choice. In one of his books, he had written that Christ expects believers to live together in prayer and confession, operating under the authority of the Scriptures and practicing "active helpfulness" that involves seeking the good of others before the good of oneself.[15] In leaving Germany, Bonhoeffer concluded that he had forsaken the costly call to stand with other believers in a time of great need. Shortly after his arrival in North America, he announced that he was turning his back on the safety of academic life in the United States and taking a ship back to Germany, to join with others living and caring in a hostile place where a madman's actions could lead to torture or death.

"I want you to know that I haven't for a moment regretted coming back," Bonhoeffer wrote later from the German prison where he spent the last months of his life. As a disciple of Christ, he had counted the cost of caring, demonstrating with his actions what he believed in his heart. He had written about the cost of discipleship; his life showed that caring costs as well.

Psychological Barriers

I have a friend who was in the midst of a doctoral program when she decided to quit. There were several reasons for this decision, but one academic requirement seemed to be the deciding factor in her withdrawal from the university. A course on cross-cultural counseling required the students to travel to some dangerous parts of the city to offer therapeutic help. My friend was scared to go, especially by herself. This was not some kind of neurotic insecurity about breaking from her own comfort zone and reaching out to people who were different. The student had legitimate fears for her safety.

Sometimes our caregiving efforts are stopped by psychological barriers. Fear is one of these barriers; pride is another. This is the feeling that getting involved in the nitty-gritty of caring is below our dignity or not the best use of our gifts, talents, or training.

At other times guilt gets in the way. I am annoyed, for example, when somebody tries to get my money or my involvement by making me feel guilty if I say no. I feel manipulated by such appeals, and usually I resist.

It also is easy to resist when we think about the motives

of people who ask for our help. Some people who ask for help are in need because of their own sin or stupidity. Others might appear to be blatant freeloaders who live off the generosity and the gullibility of naïve caregivers—like you or me. A few might be caught in the blame-game mentality, claiming (whether or not this is valid) that they are victims of injustice, and expecting you or me to provide relief.

In reading the Gospels, I've never had the impression that Jesus paused to consider motives when he encountered a need. He never refused to help because he was uncomfortable, unwilling to be manipulated, or determined to inflict punishment by withholding assistance because of a needy person's own sin, stupidity, or squandering of resources. And Jesus didn't resist people who might have been lazy, complainers, or self-centered moochers. Even though he didn't try to care for everyone in the country, whenever he met people in need, Jesus helped, regardless of their motives.

A BROADER KIND OF CARING

We need a similar mind-set, a Spirit-given willingness to provide whatever help we can give when we see a need and when we are in a position to do something—even something minor. Recently I had a very simple illustration of this in the parking lot of a restaurant. My wife and I heard a commotion and saw that an overweight elderly man with a walker had fallen. I responded exactly as you would have responded. I ran to the man, shouting over my shoulder for Julie to get one or two people from the restaurant to help. Together, we lifted the man to his feet. He claimed to be all right, and since he didn't seem to have any broken bones, we helped him to his car, gave some words of encouragement to his wife, and continued on our way. That's a caring mind-set—seeing a need and responding as soon as we can, as best we can.

According to the Bible, pure religion involves caring (people helping) and personal holiness. "Religion that God our Father accepts as pure and faultless is this: to look after orphans and widows in their distress and to keep oneself from being polluted by the world."[16]

Throughout the Bible, believers are encouraged to be kind and compassionate to one another, to encourage one another, to deeply love one another, to bring comfort, to bear each other's burdens, and to show loving words and acts of compassion.[17] The Christian love, patience, kindness, goodness, faithfulness, and gentleness that we mentioned earlier all characterize the effective caregiver. These traits exist in God the Father and in his Son, Jesus Christ. They emerge as fruit in the lives of believers who are controlled by the Holy Spirit.[18] All of this is at the core of genuine caregiving.

Even with our busy schedules, family commitments, and church or community activities, every Christian has a responsibility to give time, sensitivity, and understanding to those in need. We may feel pressed by our schedules, not greatly motivated to help, and without any reasons to feel encouraged about people in need; but for followers of Christ, caregiving is not optional. Caregiving often lifts our spirits, shifts attention away from our busy lifestyles, and rejuvenates. Such caregiving can apply anywhere; it is not limited to helping those with ongoing illnesses.

EIGHT WAYS TO CARE

I once wrote a book titled *The Joy of Caring*. It isn't available anymore, but in working on the manuscript, I began to recognize both the complexity of caring and how important caring can be for a life that is well lived. More recently, as I have studied some of the biblical references to caring and reflected on the core commitments of the Promise Keepers' movement, I wrote this Caregivers' Covenant.

CAREGIVERS' COVENANT

1. Caregivers are committed to caring about their relationship with God and dedicated to establishing a growing, vital, obedient, priority relationship with Jesus Christ, their Creator.
2. Caregivers are committed to caring for themselves by living lives of purity, faithfulness, and self-control, under the guidance of the Holy Spirit and in communion with other believers.
3. Caregivers are committed to caring for their families by granting them honor and respect; establishing a center of teaching in the home; and communicating love, acceptance, and commitment.
4. Caregivers are committed to caring for others, within the body of Christ and without, by living and growing in ways that demonstrate love, peace, patience, and gentleness through Christ.
5. Caregivers are committed to caring for their communities by being salt and light to those who live around them.
6. Caregivers are committed to caring for their leaders by praying for them, supporting them, assisting them, and submitting to them as to Christ.
7. Caregivers are committed to caring for nonbelievers and spiritual strugglers by showing love and by seeking to introduce them to the grace and peace of Jesus Christ, the one who cares about their burdens and their lives, both on earth and for eternity.
8. Caregivers are committed to caring for the world in which they live, protecting the environment, maintaining awareness and sensitivity to people who suffer from hunger, war, poverty, prejudice, and other social ills, and taking whatever action they can to contribute to the alleviation of suffering, injustice, and worldwide human need.

Caring about God

When I was a professor, I spent most of my time working in a theological seminary, where I was surrounded daily with eager, dedicated, Christian students who sincerely wanted to serve God. These young people were filled with a determination to do what they could to make an impact for Christ. Many were achievement-oriented people wanting to make a difference for God's kingdom.

Surely God is pleased with this dedication and determination to serve. Over the years, however, I've reached a conclusion that has been hard to accept: God wants us to be close to him more than he wants us to make an impact. He wants our worship more than our work, praise more than productivity, adoration more than activity, a dedication to knowing his Word more than a driven determination to do his work. In his goodness he sometimes uses achievement-centered people to touch others' lives. Often he blesses the work that we do for him and for his church. But he most wants us to be close to him.

When we have this ongoing concern about our relationship with God and when we make the effort to build this bond, then our caregiving flows from this commitment and our lives are more likely to be well lived.

Caring about Ourselves

Not long ago I met with a group of people who have agreed to hold me accountable and to help me make wise decisions about my life and work. I came to the meeting with a list of projects that I wanted to discuss, but they soon turned the focus away from these activities and centered the discussion on me. I resisted when they urged me to forget about my

projects for a while and to "think about what's best for Gary."
I complained that this was self-centered and not consistent
with what God would want for my life. In a loving but firm
way they reminded me that my health, impact on others,
future activities, and personal well-being could all collapse if
I failed to take care of myself. We talked about my need for
rest, relaxation, rejuvenation, purity, self-control, faithfulness to God. Some of the most dedicated caregivers I have
known have burned out because they cared for others and
failed to take care of themselves.

Jesus, the most compassionate person who ever lived,
cared about his relationship with the Father. We have seen
this. But he also took time to care for himself, to get rest, and
to rejuvenate with his friends.

Caring about Our Families
I could write pages about families that have collapsed
because the family members didn't pay attention to the
needs in their own households. I know some of these families. You probably know some as well. They are the families of counselors, pastors, youth workers, business leaders,
and others who have focused so much on reaching out to
other people that they have ignored or never noticed the
needs in their own homes. When life gets busy, it's easy to
slip into thinking that we have to finish our latest urgent
project, that we can spend time with the family tomorrow
or next week because they always will be here. Too many
people have discovered that this is a formula for family
collapse.

Caring for other people needs to start at home. I meet periodically with a friend who has four children, including one

ready for college and another in grade school. My friend has a busy lifestyle, but I have noticed that he purposely makes time to be with his kids, to be at teacher-parent conferences, recitals, ball games, and make occasional visits to McDonald's. And he doesn't forget to spend time with his wife. These family times add to his packed schedule, but they also pay rich dividends in terms of family support, love, stability, and togetherness. Often the best way to care is to be available, to listen, to remember birthdays and special occasions, to show by our words and actions that our families are still at the top of our priority lists.

Caring about Believers

In his letter to the Galatians, the apostle Paul makes an interesting observation about caring: "As we have opportunity, let us do good to all people, especially to those who belong to the family of believers."[19] I don't agree with Christian counselors who restrict their caregiving to fellow believers. Jesus showed compassion even to people who showed no signs of believing. This is one of the ways we can reach others for Christ.

But it is clear that we need to put a special focus on fellow believers, showing them love and care especially in times of need. Those people who cleaned our house after the flood were present when we needed them, ready to care for fellow believers—us—when we felt overwhelmed by our circumstances. Sometimes other people in the church need temporary child care, meals, money, or other tangible help. At other times caring involves praying, giving emotional support and encouragement, being willing to listen, or sometimes just the knowledge that someone is willing to be present and available in a time of need.

Caring for Communities

We've all seen it. A disaster strikes—a fire, a bad storm, a fatal accident, a tornado—and the whole community comes to the aid of the victims. Selflessly, people give money, time, support, food, possessions, energy, whatever is needed to meet the need. Scattered throughout your community, people probably are involved in acts of caring even as you read these words—people who watch a house and bring in the mail while the neighbors are on vacation, nearby families that provide meals and baby-sitting while a neighbor is in the hospital or grieving the loss of a loved one, little kids who take up collections to help a classmate in need.

The early believers were known by their love. Jesus told his followers that people would recognize them as his disciples if they showed love for one another.[20] For you this may not be an ongoing, time-gobbling involvement in the community. It may be a sensitivity to community needs and a willingness to be involved whenever needs arise.

Caring for Leaders

Most of us don't personally know many leaders in government, business, academia, or the church, and it is not likely that these busy leaders would be available even if we wanted to show our care in some way. But we can care by praying or by showing support whenever possible. And we can give practical help to leaders who are closer to where we live. Consider your pastor or the other leaders of your church, for example. Sometimes these are lonely people who don't feel much encouragement or backing for their ministries. With our prayers and our creative expressions of support, we can show that we care. Consider writing notes of appreciation to the officials in your community or to the leaders of organizations whose work you admire.

Caring for Nonbelievers and Spiritual Strugglers

I have noticed that if I ask God to give me opportunities to show kindness and compassion for people who are not believers, he answers. For example, I try to show respect and friendliness to the people who wait on me in restaurants, take my money at the store, collect my fees in toll booths, or help me when I go shopping. Many of these people in servant roles tell me that they consistently are treated with rudeness. It does not take any extra time to give a kind word, a smile, or a few words of encouragement. Commenting on a parable, Jesus said that in caring and doing things for others—and this presumably included nonbelievers—we were doing this unto Jesus himself.[21]

Caring for the World

We've said it before: nobody can care for the whole world. God doesn't expect the impossible. But he does expect us to show compassion for people in need. Jesus was concerned about the poor and suffering, so doubtless he is pleased when we make a contribution, however small, to relieving suffering in other parts of the world. Sometimes this involves money or the collection of supplies for needy countries; it may involve an occasional trip abroad to give practical assistance if we can. In our house we recycle everything we can, in part because we believe God wants us to do our part to care for this planet and to keep it from further destruction.

This list and the more formal expression of it in the Caregivers' Covenant are not intended to be some overwhelming, rigid, or confining formal treatise. Instead, the covenant is one person's initial attempt to summarize what caring really means. It is a set of goals that we all can shoot for, a list that can and probably will be revised and refined.

A MINISTRY OF PRESENCE

Each believer has been given spiritual gifts for the purpose of making the church stronger. Biblical writers don't include *caregiving* in their lists of spiritual gifts, but we are told that some people are especially equipped for serving, encouraging, showing mercy, and contributing to the needs of others.[22] Some among us have been specially endowed with a unique ability to care for others. That doesn't let the rest of us off the hook. We are all called to love one another; if we never show love, then we aren't Christians, regardless of how we describe ourselves.[23]

In one of his books, management consultant William Diehl describes his wife's history of attracting all kinds of women who have problems and frustrations, even though she makes no effort to do this. For many years, Diehl complained that it was terribly unfair to his wife when "all the women in the neighborhood came to her with their tales of woe." Frequently he urged his wife to tell these women to keep their problems to themselves. She didn't (or maybe couldn't) do this, and the pattern continued.

Eventually the frustrated husband began to realize that there was something about his wife, Judy, that encouraged these people to share their concerns. He thought it might have been her nonjudgmental nature, her unusual ability to listen, her refusal to lay guilt on others, or her unwillingness to assign blame. In the end he decided that "the ministry Judy was doing within the context of her primary role as mother and homemaker was a *ministry of presence.*"[24]

All of us have the potential for a Christian ministry of presence. We can "be there" or "show up" when we hear of a need. We can let God use us when somebody is hurting, needs help, or wants to talk. It's the most basic way that we care, serve, and show the love that Jesus described in the second great commandment.

Caregiving in Action

In all of my life, I have never met another man like Ralph Hamburger. When a Christian relief agency invited me to travel overseas, they asked Ralph to meet me in Europe, travel along, and give me help. Gently and efficiently, he anticipated and took care of every possible need that I might have had. Never before had I met a man so sensitive, so caring, so giving, so unimpressed with himself. From the start, I knew that I was in the company of a uniquely special servant, a Christlike caregiver who personified the ministry of presence and caregiving as I had never seen it demonstrated before.

Imagine my surprise, several years later, when I discovered a book about a group of deeply committed Christians in Hollywood after World War II. Ralph Hamburger was a member of that group. Each of them had decided to live his life "as an expendable for Christ," and together they decided to travel to war-torn Europe to serve, inconspicuously, in three different work camps. Ralph had been a postwar refugee who came to the United States with a heart filled with hatred for the Nazis. But "I am learning to forgive," he told his group a few weeks after his arrival. "I am learning the meaning, the reality of unconditional love. Christ is releasing me from the bondage of hatred."

The words in the book, which described Ralph Hamburger half a century ago, were equally descriptive of the Ralph Hamburger that I met on that trip years later: "Ralph was everywhere, doing everything from securing charter air flights to making packing lists. Weekly he published and distributed bulletins in which he encouraged, admonished, cajoled and corrected the group, expressing a tremendous sense of humor and keen insight. Watching him, Harriet [a member of the group] summed up my own feelings: 'All that planning! All those contacts! He's a genius!'"[25]

For most of Ralph Hamburger's adult life, he has traveled to and from Europe, often making dangerous trips behind the former Iron Curtain to bring help, encouragement, and a servant spirit. His life has been very busy, but it is not breathless. He is genuinely other-centered, consumed by caring.

People like this aren't mentioned in time-management seminars and workshops. Most often those programs are centered on how I can get things done, how I can be more efficient, how I can find time to do what I want. There isn't much emphasis on caring or compassion for others.

But I sense that this attitude is changing, especially as people try downshifting and reevaluating their lifestyles. You and I will not have the opportunities and experiences that Ralph Hamburger had. But we do have opportunities to be like Christ, to reach out and give encouragement to people who have no hope, to practice a ministry of presence. In so doing, we become people with lives that are well lived.

TAKING A STEP TOWARD
Developing Compassionate Caring

As you reflect on this chapter, take some time to answer these questions. You may want to do that in a journal, with a friend, or in a group. Allow the questions to help you focus on the next step God is calling you to take in living a life of servanthood and caring.

1. In what ways have you experienced compassionate caring from other people? How has that affected you?
2. In what ways do you presently demonstrate caring?
3. What are your obstacles to caring for others compassionately? What can you do to reduce those obstacles?
4. What example of compassionate caring from Christ's life would you most like to emulate?
5. Which commitment in the Caregivers' Covenant would you most like to develop at this point in your life? How will you do that?
6. To whom can you extend the ministry of presence?

CHAPTER 5

Character
Writing Your Own
Book of Virtues

THEY CALLED HIM a legend, an inspiration to his teammates, the great Yankee slugger. Everybody recognized the name of Mickey Mantle. "When Mickey Mantle stepped to the plate, No. 7 embroidered among those coldly efficient pinstripes that spread at the shoulders, it was high drama. The Mick would either strike out, hit a 500-foot home run or do something in between."[1] He got standing ovations wherever he went.

But Mickey Mantle became a drunk. He learned to drink, to carouse, and to be irresponsible. In turn, he encouraged his sons to drink, and they became alcoholics like their father. Liquor destroyed Mantle's marriage, his family, and his body. When he reached the end of his life, he was crippled by liver disease, hepatitis, and cancer. "God gave me everything and I blew it," Mantle said, reflecting on his life. "It seems like all I've done is take—have fun and take. . . .

I'd like to say to kids out there, if you're looking for a role model, don't look at me."[2]

Unlike some of his headline-grabbing teammates, Mickey Mantle was a humble man. He rarely called attention to himself, and he never acted like a superstar, despite his reputation as one of the best baseball players ever to play the game. But in the fast-paced, breathless world of professional sports, he forgot about character and slid into a self-destructive lifestyle of debauchery, lust, and irresponsibility.

When our fast-paced lives are driven by the clock and by incessant demands, character sometimes gets pushed aside. In our rush to get things done, we strive for efficiency and excellence, but we forget to give encouragement, to say thanks, to show loyalty. We applaud and admire people who are competent and creative, but often we're too busy to show understanding for people who struggle, or we are too wrapped up in our own schedules to extend compassion to those who are weak. We genuinely believe in good character, and we sing the praises of honesty and traditional values, but we don't have time to cultivate these values in our own lives or to instill them in our kids.

I'm not pointing a finger of blame. We are all in danger of neglecting character. It takes all the energy we've got to keep our families intact, our jobs secure, and our checkbooks balanced. Busy meeting deadlines, keeping ahead of demanding schedules, pleasing our employers, or preparing for the future—who's got time to think much about character?

CHARACTER AND COMPETENCE

Rick Love wasn't encouraged to think much about character when he was learning to be a missionary. He and his wife

sat at the feet of some of the most respected missionary teachers in the country as they studied theology, evangelism, mission strategy, and cross-cultural communication. Soon after
getting their diplomas, Rick and his wife headed for Southeast
Asia. They were overflowing with enthusiasm, confident
because of their education, and excited about the challenge
of planting churches among unreached Muslim people. Very
quickly they made a disturbing discovery. Their teachers had
overlooked a significant key to reaching non-Christians: competence is important, but *character is crucial.*

The Bible said that, of course.[3] The apostle Paul emphasized character when he listed the qualifications of church
leaders, but somehow that didn't seem to be of much practical relevance when the Loves studied modern church planting. They had to learn the hard way.

"Certainly we need gifted, competent people to start and
maintain church planting movements," Rick Love wrote with
insights that can apply to us all. "We need to know how to
be competent to perform our ministries if we expect to see
breakthroughs occur among unreached people. However,
*character and competence are vitally linked. The road to true
competence leads through the valley of character development.*"[4]

The Loves found themselves working among people who
were easily offended and inclined to hold grudges. Forgiveness was not part of the culture, and the residents of their
Indonesian village were experts in getting even. When a little
church was established, the congregation was weakened by
bickering and split over character issues. The young missionary couple learned that a loving, caring, forgiving,
vibrant church could come only if the people consistently

heard about moral values and saw them modeled by men and women of Christian character. Because of their competence, the Loves were able to learn a new language, adapt to a new culture, and plant a new church. But their hardest task, and the one for which they had been least prepared, was the development of character in the little band of believers they were seeking to nurture.

Character is not built quickly, and it doesn't come through time-management programs and career-building seminars that focus on competence. These tell us how to get control of our schedules and build success into our lives. They may even be inspiring, encouraging, and useful in teaching practical principles for living. But competence without character leads to efficiency that is cold and empty.

I have seen this in my own profession. Counselors can know all the methods, medications, theories, and explanations for personal problems. They can radiate competence, say all the right things, and give the best counseling. But the most effective counselors also show compassion, demonstrate that they genuinely want to understand, and aren't afraid to talk about right and wrong. Good counselors combine competence and character. The same is true of good parents, teachers, business people, or athletes. Whatever your work or place in life, competence is important, but character is crucial.

PRACTICAL CHARACTER

Character is an old-fashioned word that is easy to describe but hard to define. D. L. Moody described character as "what you are in the dark." The philosopher-psychologist William James expressed something similar when he wrote that your character is something inside you that says, "This is the real me." Your character is what you are when nobody is looking. It is the foundation that each of us builds to undergird our lives.

Whenever prominent and previously respected public figures are caught doing something illegal or immoral, almost everybody is surprised. I remember discussing this with my wife several years ago, following the fall of a well-known leader. We concluded that people of character are those whose actions and behaviors are the same at home and in public, when they are by themselves and when they are with others. In such people there is no phoniness, no need to "put on a front" when they are with other people. These are authentic, reliable, trustworthy people. They become known as people of character.

The core of such character is self-discipline, suggests Daniel Goleman. "The virtuous life, as philosophers since Aristotle have observed, is based on self-control."[5] People of character are able to control their impulses, appetites, and passions. These are people others can count on to be faithful, trustworthy, dependable, beyond reproach, consistent in their sensitivity to others. This does not become part of "the real me" overnight, and it does not come without effort. Character is formed over time. It comes to people who learn to motivate and guide themselves whether they are doing homework, finishing a project, sticking with an exercise program, or turning off the television late at night. Character comes when we see it modeled in others. Often it is shaped in the midst of crises. And character develops in its richest form among those who allow God to work within to mold their lives.

Jesus showed such character. Probably it was first formed when he grew up in the humble home of a Judean carpenter. It was molded by his determination to please the heavenly Father and was tested when he was in the desert for forty days being tempted by Satan.[6] Character was demonstrated when he was so willing to be open and honest that he dared to form a little band of disciples who could watch his every move.[7] We see character in Jesus when he showed his determination to accomplish his life purpose despite the distracting adulation and presence of applauding crowds.[8] Read though the Gospels, and you see this character again and again. Jesus did not hesitate to challenge the errors and inconsistencies in religious leaders or to publicly criticize King Herod himself.[9] When some critics tried to discount Jesus' teaching, he didn't hesitate to point out, with confidence and without apology, that these smug legalists were in error because they did not know the Scriptures or the power of God.[10] He was not afraid to touch lepers, talk with sinners, teach unpopular lessons, and tell stories that might be misunderstood but that illustrated the core of his message to the world. In the time of his trial, when his band of supporters had forsaken him and fled, Jesus stood alone in the courts of his accusers and never backed down on his beliefs, his values, his life purpose, or his determination to obey the Father's will. Jesus consistently modeled impeccable character and showed a life of virtue.

WRITING A BOOK OF VIRTUES WITH YOUR LIFE

I wonder if the publisher was skeptical when William Bennett suggested putting together a *Book of Virtues*. A political figure who had long championed moral education,

Bennett wanted to compile a collection of "great moral stories" that would teach children about self-discipline, courage, compassion, responsibility, loyalty, and other character traits. Bennett argued that children need training in good habits. They need to see what morals look like, how they work, and why they are important. Kids need to hear stories and be around adults who take morality seriously.

When the *Book of Virtues* appeared, it became an immediate best-seller, despite its length of almost nine hundred pages. The stories and poems—many written by some of the greatest writers of history—caught the attention of parents, teachers, young people, and child psychiatrists like Robert Coles. He concluded that the stories would be "of enormous help" in filling "an aching void in this secular society."[11] The book was intended as a moral point of reference that would help to anchor children and adults in their culture, their history, their traditions, and their ideals. The book's success showed that even in our super-busy age, character still matters to many people.

Character refers to the principles and values—Bennett calls them virtues—that govern our lives for most of our waking hours. Obituary notices describe the things we've accomplished, but the people who know us best look past our achievements and see what we really are like as people. What character traits permeate our lives and radiate from all we say and do?

Julie and I have a little motto on our refrigerator: "What you are is God's gift to you. What you become is your gift to God." We all bring traits and predispositions that are based on our genes, but what we become is determined by the moral decisions we make every day of our lives. Will we be

honest, fair, caring, willing to listen, persistent, courageous? Will our lives be dominated by ambition, cynicism,
worry, insensitivity, self-promotion? You and I might not
write a volume like *Book of Virtues,* but we are involved in
something more significant. We are each writing our own
book of virtues. By the decisions we make and the values
we embrace, we are writing our life stories with the characteristics that will form the core of our being and that will be
read by others.

Whom Do You Please?

I thought about this question recently when I picked up a
special section of the big-city newspaper that comes to my
house every day. My eye caught the lead story with its foot-
high photograph of a singer-songwriter who apparently is an
up-and-coming star. The article began with these words in
bold print: Pleasing herself is the key to offbeat singer's
success.

Accepted at the Peabody Conservatory in Baltimore when
the singer was only five years old, she resisted the training
from the beginning. She did not like classical music, didn't
want to read music, and resisted doing what her teachers
expected. At age eleven she was kicked out of school, apparently for disciplinary problems, but she went on to become a
musical success whose concerts are selling out all over the
country.

The singer has a motto: "If it's too loud, turn it up." She
likes to push the boundaries and to forget about keeping
other people happy. "I gave up trying to please others and
started playing for myself," the singer said in the article.
"Things naturally happened then." Her career soared.[12]

This story conveyed an interesting message to me and probably to its young readers. If you want to be successful, please yourself. Resist discipline. Don't pay attention to adults, especially teachers. Do what you want, and then wonderful things will happen—naturally.

I can appreciate the singer's independent streak. Many of the people who make the greatest impact in this world are those who take risks and are willing to challenge the status quo. But a please-yourself, resist-authority, dump-discipline, snub-teachers approach to life usually backfires. Live a life built on self-indulgence and self-satisfaction, and you are likely to self-destruct. Take it from Mickey Mantle. Better still, read through the Old Testament books of Psalms and Proverbs.

In preparation for a major convention about the state of the family, I spent almost a year reading books and articles about family relationships, family strengths, and family problems. As the weeks passed, I began to see some trends and reach some overall conclusions. One of these surprised me: the families that were strong were not focused on themselves. Of course, they tried to do things together, and the members of healthy families didn't ignore or snub each other. But they learned to work together, to give to one another, to express appreciation, and to reach out to others. The children in these families were learning about good character by seeing it demonstrated, especially in their parents, and by being part of efforts to put character into action. When the kids from these families get into hectic work environments in years to come, they are likely to handle the pressures better because, at the core of their lives, they are guided more by their character than by their clocks.

Character in Leaders

When fifteen hundred busy managers were asked to select the traits that were crucial to leadership, *competence* ranked high on the list. Good business leaders, according to the survey, are people who show competence, efficiency, and the ability to get things done. We admire, vote for, and follow leaders who are inspiring, decisive, and confident.[13]

According to the survey results, however, another characteristic is admired even more than competence. At the top of the list came *integrity*. In business, politics, religion, and education, we want leaders who are truthful, trustworthy, dependable, and willing to stand up for their convictions. Lists of virtues can be long and seemingly endless, but most of these can be grouped under the one overarching trait that we most admire in others and most need in ourselves. To rise above our breathless circumstances and have lives that are well lived, we need to be people of integrity.

INTEGRITY: THE CORE OF A LIFE WELL LIVED

Stop reading for a minute and ask yourself these questions: Who are the heroes in your life? Who has inspired you, shown what it means to have a well-lived life, been a model whose words or lifestyle urged you to try greater things than you might ever have attempted otherwise?

You might think of a relative, a teacher, somebody in your church or community. I suspect, however, that for many of us there are no heroes, at least not now. Maybe we have some Bible heroes and historical figures who infuse us with admiration and even motivate us toward greatness, but there are few modern giants who fill us with admiration and determination. Many people who appear on popularity lists—sports figures, entertainers, politicians, military commanders, people of achievement, or those who have done something admirable or overcome great odds—find that their popularity fades almost as quickly as it appeared. Only a few persist over time, and often these are prominent religious figures. Mother Teresa still makes most of the "admired-people" lists, and so do Martin Luther King, Jr., Pope John Paul, and Billy Graham.

These people have been respected for their integrity. They didn't hedge on the truth, waver in their commitments, or vacillate in their values. Most were not rigid, refusing to engage in debate or unwilling to hear criticism. But they knew what they believed, and they showed the courage to stand firm and keep their commitments and their convictions in the midst of disapproval, protest, challenge, or risk.

Many years ago I asked Billy Graham's son-in-law to tell me about his famous relative. The answer was so concise that it has never left my mind. "Mr. Graham decides what is right, then he does it."

When Yale professor Stephen Carter published a whole book about integrity, his definition was almost identical to the description of Billy Graham. Integrity requires three steps, according to Carter.[14] First, integrity requires that we need to be *discerning* about what is right and what is wrong. This takes time, emotional energy, and courage to do the work of soul-searching to clarify our values. For Christians, this discernment involves knowing the Scriptures and learning from others who are mature and established in the faith.

Second, integrity involves *acting* according to our beliefs, even if this involves great personal cost. Third, integrity means *saying openly* and honestly why we are speaking or behaving in the way we do. This step can be difficult because openness invites criticism and adverse publicity when most of us prefer to be approved of and accepted.

The opposite of integrity, according to Carter, is corruption—getting away with things we know are wrong and lacking the courage to stand up for what is right.[15] In contrast, the person of integrity has a serenity and self-assured confidence in the knowledge that he or she is living rightly. This is the kind of confidence that Jesus showed repeatedly.

One of the greatest enemies of integrity is a lack of time. Many of us are too busy to think about moral questions; we find it easier and quicker to go with our instincts, follow some persuasive leader, or move with the crowd. When there is no time to think about right and wrong, we don't arrive at clear standards for living. Without standards we can't act with integrity. Carter concludes that the lack of time undermines our morality and hurts our families. Simply put, "If we do not have time to stop and think about right and wrong . . . we do not have time for lives of integrity."[16]

Standing Firm for the Truth
In an earlier chapter I described a rally in Poland, where I was asked to speak before a concert by a popular singer named Tomasz Żółtko. One year later, after I started work on this book, I returned to Europe and spent almost a week at a conference that Tomasz and his wife also attended. Unlike my first visit, when our paths had crossed briefly, this time Tomasz and I were able to talk.

From a mutual friend, I discovered that the singer's fame had plummeted while I was gone. Tomasz had written and performed songs for a new album that was expected to expand his already impressive impact. It was powerful music with captivating, sometimes penetrating lyrics that drew enthusiastic applause from his audiences.

But after Tomasz made a few references to his Christian faith in the lyrics, his producer announced one day that these words would have to be toned down before the album could be produced. Tomasz refused. To compromise would have meant a loss of integrity. Instead, he stood for what he believed and gave away his number one ranking on the Polish hit parade. The acclaim faded quickly; so did the invitations for concerts and, I suspect, the income.

Through an interpreter (Tomasz does not speak English), we talked about achieving success, getting ahead in the world, and learning to live with disappointment. He had the courage to stay with his convictions, and he is paying the price of integrity.[17]

Jesus tells us to toss away the world's book of values—the emphasis on greed, selfishness, hatred, and compromise. In a book written several years ago, Bill Hybels warned about the danger of human applause and stressed the importance of making people, not things, our priority. He warned about wasting the lives God has given us in trivial pursuits: "I have only one chance to live, and I want to make it count," Hybels said.[18] Tomasz would agree, and so do I.

Keeping Our Lives on Track

A wise older pastor once talked with a young seminary student about the dangers of ministry. "It has been my observation that just one out of ten who start out in full-time service for the Lord when they are age twenty-one are still on track by the age of sixty-five," the pastor said. "They're shot down morally. They're shot down with discouragement. They're shot down with liberal theology. They get obsessed with making money. But for one reason or another nine out of ten fall out."

The seminarian, twenty-one years old at the time, was shocked.

He went home, turned to a blank page in the back of his Bible, and listed the names of twenty-four young people who were his peers, preparing for ministry. These were enthusiastic and deeply committed believers, burning in their desire to be used by God, overflowing with potential. Today, a little more than thirty years later, only three of those people are still serving. The rest have left their places of ministry—just as the older pastor had predicted.[19]

When I read that story, I was shocked. I pulled out a little card, wrote down the names of thirty people whom I know well, and taped the list near the screen on my computer. Some of the people on my list are pastors; some are involved in nonpastoral ministries. Others are counselors, teachers, and people who work in the secular world. I pray for them by name almost every day. I know how easy it is to run out of energy, be tempted by immorality, face intimidation from critics, or get bogged down in discouragement. When we see our careers and ministries growing, it is easy to get distracted by the crowds, enamored by our own capabilities, distracted by the sweet smell of success, and inclined to pursue fame and riches. The history of Christianity is filled with people who allowed success and stardom to erode their intimacy with Christ. When life is moving quickly, we can forget that we are serving Christ. We can allow ourselves to be overwhelmed with work and busyness, so that we fail to get needed rest and spiritual rejuvenation. My computer list has been taped up for only a couple of years, and all the people are running strong. I pray that none of them will leave the ministry and that all will look back someday on lives of integrity, lives that were well lived.[20]

Finishing Strong
The apostle Paul could look back on his life and conclude that he had kept the faith and had finished the race without stumbling.[21] He didn't get there by luck. He lived his life with an awareness of the dangers of falling. He was diligent in watching his own life lest he preach to others and then stumble himself.[22]

In busy times like ours, how do we build character, maintain integrity, and live according to biblically based values? Much of the Bible gives guidelines for a life well lived, but the topic gets special attention in one of Paul's letters to his younger protégé, Timothy.

1. Train yourself to be godly.[23] The culture in which Timothy lived was steeped in strange teachings that were promoted by persuasive leaders and embraced by uninformed or easily impressed followers. The situation is not much different today.

Paul's instructions to Timothy are equally effective for us. Avoid all of those "godless myths and old wives' tales," Paul wrote, and focus on what you know to be good teaching. Paul told Timothy to be thankful for what God had given, to be discerning in a culture of false teaching, and to be dependent on the living God, who is the source of our hope.

Just as athletes follow diligent training programs to build and strengthen their bodies, we must be diligent in building our spiritual lives. That is a tough assignment for busy people. Who of us takes enough time to pray, read the Bible, participate in corporate worship, spend time in quiet reflection, or serve the Lord in compassionate ministries? Many Christians want to be godly, but they allow their time to be gobbled up with so many other things.

What would it take for you to set up a spiritual training program? Start by setting realistic goals for yourself. Maybe you can carve out fifteen or twenty minutes from a schedule that feels very tight. Then find an accountability partner, somebody who will hold you responsible for your spiritual training program.

2. Set an example for believers.[24] Timothy was a young teacher who might have been discounted by some people because of his youth. Paul dealt with this in one powerful sentence of his letter: "Don't let anyone look down on you because you are young."[25] Young people need encouragement to build lives that are well lived; they don't need condescension, ridicule, or indifference from people who are too busy or disinterested to invest in the next generation.

At every age, a well-lived life involves admirable behavior that others can see. Even when our lives are busy, we can set an example for people—including our children—in the way we talk, live, love, express our faith, and keep our minds and bodies pure.

3. Do not neglect your gift.[26] Long before Paul wrote his letter, apparently the church leaders had held a commissioning ceremony in which they put their hands on Timothy and prayed for his ministry. In the process he must have discovered the areas of expertise that God had given him for the purpose of strengthening the church.

I have never had this kind of ceremony, and maybe you haven't either, but I know that every believer has been given special gifts.[27] These are divinely bestowed abilities that come to each of us for the purpose of building up the church. The gifts include encouragement, hospitality, giving, administration, leadership, healing, evangelism, teaching, and preaching. Probably you know already what gifts God has given to you. If not, ask him to show you, and talk it over with a few people who know you well. They will have spotted what you do best, and their observations will have relevance to how you live.

I know people who are gifted in one area but are trying desperately to succeed in some other. When life is busy and time is limited, it makes sense to focus on what you do best. If you are a gifted administrator but a not-so-gifted public speaker, then focus your time and attention on some aspect of administration, and don't try to be a teacher or an evangelist.

4. Watch your life and doctrine closely.[28] This statement summarizes not only Paul's guidelines for Timothy but also the message of this chapter. Keep an eye on what you do and what you believe. If you are able to maintain integrity between what you believe and what you do, there will be two results. First, others who might be watching you will see a consistent life that is free of hypocrisy. Second, you are more likely to have a life that is well lived, even if you are pressured by time constraints.

THE REST OF THE STORY

A few weeks before Mickey Mantle died, he met with a group of reporters who asked if he had wasted his talent. "God gave me a body and an ability to play baseball," he said. "God gave me everything and I just . . ." He stopped in midsentence and gestured as if he had thrown everything away. Despite his career achievements, Mickey Mantle's life had not been well lived.

But Mickey Mantle finished strong. He allowed a former teammate to talk with him about Jesus Christ and about the message of forgiveness. Mantle confessed his sinful lifestyle, accepted God's forgiveness, and became a new man. When he was asked why God would ever let someone like him into heaven, he smiled and gave an answer. "I'll just say, 'For God so loved the world that he gave his one and only Son, that whoever believes in him shall not perish but have eternal life.' I am trusting Christ's death to take me to heaven."[29]

The great baseball player had only a few weeks to live, and his formerly robust body was weak and emaciated. Nevertheless he announced that he was "going to start giving something back" and vowed to spend the rest of his life trying to "make it up" to the people whom he had disappointed. He apologized to the young people of America, established a foundation for organ donations, and demonstrated genuine integrity.[30]

Mickey Mantle showed that despite failures and stumbling, any of us can finish life on a strong note, even if our lives to this point have not been well lived. It is never too late to pick up and start over.

TAKING A STEP TOWARD
Strengthening Your Character

As you reflect on this chapter, take some time to answer these questions. You may want to do that in a journal, with a

friend, or in a group. Allow the questions to help you focus on how you will live a life that strengthens character and maintains integrity.

1. In what ways are you concentrating more on competence than character?
2. What are the character traits your family sees in you? What are the character traits your friends see in you? What are the character traits your co-workers or church members see in you?
3. What character traits would you like to have people see in you?
4. How does your integrity express itself in your life?
5. Of the three aspects of integrity Stephen Carter mentions in his book (discerning what is right and wrong; acting according to our beliefs; and saying openly why we do what we do), which is the hardest for you? What steps can you take to work on that area?
6. When it is hard for you to stand firmly for something you believe in, to whom can you look for help?
7. What can you do to make sure that you keep your life on track? Whom can you ask to help you in that task?
8. What person can *you* help to stay on track—a family member, a friend, a co-worker, a church member?

CHAPTER 6

Balance
Keeping Your
Life Equilibrium

SOMEBODY ONCE sent me a greeting card showing a perplexed-looking cartoon character standing next to a sign with these words: "God put me on earth to accomplish a certain number of things. Right now I'm so far behind, I will never die." I can relate to this statement, and maybe you can too. It is easy to get so far behind that we feel as if we'll never catch up and get our lives in balance.

For years I've been hearing about balance. Everybody knows that we need a healthy mix of work, leisure, love, and learning if we're going to have physical and psychological health. I've even talked about this in seminars and watched all the people in my audiences nod in agreement.

Talking about balance is easy. But finding balance in our lives is hard. It isn't easy juggling all the things that comprise and clutter our modern lives. Like a circus performer who can't get distracted, even for a minute, lest one of the juggled objects fall to the sawdust floor, I feel sometimes that my attention must stay riveted on the cascading demands that keep my life lively and exciting. Those of us who live like jugglers often are surrounded by other jugglers; we can't let down because we're all afraid of "dropping the ball." We are jugglers who are too busy to help each other, and we can't seem to slow the pace and stop performing.

The *Wall Street Journal* recently described a program for busy executives who pay up to a thousand dollars a day for help in slowing down and getting their lives back into balance.[1] Many people who enroll in this program offered at the Menninger Clinic in Kansas have become so busy and so driven that they don't know how to step back and reduce the pace of their high-strung lives. They come to Kansas controlled by their careers and calendars. There, far away from offices and daily demands, they are forced to stop, talk about the pressures, share with others who have similar struggles, think about the never-ending demands in their lopsided lives, and find ways to bring equilibrium into their lives.

This may be wonderful therapy for those who can pay for it or for people whose companies can pick up the bill. But what about the rest of us? Without spending thousands of dollars and time in a clinic, how can we have balanced, well-lived lives that are not pulled in a multitude of directions or dominated by juggling priorities?

TWO STARTING POINTS

We must recognize, first, that *balance—the right mix of work, family, worship, relaxation, and other parts of life—varies from person to person and depends on one's stage in life.* When I was a graduate student, I was young, energetic, and single. I also was living hundreds of miles from my family and was able to focus solely on completing my degree. Working twelve or fourteen hours a day was normal and invigorating for me. I tried to get rest and exercise. I taught a Sunday school class and fit in time for worship. On Sundays I sometimes squeezed in time for recreation. Even so, the academic program ruled my life. Family time was not an issue in those days because I had no family; completing my education with a minimum of expense and delay was a high priority.

Was my life out of balance? Absolutely. Was this unhealthy? Probably not, because it was temporary and because I did not let this one part of my life so dominate me that other parts—my spiritual life, for example—were neglected or destroyed. It wouldn't be healthy to continue an all-consuming study routine for the rest of my life. But for a few years maybe it was all right to let one passion (getting that degree) dominate my time. Later, when I got the diploma, my time allotments changed and I had more room in my life for other things. I turned my attention to finding a wife.

Young couples have a similar lack of balance when they first become parents. A newborn baby dominates all of life, quickly throwing everything out of balance. If that child cries all night or gets sick, everything else is pushed aside until the emergency passes. As the children grow up, the parents are freer to give increased attention to other things. When our kids were small, we felt it was important for me to turn down weekend speaking engagements and stay home with the family on Sundays. Now that our children are adults, I am more able to travel, and my wife can go with me.

At times we all find ourselves at seasons in life when

balance may not be possible or desirable. Because of these variables, none of us can dictate what healthy balance will be like for somebody else. And none of us can pin down a concise definition of a balanced life. For most of us, living involves a continual juggling act, and healthy balance is an ever-changing, moving target.

This leads to a second starting point: *we need to acknowledge that, for most of us, balance is not an ideal state of equilibrium that can be reached and kept the same forever.* Even when our days are organized meticulously, unanticipated crises and life events can throw us off balance, hijack our time, hit us with new demands, and pull us in directions that we were not anticipating. It is then that we need to make corrections, dropping some things and adding others to bring a return to equilibrium. Some people have to do less of this because they have fewer life disruptions than others. If your life is not bombarded by many changes and interruptions, it is easier to keep balance. Others, probably including many of the people who read this book, find that life-altering influences come frequently, so the challenge to maintain balance is more of an issue. For all of us, however, balance is always something to pursue. Realigning life when it gets out of balance is a continual process.[2]

The balancing process involves at least three parts: our *attitudes, boundaries,* and *cushions.* These are the ABCs of balance.

BALANCING ATTITUDES

Angel Wallenda died recently. I might have missed the death notice had my eye not caught the six-word obituary following her name: *performed with famous high-wire family.*

The Flying Wallendas had few equals during the years
that they dominated the circus world. They were known for
their ability to walk on wires strung between skyscrapers,
over canyons, and between speeding cars. For generations,
children born into the Wallenda family learned the balancing
skills of walking on wires almost as soon as they could walk
on the ground. When "Karl the Great," modern-day patriarch
of the Wallendas, fell to his death from a cable strung
between two Puerto Rican hotels in 1978, the celebrated
family of aerialists continued with the show, living by their
family motto: "Life is on the wire. The rest is just waiting."

Elizabeth Pintye was just waiting for the show to begin one
day when a handsome young Steve Wallenda picked her
from the crowd and invited her to assist in his performance.
Weeks later, she became Angel Wallenda and joined her
new husband on the high wire. But their career together was
short. Two years after the wedding, she was diagnosed with
bone cancer, and her right leg was amputated below the
knee. With show-business determination she relearned to
walk the wire, inching along on her one good leg and an artificial limb. Soon, however, the cancer spread to her lungs,
and doctors found it inoperable. No longer able to support
the thirty-five-foot balancing pole, she was forced to quit
after a final performance in 1990.

Steve Wallenda could balance his body to walk across
wires strung at dizzying heights. But he was unable to balance the stresses of his life when the progressing illness of
his wife scuttled their careers and disrupted their future
plans. Wallenda became abusive and tried to hang himself
while imprisoned on charges of violating a restraining order

that had been issued to protect his ailing wife. When she died, Angel was only twenty-eight.[3]

Quality and Character

Shortly after I read the story of Angel Wallenda, I came across a statement from Samuel Brengle, a Salvation Army revival preacher who was popular early in this century. In words that could apply equally to males or females, Brengle concluded that in the end, "History cares not an iota for the rank or title a man has borne, or the office he has held earlier in this century, but only the quality of his deeds and the character of his mind and heart." The Wallendas were remembered for their performing abilities and high-wire balancing acts, but we don't hear much about the quality of their lives, the character of their minds and hearts, or how they balanced their emotions and attitudes. In the end, those were the things that really counted.

In our chaotic times of global competition, fast-changing technology, virtual reality, and downsizing corporations, we have come to place a high value on performance, flexibility, innovation, competence, and life balance. Buffeted by change and demands for our time, many of us strive for a sense of stability, and forget that in God's eyes and in the light of eternity, "character of . . . mind and heart" is infinitely more important.

I have struggled to remember this for much of my life and have seen similar struggles in many of my friends. We really want to be servants, to live balanced lives, but we get distracted by a strong urge to be successful. We know that God values faithfulness and humility, but our careers are driven by some inner compulsion to be acclaimed, influential, and

financially secure. We want our lives to honor God, but our
actions suggest that we are more ego-driven and committed
to getting recognition and honor for ourselves. These struggles sound like a modern version of the inner turmoil that
Paul described in Romans 7:15-24; he knew what was right
to do, but he had such a hard time doing it.

Some time ago I wrote a list of attitudes that God clearly
wants in any life, in contrast to attitudes that naturally and
too often drive my behavior.[4] I've learned that I can't change
the natural inclinations on my own. If my life is to be balanced, I need God's help to genuinely want these things:

faithfulness	*rather than*	fame
humility	*rather than*	honors
sincerity	*rather than*	success
gratitude	*rather than*	glory
servanthood	*rather than*	self-service
vision	*rather than*	visibility
passion	*rather than*	popularity

I must be

focused	*rather than*	fractured
deliberate	*rather than*	driven
accountable	*rather than*	autonomous
generous	*rather than*	greedy
content	*rather than*	complaining

It is easy to focus on the items that appear on the right side of
this list. Many of these—fame, honors, success, popularity—
are goals that attract people to success-building and time-
management seminars. I have noticed that when we focus on

99

the items on the right side of the list, the attitudes on the left rarely appear in our lives. When we seek to develop the features on the left, however, the items on the right sometimes appear, but we are not greatly concerned about whether or not they come. When we push to be famous, for example, faithfulness rarely follows as a basic life attitude. When we determine to be faithful, however, fame sometimes comes, but whether or not this happens does not really matter.

As Christians we will not find balance unless we start with our core attitudes. Most often we drift to the right column on the list. Some of what we find there—a desire for visibility or autonomy, for example—is not innately wrong, but these might be considered "natural desires" that distract us from what God wants for our lives. Only he can work within to revolutionize my thinking, desires, and attitudes so that items like those on the left of the list become ingrained as a part of my being, just as they were ingrained in Jesus' life. "Those who live in accordance with the Spirit have their minds set on what the Spirit desires," the Bible states.[5] When the mind is controlled by the Spirit, our attitudes are different from what they would be otherwise, and we are less inclined to be torn by competing pressures and divisive demands for our time. We experience inner peace, and life is more balanced and well lived.

BALANCING BOUNDARIES

A second area in which we need balance is in setting boundaries. When I was growing up in southern Ontario, our family would occasionally take an afternoon drive across the border into the United States. Getting from one country to the other was easy in those days. We pulled up to the immigration officer, answered a couple of questions, and drove on.

Years later, when I had a family of my own, we traveled from Vienna to Prague and had to cross the Czech border. This was at the height of Communism, and border crossings were a lot different from what I had experienced as a child living in Canada. The Communist border guards all had rifles. They searched our car, our luggage, our clothes. They used mirrors to look under the car for hidden contraband, and they questioned us without any hint of friendliness. It was easy to understand why the tourist industry didn't thrive in those days.

Borders between countries, like boundary lines between the yards of neighbors, can be either easy to cross or protected by high fences. Some boundaries are clearly marked. Others are like the property lines in the neighborhood where I live—fences are illegal and most of us aren't sure where one person's property ends and another's begins, but nobody is concerned about it. In other places, people argue or even go to war about borders—especially about disputed borders.

Like countries and neighborhood property, each of our lives has boundaries. My skin is a boundary between what's inside of me and what's outside. The walls of my house serve as a boundary between the private space where my family lives and the rest of the community. My telephone can be a flexible boundary that lets me open myself to the world or shut myself off from any except the people whose voices get past the screening of my answering machine. Whether or not we have balance in our lives depends, to a large extent, on what we do with the boundaries of our lives.

Divine Boundaries

Jesus had clear boundaries in his life. Perhaps they even were put there by the Father, who gave Jesus only three years for his public ministry. If Jesus had started early, maybe as a teenage prodigy at the age of fourteen, and continued until he died at age thirty-three, Jesus would have had nineteen years to do his work rather than only three. Or, God could have chosen to have Jesus start a public ministry at age thirty but then be active until he was sixty-five, netting thirty-five years of time to get his message across to a dull and stubborn humanity. Our contemporary culture would have understood those choices because we feel a need to optimize every possible moment. But God didn't make those choices. He set boundaries. And he was content with them.

Jesus also set boundaries on himself. When the disciples came to his solitary place, they probably assumed he would return with them to the crowd that was waiting expectantly. To their surprise he said no and indicated that he planned to "go somewhere else." Because he had boundaries, he did not meet, touch, heal, or teach every person living on the earth during his three years. He did not feel the pressure to do everything or to have all the loose ends tied up before he died. While he was a young carpenter, a small-group leader to the Twelve, a teacher, a family member, and a Son to his Father, apparently he did not feel any pressure to be a lawyer, to be a city leader, or to play any role other than what his Father told him to do. Because he had clear boundaries and was content within these boundaries, he did not let the enthusiasm of the disciples or the demands of the crowds overrun his life.

In our lives today, we need boundaries that are clear, respected, and controlled.

Clear Boundaries

To maintain balance, we need clear boundaries in our speech, our thinking, and our behavior. *In our speech,* for example, my wife and I can talk freely to each other about sex or finances. We have no boundary between us to stop discussions about these or any other issues, however private or sensitive. But as a couple we have a boundary that says "nobody else talks to us about these personal issues." If we were to see a counselor, we might let that person cross this boundary and come into our lives verbally to discuss some personal issues, but only with our permission and only temporarily. In turn, I do not have the freedom or permission to cross your personal boundaries and ask about the details of your sex life or your money management.

Many lives get out of balance because we don't have clear boundaries in what we talk about and with whom. Some of the worst and most titillating television involves talk that sweeps past personal boundaries and leaves talk-show guests exposed and vulnerable before an audience of millions. When they walk away from the studio, these verbally abused victims of voyeurism are left on their own to reestablish the boundaries that have been violated so publicly. Careless speech that lures out secrets or destroys personal privacy can create chaos and lead to a multitude of moral, emotional, and other problems.

In addition to boundaries in our speech, we also need clear boundary limitations *in our thinking*. It is difficult to put a fence around a mind, but it can be done. To start, we need to monitor what comes into our minds. How can we expect to think about things that are noble, pure, excellent, praiseworthy, and admirable if we open our minds to sexually explicit films or novels, media violence, or perversity in soap operas and talk shows? Jesus clearly believed that what we think on the inside is what we really are like—even if our outward actions are pious and beyond criticism. Of course, sinful ideas pop into our minds without warning. That does not surprise us. But the biblical instruction to guard our hearts surely involves shifting our thinking away from invading thoughts, replacing them with more noble ideas so that we don't dwell on the mental immorality that nobody else sees or knows about.[6]

Impure, hypercritical, bitter, envious, and judgmental thoughts can churn up the mind in the same way a plow breaks open the soil in a pasture. Later, when seeds of opportunity come our way, they are more likely to take root and grow into unhealthy and unwholesome behavior when the mental soil has been prepared—especially when it has been plowed repeatedly. Mental boundaries keep out—or kick out—the invasive, sometimes enticing ideas that steal across the unprotected borders of our minds and force their way in. The Holy Spirit, living in the Christian and guarding his or her mind, keeps these ideas at bay when we are serious about keeping them out.

Along with speech and mental boundaries, the life well lived has boundaries *in behavior*. Recently I was invited to serve on a church board in a position that would have been of great interest to me. But it did not take me long to say no. When I am as busy as I am and when I travel as much as I do, I have to set some boundaries on what more I let into my life. Serving on boards or church committees, volunteering to work with a community youth program, or joining a reading

group at the library can all be worthwhile and enjoyable. But
I have some self-imposed boundaries that keep me from getting involved in these activities. By saying no to these, I can
participate in other things that I want to do more.

Your boundaries, of course, will be different from mine.
But you and I need to realize that without boundaries, our
lives are invaded by interruptions and voices. Many of these
are from sincere people with good intentions, but they can
clamor for our attention, pressure us for compliance, and
encourage us to "cave in" so we agree to another commitment. Before long, we are running from one activity to
another. If we do not put boundaries in place, we will allow
our lives to be pulled further out of balance.

You may not struggle with invitations to join committees
or library reading groups, but you have other pressures that
will overwhelm your schedule if you don't decide where to
draw the line and say no. If you have trouble drawing boundary lines (many of us do), find some supportive friends who
will help you. At the urgings of some friends, for example, I
got an unlisted telephone number, because I do not want to
open my life to calls from strangers when I am home. That is
a clear boundary.

Respected Boundaries
Our boundaries must be not only clear but also respected. In
my appointment book, I have written the home telephone
numbers of several people who have given me their numbers
and urged me to call them at home if necessary. I rarely do
so because I want to respect their privacy when they are
away from work.

When we respect the boundaries in other people's lives,

they in turn are more likely to respect our boundaries. As a result, all of our lives are more balanced. If I invite people to participate in a project and they turn me down, I try to respect their right to say no. This is a way of respecting the boundaries of others. I also try to respect the fact that other people have boundaries that are different from mine.

For many years, I taught counseling to graduate students. These courses always urged counselors to have clear boundaries in their own lives and to respect the boundaries in the lives of their clients. If clients can phone their counselors at any hour of the day or night, have visits in each others' homes at will, exchange gifts, or socialize together, then the counselor-client boundaries have broken down and the counseling is likely to be less effective. In counseling, as in life, boundaries are to be clear and respected. They also need to be controlled.

Controlled Boundaries

Boundaries are useless if they are ignored or so fuzzy that they can't be seen. Some people's boundaries are so flexible and permeable that anybody can come in to make demands. As a result, balance is impossible. Others have boundaries that are so firm and so rigid that they are constrictive and lead to lives that never grow or allow the entrance of new ideas or challenges.

Jesus was able to strike a balance between boundaries that are too flexible and those that are too firm. The disciples were surprised, for example, to see that Jesus sometimes crossed boundaries that they would not have expected him to cross. Once they found him talking with a Samaritan woman at a time when Jewish men didn't talk to Samaritans or to women, especially about marriage and spiritual issues.[7] Apparently he chose consciously to overstep a cultural boundary for the special purpose of ministering to this woman. At other times Jesus challenged the boundaries of people like the religious leaders who remained aloof, self-righteous, and impervious to anything that Jesus would say.[8] They had put such rigid boundaries around their minds that they weren't even open to learning from the Scriptures.[9] When we have too few or no boundaries, we can be overwhelmed by the pressures of life and the demands of others.

Parents often walk this fine line. If we don't put some limits on our children and on our time, we can become like full-time servants, perpetually subject to interruptions, expected to do whatever we are asked to do. Teenage family members might need to learn, for example, that they don't walk into their parents' bedroom without knocking, don't open other family members' mail, or don't take the car without asking. But boundaries like these cannot be overly rigid. We must be flexible enough not to pounce on our children if on occasion they burst into our bedrooms or open a piece of mail without asking us, or use the car for a short errand without checking with us first. When there is mutual trust and respect, we can form boundaries that are firm without being rigid.

In one of the apostle Paul's epistles, he quoted from a Greek poet who wrote that bad company corrupts good character.[10] Stated differently, we could say that without boundaries separating us from people of bad character, our lives will be affected adversely. We all have the responsibility for determining and controlling the boundaries of our lives. If we fail to do so, we can't have balance, and we'll never have lives that are well lived.

BALANCING CUSHIONS

Physician Richard Swenson thinks we've all got a problem that is inescapable. In one form or another, it happens almost daily to nearly every one of us. Swenson calls it the problem of *overload*.[11]

Overload

Think about it. We have a cultural tendency to keep adding things to our lives: one more project, one more charge on the credit card, one more appointment on the calendar, one more commitment at church. Each of these additions can be energizing, and each is doable. Sooner or later, however, we realize that these additions to our lives have piled up and are weighing us down with what Swenson calls the *overload syndrome*. Swenson has even identified some parts of the overload. Most common are activity overload, commitment overload, debt overload, expectation overload, hurry overload (that comes when we try to do things faster and in less time), competition overload, ministry overload, education overload (seen in people who never stop taking courses), possession overload, and work overload. Our society adds a few others, without our approval and often without our awareness. These include change overload, choice overload (think of this next time you're in the supermarket), pollution overload, information overload, media overload, noise overload, technology overload, traffic overload, junk overload (look in your basement), and even people overload.

Nobody deliberately sets out to overload life. Overload just happens. The progress that characterizes our age consumes more of our time and sweeps us toward increasing stress, complexity, and overload.[12] This overload, in turn, breaks down boundaries. It leads to mental and physical exhaustion. It hurts our spiritual lives because there is no time or energy for prayer and meditation. Overload hinders our relationships and puts strain on our marriages and families. It leaves our energies depleted, but we keep trying to run on empty and wonder why we feel so listless and overwhelmed. And overload breaks down any semblance of balance that we might try to bring into our lives.

Because overload fills our lives to overflowing, we have no "give" in our schedules, not an ounce of extra time, energy, or money. With life filled to the brim, there is no way to cope or adjust when we face an unexpected emergency. Overload is a threat to our goal to have lives that are well lived.

Margins and Cushions
Richard Swenson's prescription for the overloaded life is simple to state and difficult to apply: We need *margin* in our lives—emotional, physical, spiritual, financial, and time reserves that are kept for contingencies or unanticipated situations. Consider money, for example. When every cent of a paycheck is committed to existing bills and when credit-card debts are at their limits, there is nothing available for unexpected expenses. In this situation, a person needs financial guidance so funds can be held as a margin or cushion for unanticipated needs.

To mature spiritually and maintain well-lived lives, we need more margin, suggests Dr. Swenson. The most important of these is emotional margin. "Of the four margins—emotional energy, physical energy, time, and finances—margin in emotional energy is paramount. When we are emotionally resilient, we can confront our problems with a sense of hope and power. When our emotional reserves are depleted, however, we are seriously weakened. Emotional overload saps our strength, paralyzes our resolve, and maximizes our vulnerability, leaving the door open for further margin erosion."[13]

If you feel overloaded, you have all the needed evidence to show that you have not kept margins in your life, despite all your best intentions. Recently I attended a seminar intended to help us set margins and reduce overload. The speaker gave a list of helpful suggestions, including these:

- Plan ahead; don't wait until the last minute to do what needs to be done.
- Set realistic expectations; don't overbook by scheduling more than you possibly can do.
- Find some people who will help you to keep focused and avoid distractions.
- Work with your physical rhythms. If you are a morning person, for example, schedule the most demanding tasks for early in the day when you are most alert.
- Work to build routine in your life, including small things like eating meals on schedule, going to bed at the same time each night, disciplining yourself for exercise. If every day is different, life is likely to be less organized and more overloaded.

Despite helpful lists like these, there are no never-fail formulas for bringing margin into overloaded lives. It will take your time, energy, creativity, and determination, along with the help of caring friends, to restore the cushion or to bring it into your life for the first time.

We all need to be nourished. We need nourishing families, friendships, churches, and communities. We need human contact, support, people to give us encouragement, opportunities to serve others, and friends to hold us accountable. We need other people to remind us to rest, tighten up our boundaries, build attachments, and work to restore margin in our overbooked lives.

Restoring Margin

When I was in the midst of writing this chapter, I had breakfast one morning with a young church leader. At one point in our conversation, he mentioned that I looked fatigued. We talked about why I needed more rest and the importance of vacations. This Christian brother challenged me to take better care of myself and urged me to build physical margin in my life— exactly what I was urging others to do but forgetting in myself.

My friend's comment about rest points to the most obvious place to build margin. We need to give ourselves permission to take time off, get more rest, watch our diets, get exercise, and do the other healthy things that we tend to ignore. Other people can encourage us to do these things, but we are the only ones who can take care of our own bodies. If we refuse to take this responsibility, we can forget about margins, cushions, balance, and well-lived lives.

In addition to the physical margin, we also need financial cushions. These come when we learn to decrease spending, resist impulses to add debt, change attitudes about possessions, increase income if possible, and develop a giving mind-set. Competent financial planners can help us look at our financially overloaded lives and make the necessary changes.

Time cushions are tougher to put in place. "Timesaving" technologies like cellular phones, fax machines, E-mail, and conference calls rarely give us the additional free time that they promise. It is difficult to find more time margin when we live in a society where, in a lifetime, the average American will

- spend six months sitting at traffic lights waiting for them to change;
- spend one whole year searching through desk clutter looking for misplaced objects;
- spend eight months opening junk mail (not including the disposal of junk mail on the fax machine and E-mail mailbox; on average we receive six hundred advertising messages every day from television, newspapers, radio, billboards, and magazines);
- spend two years trying to call people who aren't in or whose lines are busy;
- spend three years in meetings;
- be interrupted an average of seventy-three times every day.[14]

Articles and seminars that tell us how to reduce the time pressures in our overloaded lives sometimes make useful suggestions. They tell us to learn to say no (that involves firm boundaries), schedule buffer time into the calendar, unplug from some of the time technology like cellular phones or beepers, develop the mind-set that says interruptions are all right, ask God to remind us that each of us has all the time we need to do all that God wants us to do. When you do take a break, try not to think about the time you are losing or the things that you could be doing if you weren't trying to relax.

Earlier we suggested that time management is a misnomer; nobody can manage time. It keeps moving at a consistent rate no matter what any of us does. What we manage is ourselves—our own attitudes, boundaries, and cushions.

THE IMPOSSIBLE DREAM?

You won't find these listed as mental disorders in any psychiatric textbook, but a lot of us seem to suffer from problems with "overwork intoxication," "time trauma," "downsizing terror disorder," or "balance despair." We look at our lives and conclude that we'll always be pressured, always overloaded, never able to achieve the seemingly impossible dream of living with balance.

Don't believe it.

Events beyond our control will always demand our attention. We will all have times of feeling pressured with too much to do, strapped for funds, emotionally depleted, and drained of energy. Even the most dedicated Christians have spiritually dry spells, struggles with temptation, and disappointment with God. These may throw us off balance, but we don't need to stay off balance.

Whenever I read through the Gospels, I am struck that Jesus never rushed. He came to redeem the whole world, for all of eternity, and he had only three years of ministry time to do it. Even so, he never hurried. He seemed to have enough margin in his life to relax with his friends and to be interrupted without becoming annoyed. He had clear enough boundaries that he knew how to live without being invaded by the crowds that pressed into his life. Most important, he had the right attitudes. He came to do the will of his Father, to please the Father, and to let the Father lead. As a result, Jesus had a life of balance.

Maybe our persisting breathless lifestyles should remind us that we can't reach a healthy level of balance with our own creativity and in our own strength. In a remarkable statement, Jesus told his followers—that includes us—to come to him with our weariness and our burdens and to expect that he would give us rest.[15] He is the sole source of genuine peace in busy times like ours, and ultimately he alone lets us find life balance and the ability to have a life that is well lived.

TAKING A STEP TOWARD
Equilibrium

As you reflect on this chapter, take some time to answer these questions. You may want to do that in a journal, with a friend, or in a group. Allow the questions to help you focus on how you will move toward more balanced living.

1. In what areas of your life do you feel the most balanced right now?
2. In what areas of your life do you feel the most unbalanced right now?
3. Using the list on page 99, point out an attitude (left column) that you would like to develop with the Lord's help. What people might he choose to help you develop this attitude?
4. In what area of your life would you like to establish a new boundary? What action will you take toward making that happen?
5. What areas of your life need more cushion, more margin? What will you do about that? Whose help will you enlist?
6. How can you help your family members or friends maintain balance in their lives?

CHAPTER 7

Purpose
Living a Focused Life

H E CAN STILL remember the details, years after it happened. "I went to my room and closed the door and I cried. For a while I couldn't stop. Even though there was no one else home at the time, I kept the door shut. It was important to me that no one hear me or see me."[1]

He was a teenager at the time, passionate about basketball, determined to earn a place on his high school team. For two weeks every boy in the school knew when the list would go up and the selected players would be announced. If his name was on the list, he had been chosen for the team. If his name didn't appear on the list, he had been cut.

Feeling hope mixed with fear, the young man made his way to the gym and jostled past the other kids to read the list. His name was not there. He wasn't good enough to make the team. All day he hid the disappointment, and when school let out, he rushed home and sobbed.

Weeks later, when the team was going to a tournament, he asked the coach if he could ride on the bus. The coach said no, but the young man persisted and was allowed to go if he would agree to carry the players' uniforms into the arena.

"So that's what I did," he said, years later. "I walked into the building carrying the uniforms for the players who had made the team. What made me feel the worst about that was that my parents had come to watch the tournament, and when they saw me walking in carrying the uniforms, they thought I was being given a chance to play. That's what hurt me. They thought I was being given a chance, but I was just carrying the clothes for the other players."[2]

That young man, Michael Jordan, went on to become the best basketball player in the world, maybe the best who has ever played the game. He is a hero to millions and an inspiration to young people everywhere. His name appears on T-shirts and baseball caps worn by kids all over China, in remote parts of Africa, and in tiny villages of South America. He is known for his persistence, hard work, and genuine concern for school kids who want to be basketball stars. At one time, he wasn't good enough to make the team. But he persisted, moved along by a determination and a life mission that he never abandoned.

In these days when demands seem to pull us in every direction, it is good to think about somebody with a life mission that gives focus and direction. No other person has ever had the determination and life focus that Jesus modeled. He astonished and infuriated the people in Nazareth when he went to the synagogue and announced that he had come for the purpose of fulfilling a prophecy that had been written centuries earlier by the prophet Isaiah.[3] Jesus came to earth to do his Father's will and to preach a message of good news. "I came to preach," he told the demanding disciples. "That is why I have come."[4]

The core of his message was simple. Motivated by love, Jesus came to give us life—abundant life on this earth and eternal life in heaven.[5] When he walked on the earth, he showed us how to have lives that are well lived. When he died on the cross, he took on himself the penalty for sin that should have come to you and me. In so doing he made it possible for anyone who believes in him, anyone who trusts him for forgiveness, to find freedom and a sense of relief that could never be possible without him. His whole life moved toward the Crucifixion, when he would accomplish his purpose. Healing people like Peter's mother-in-law or the man with leprosy were demonstrations of his lordship and further fulfillments of Isaiah's prophecy that he would bind up the brokenhearted, bring freedom to prisoners, and proclaim a message of salvation. But Jesus' ultimate goal—the focus of his life—was to do the Father's will by paying for the sins of the world and making forgiveness and salvation possible for human beings.

After Christ's return to heaven, some of his disciples also had clear life missions. Paul, for example, knew that his goal was to preach to the Gentiles, regardless of any opposition he might encounter. In contrast, Peter, James, and John had the mission of preaching to the Jews.[6] These people knew what they had been called to do. They had clear direction in their lives, unlike many of us who find that bringing life into focus and clarifying a life mission can be a lot like peering into the fog.

117

SEEING THROUGH THE FOG

Some of the world's most beautiful scenery is in South Africa, near Kruger National Park, three or four hours' drive north of Johannesburg. People have described it as a sight that rivals the Grand Canyon in sheer spectacular beauty.

On a recent trip to South Africa, friends showed Julie and me photographs of this area and invited us to view these awesome sights with them. On the morning that we were supposed to hike to the lookout, however, torrential rains poured from the saturated skies. Undaunted, we took umbrellas and went to the viewing spot where thousands have taken pictures and marveled at the beauty of the landscape. All we could see was fog.

I looked at my disappointed South African host, standing in the rain, his spirits drooping. Suddenly I saw him in a new light. "Stop!" I exclaimed to his surprise. "Don't forget this moment." Julie and I could not see what was beyond the mist, but my friend could envision things that were hidden to his visitors. He saw beauty, God's handiwork, inspiration, and a landscape that stretched far into the distance.

Julie and I saw fog. But we also saw a man who is one of the eight or ten true visionaries that I have known. My friend who stood in the mist that morning has a God-given ability to see opportunities, possibilities, and realities that others don't see. Not yet!

If you go to a bookstore or library and skim books about leadership, you will find that almost all of them have at least a chapter or two about vision. Those books tell us that the most effective leaders can evaluate the present reality and see into the future, through the fog. These people are able to share their visions with clarity and enthusiasm, move forward courageously, transform their visions into reality, and inspire others to come along. True visionary leadership appears to be a God-given characteristic of some people, but not everyone.

No matter how hard some people try, they can't see the big picture. Their perspectives don't go beyond their present problems. They can't look past the fog into the future, and they aren't able to inspire others to action. These people may have great capabilities and potential, but they lack vision.

While not everyone has vision, each of us has a mission—a God-inspired life purpose that draws on the unique gifts, abilities, and opportunities that he gives each of us. Your mission is a summary of where you want to be headed with your life. It is the passion that drives you, that keeps you moving, that gives meaning to your life. It is like a road map that shows you the way to go. Your mission can be a standard against which you evaluate all of your hectic activities. The most productive, fulfilling, and sometimes challenging activities in life are those that move you closer to accomplishing your mission. A life well lived is a life motivated by mission.

Some of you may feel as if you don't have a mission. Maybe you feel that your mission is merely to get through the pressures of this day without collapse or bankruptcy. For many people, including Christians, managing to survive seems more important than trying to define a mission statement.

But let me encourage you. You *do* have a mission. You may not be aware of what that mission is, but when the fog lifts, you will find that your mission can motivate you in important ways. A mission is a rock-bottom essential for a life that is well lived.

FINDING YOUR MISSION

Michael Jordan had no trouble finding his mission. His height, speed, and passion have determined his life purpose—at least until he moves past age forty and is too old to compete. For most of us, finding a mission is harder.

Have you noticed that some of our most difficult birthdays come when we "hit the big 0"? It doesn't matter whether we are turning thirty, forty, fifty, or sixty; moving into a new decade seems to be a fresh reminder that we aren't as young as we once were and that our time on earth is getting shorter.

It happened to me recently. My wife and I went to a remote resort to celebrate my sixtieth birthday, far from telephones or from any "over the hill" parties that might have come from well-meaning friends. During those days next to the ocean, I struggled with my age. After we returned, I mentioned my concerns to a business consultant, who suggested that I needed a fresh look at my life direction. Part of his work is to assist individuals and groups in finding and aligning their lives with value-based, vision-driven missions. As a gift he offered to help me take a refreshing new look at where I was going with my life. Over a period of weeks we dealt with several questions that helped me refocus and redefine my mission.[7] I will discuss five of those questions here.

What Do You Do Best?

We started by looking at my abilities and skills. Most of us know what we do well and where we are less capable. We know what interests us, what motivates us, and what brings the greatest fulfillment. It is difficult to stay enthusiastic about or to excel in tasks that we don't do well or don't find interesting. We're not likely to have maximum impact and satisfaction in life if we let parents push us into vocations for which we are not well suited or if we allow ourselves to be pulled into being a part of somebody else's mission. Our interests and God-given abilities should be important considerations when we think about the direction of our lives.

For Christians it also is crucial for us to know our spiritual gifts. These are the special endowments God gives to all believers, not for the purpose of advancing their careers (although that may happen), but for the purpose of serving and building up the church. The Holy Spirit gives us the gifts and reveals them to us. You may already know what your gifts are, or you may want some help in clarifying them.[8]

Some of the best help in clarifying your gifts can come from fellow believers who know you well. Find two or three of these people and ask them to read through Romans 12 and 1 Corinthians 12 and then identify your spiritual gifts. When I asked some close friends to do that with me, everybody came up with the same three or four characteristics, and several people even listed them in the same order of priority. That was an encouraging exercise for me. What was *not* on their lists was as important to me as what was on the lists. These friends helped me refine my mission statement and understand how I can have a life that is well lived.

What Have You Done Consistently and Well?
What have you achieved? When you think back over your life story line, what things have you done consistently and what things have you done well? When I look at my life, I see several things that have appeared again and again. These are the things that excite me, that I clearly do well, and that God seems to have blessed. They seem to be the things that I am uniquely capable of doing.

When I was in high school, I taught a Sunday school class of younger kids who probably saw me as a teenage role model. As a graduate student, I found myself encouraging undergraduates who were getting started in their college careers. When I was a professor, Julie and I had students in our house for every holiday, for frequent meals, and for special times of encouragement and decision making. After I left teaching, Julie and I were very much involved in working with a church group of young married couples. Now I meet often with young professionals and others who are getting established in their careers. Looking back and listening to the people who know me best, it isn't hard to discern that mentoring and encouraging the generation that is coming along behind me has always been exciting and fulfilling for me.

What things have surfaced repeatedly in your life? You may want to make a list. Discuss this with people who know you well or have known you for a long time. Sometimes it can be interesting and revealing to draw a timeline and start marking off the events that have been significant in your life. Do you see consistencies? Do you see things that have attracted your attention repeatedly? These common threads may not be apparent when you begin, but as you and others reflect on the timeline of your life, you can begin to see things you have done consistently and well. You also are likely to see what you haven't enjoyed and what you have not done successfully.

What Do You Care about Deeply?

I have a friend, not yet thirty, who wants to be a novelist. He reads avidly, writes every day, has a file of short stories that he has crafted, and has completed several novels that he considers to be practice for the time when he can write for publication. For my novelist friend, writing is a passion. If he gets to be ninety and still hasn't published anything, I suspect he'll still be writing. When I asked him about that after writing this paragraph, he quickly agreed that my description was accurate.

The word *passion* has its roots in the Greek and Latin words for suffering. Passionate people are willing to pay whatever price is needed, even if this involves suffering, to fulfill their passions. They are willing to risk their independence, their fortunes, their health, their relationships, even their lives for people or a purpose beyond themselves.[9] Your passion concerns both people and issues: passion involves *who* fires you up and *what* genuinely excites you.

Rick Warren gets fired up about the church. His book about the purpose-driven church exudes his passion for building vibrant congregations that penetrate our materialistic, humanistic culture with the transforming message of the gospel.[10] Warren is passionate about evangelism, about prayer, and about challenging people to commitment. He believes that "God always uses imperfect people in imperfect situations to accomplish his will."[11] His writings talk about the difference between a *belief* and a *conviction*. A belief is something you will argue about; a conviction is something you will die for.[12] A belief is what you hold; a conviction is what holds you, someone has said. "The people who have made the greatest impact on this world, for good or evil, have not been necessarily the smartest, wealthiest, or best-educated people; they have been the people with the strongest, deepest convictions."[13] These are people with passion. Rick Warren's writings ignite the enthusiasm of his readers because they show strong convictions and they radiate passion. I would guess that his life exudes something similar.

People with passion have a mental grid through which they can pass many of the demands for their time and attention. Passions help us sift out less important things, determine what really matters, and better manage our lives. Our passions also determine whether or not we will have lives that are well lived. Drug addicts or people addicted to pornography have passions that have gone awry. They care most deeply and most passionately about satisfying their addictions. This kills growth and blocks progress toward well-lived lives.

The nature and strength of your passions, and even whether you have passions, depends on your personality. Some people live quiet lives without much drive, enthusiasm, or passion; others are more dynamic, energetic, and forward looking. Maybe God chooses to give some people an intense passion and a drive to go with it, like Rick Warren's passion for the church or my young friend's ardor for writing novels.

What do you care about deeply?[14] What might you be willing to die for? The answer to those questions will have a bearing on how you live.

What Is Your Style?
I have a business partner who handles his life and work differently from the way I do. He likes to deal with issues verbally, on the phone; I prefer to write memos. He is extroverted and gets invigorated by people; I relate well to people but prefer to pull away to reflect and to read voraciously. He doesn't express his deepest emotions very often; I have trouble hiding how I really feel. He likes to autograph books, promote our business, and do radio interviews; I'm

more comfortable with a low-key, lower-visibility approach. He is an excellent salesman who likes to move products; I prefer building relationships and selling ideas.

My colleague and I share a deep commitment to Christ and have similar theological perspectives, but we're involved in churches that have very different styles of worship. He is willing to get involved in political issues and handles himself very well in that arena; I tend to avoid the political world. My partner and I both work hard. He takes frequent vacations and often goes away for the weekend; I stay home unless I am involved with a speaking or business trip. He likes golf; I do not.

Whose style is best? The answer, of course, is neither. God uses different people with different preferences and different ways of doing things to accomplish his different purposes. Our styles in life aren't about our passions or about whom we serve. Style concerns *how* we serve. That, in turn, will be reflected in our life missions and in the ways that we live.

When my friend and I feel pressured by the demands of life, we automatically respond in different ways that reflect our styles of life. Because we understand and respect each other's approach to life, these differences do not create problems. But you and I know that when we try to work with a colleague, a fellow church member, or a spouse whose style is different, we often feel the potential for conflict and misunderstanding. If we are working under pressure, facing deadlines or other demands, contrasting styles can hinder our progress, increase tension, and add more pressure for everybody. If you go to a time-management seminar to get help with a breathless lifestyle, the speaker's message is more likely to be of value if it resonates with your style of doing things. It is useful, therefore, to look at your life and become aware of your personal style if you hope to live a more focused and less distracted life.

What Are Your "Toe" Values?

Virtues and values often get confused. Both words refer to human characteristics—like honesty, fairness, courtesy, compassion, and sensitivity. But the word *values* implies something of greater intensity. Stuart Briscoe says that values are beliefs so deeply held that they turn into commitments that are fiercely defended.[15] Values are firmly entrenched standards and guiding principles that keep us focused on issues that really matter. They are at the core of our lives. They influence our decisions and determine our friendships. We hold our values so deeply that we often resent others who do not treat our values with respect.

My friend who helped me with a mission statement repeatedly talked about "toe values." These he defined as the values that are so much a part of us that they "go right down to our toes." Not only are they principles worth living for, but they also are things worth dying for. When the American Declaration of Independence was signed in 1776, the Founding Fathers pledged "our lives, our fortunes and our sacred honor." For them, liberty was a "toe value," and they were willing to stake everything on their commitment to freedom.[16]

Our toe values are obvious to others. They can be seen in our behavior. For Christians, these values don't just grow from our personalities or past experiences. Christians willingly allow God to plant and nurture the values that are revealed in Scripture. These are values like compassion, humility, purity, and avoiding even the appearance of evil.

They are crucial values for any life that is well lived and pleasing to God.

When I was writing this chapter, the coach in a nearby community high school was getting his team ready for the football season. Winning was a very high value for coach Joe Petricca, but something else was at the core of his being. He valued the painstaking process and goal of turning teenage boys into responsible young men.

The school district where he coached had a policy that would not allow any player to stay on a team if he was caught drinking or using drugs. Petricca convinced the school board to change its athletic code and allow kids to remain with the team if they came forward, confessed a violation, and agreed to do personal restitution. Before the most recent season began, twelve football players admitted violating the code by using alcohol or drugs.

"Turning myself in was the hardest thing I ever had to do," said one six-foot-two-inch, 270-pound starting guard on the team. "I could have gotten away with it," said another, "but I didn't want to go through the entire season, getting here at 6 A.M. for early practices and pretending to be part of a drug-free program. I'd know I wasn't being true to myself." Another admitted that he "did things that weren't right" during the summer, "but I felt like a different person after I admitted what I did. It felt like I had grown up."

Coach Petricca put his team through rigorous athletic drills to prepare them for their games. Unlike other coaches, he also took them to the inner city to share brown-bag lunches with the homeless. They've spent time working on broken-down homes in poor communities, delivering food to shut-ins, adopting residents of a senior citizen home as "grandparents," and listening to corporate executives describe the dog-eat-dog business environment.

Did the coach want to win a state championship? You bet. But at the core he wanted his players to be instilled with knowledge of "the real world and some of the exciting things you can do without drugs or alcohol." Turning impressionable suburban kids into exemplary young men was a mission for Joe Petricca. His toe values included honesty, integrity, and commitment to mentoring.[17]

GETTING TO THE MISSION

After working for several weeks to sharpen my answers to the five questions, my consultant friend helped me write a mission statement. In the process he asked two more thought-provoking questions that you might want to consider: If I had only six [or one, or three] months to live, what would I focus on if I knew I couldn't fail? and When I am gone, how will the world be different because of my life? These are not meant to be morbid topics. Instead, they can help us to focus on what really is important in life.

Ask yourself, When people hear my name, what thoughts do they think about me? When we hear the name Moses, we think of a leader. When we hear the name Barnabas, we think of an encourager. Solomon is still remembered as a man who was very wise (except in his relationships with women). In modern times, Billy Graham's name has come to be associated with evangelism. The name Jim Dobson is tied to families.

What about you? What do people think about you? What are you remembered for? What would you like to be remembered for? The answers to these questions can help capture our deep purposes, concerns, and directions.

Eventually, I was able to write a one-sentence mission statement to describe the current focus of my life. As my thinking continues to develop, I will refine and develop the statement further. It is likely that I will still remain committed to stimulating churches that care and building excellence in Christian counseling. But on a more focused level, *I want to be a catalyst, stimulating and equipping people who have potential to honor Christ and to have an impact as competent people helpers.* A catalyst isn't always seen but makes things happen. Somebody who stimulates and equips others is an encourager who provides the tools and gives the training to people who want to accomplish some purpose. I can't give my attention to everybody, so I have chosen to focus on people with potential. For me that means emerging leaders, people building careers as counselors, and others who are committed to helping people with as much competence as possible. I want to stimulate others to have an impact—not just any impact, but an impact that honors Christ and relates to people-helping and caregiving.

Caleb, part of the group of spies sent to explore the land of Canaan, is described in Scripture as someone who followed God wholeheartedly.[18] At age eighty-five, Caleb was still vigorous, strong, and eager to serve. Recently, it occurred to me that if God gives me good health and opportunities, I will be eighty-five in the year 2020. I have been thinking, therefore, of a 20-20 vision for that year—some challenges and goals that can be reached by my eighty-fifth birthday or before. God alone knows the length of our lives and the things he has for us to do, but I want to be guided by my mission statement, moving through productive and faithful service as I grow toward 2020. Maybe then I'll retire. For now, clearly I am less concerned about age than I was on that recent birthday.

How does anyone develop a mission statement? It isn't something done quickly; it comes after a lot of thought, reflection, and discussion with close friends who can help us answer questions like those we have been discussing. Developing a mission statement involves pondering issues like why we are in this world, what our overarching purpose might be, how the world will be different because of us, and how we're going to get where we're going. A mission statement is like a road map that summarizes where we are and where we are headed. It needs to be something concise, clear, and doable. Your mission statement should be consistent with your toe values, and it probably will be motivating once you get it on paper and summarized concisely.

Thinking through a mission in life can be challenging and even fun. It involves focusing on ourselves and even talking about ourselves, something that most of us enjoy even though we might not admit this. Maybe you will choose not to work at this, but if you do, the exercise can help you decide when to say no to the demands of others. Working on a mission statement also helps you feel that your life is more focused, having the sense of direction that so many people lack.

MANAGING WITH YOUR MISSION

Sometimes we can spend so much time thinking about a mission statement that we never do anything with it. We can write a mission statement as a guide but have no idea how to put it into practice. We even can use a mission statement as an excuse for doing nothing, telling others that we can't serve where there is a genuine need because this does not fit our mission.

A mission statement is meant to be a practical guide. It can be used in several ways. First, when you are making decisions about the future or dealing with continuing life demands, a mission statement can help you set boundaries to decide what is worth doing and what can be put aside. This is easier if you have two or three friends with whom you can discuss major decisions, friends who can help you decide how to live in accordance with your mission.

Second, your mission statement can help you evaluate what in your life is strategic. I expressed this idea one morning when I was having breakfast with an insightful young pastor from Singapore. When he asked me to define *strategic*, however, I couldn't do it, so we pulled out a paper napkin and worked on this together. The following chart summarizes our discussions.[19]

WHAT MAKES SOMETHING STRATEGIC?
Strategic issues, projects, meetings, and activities

1. Have long-term influence, not momentary impact
2. Empower others, not simply entertain
3. Advance God's purposes, not human agendas
4. Are intentional, not incidental
5. Are done at the most opportune time, not just anytime[20]
6. Are distinctive, not simply doing the same old thing
7. Embody our unique gifts and abilities, not copy what others do
8. Respond to current needs, not done just because "we've always done it"

Focusing our energies on the things that are strategic is a way to fulfill our missions and have well-lived, Christ-honoring lives. In reality this is an ideal that we can't always reach or apply. There are routine, necessary, and sometimes boring demands that rob us of our time and aren't very strategic in terms of a life mission. Paying the bills and doing the laundry are examples. When we have a mission, however, we can have clearer goals and guidelines for making major decisions.

When I have to make major decisions, I ask myself a set of questions that helps me determine what is strategic, where my boundaries should be, and how the issue about which I have to make a decision fits into my mission statement. You may find these questions helpful, or you may want to use them as a springboard to develop a list of your own.

DECISION-MAKING QUESTIONS

Concerning the issue, project, meeting, activity, or other decision that I am considering:

1. Is it consistent with biblical teaching?
2. Is it Christ-honoring?
3. Is it consistent with my life goals and mission?
4. Does it make best use of my abilities and spiritual gifts?
5. Can (or does) somebody else do it as well as I can or better? (If so, then maybe I should devote my energies elsewhere.)
6. Do fellow believers who know me agree it should be done?
7. Is it feasible (in terms of my time, finances, schedule, energy, etc.)?
8. How would it affect my marriage and family?
9. What are the advantages and disadvantages of doing it?
10. What are my motives for doing it?
11. How might I be manipulated by others in doing this?
12. Do I feel like doing it?

DESTROYED BY YOUR MISSION

Ken Blanchard is an internationally known management consultant and coauthor of *The One Minute Manager*, which sold more than seven million copies. The business environment today is like a turbulent river, Blanchard wrote recently. In life, as in business, we must learn to navigate through constantly churning waters, knowing where we are going and having a willingness to change direction and be what he calls "what if" people.

"What if" people don't go through life burdened with a boatload of dire and pessimistic worries, but they are realistic enough to anticipate some of the difficulties of life. As they plan for the future, for example, these people sometimes ask "what if" questions like these: What if I am disabled? What if I run out of money? What if I don't prepare financially for my retirement? What if I have a "2020 vision" and don't have anybody to help me or to take it over if I can't complete it? Or consider this question: What if I develop a mission and learn to live by it but then discover that my mission is destroying me? This could happen in at least two ways: your mission could trap you, or it could distract you.

Trapped by a Mission
Decades ago, one of the pioneers in American psychology told his students to develop theories of personality, to let those theories be their guide in the counseling room, but always to hold those theories lightly. A mission statement is a guide, not a rigid formula. It is a humanly crafted blueprint for controlling pressures and helping us have lives that are well lived; it is not a rule book, set in cement and impervious to the winds of change.

Sometimes, in his wisdom, God takes our best plans and turns them upside down. Moses and David were both shepherds taking care of flocks when God gave them new missions as leaders. Saul of Tarsus was an anti-Christian religious zealot when God gave him the new mission of taking the gospel to the Gentile world. In our own day, Joni

Eareckson Tada's life plans were changed forever when she dived into waters that were too shallow, became paralyzed for life, but sailed into a powerful ministry that might not have been possible otherwise.

We need to develop our missions, pursue them passionately, but hold them lightly with the awareness that God sometimes has other plans for our lives as we get older. The Bible prepares us for this. When people are faithful in little things, God sometimes gives them larger missions.[21] When a believer is humble, God lifts that person up, sometimes to a place of higher visibility and impact.[22]

Sadly, the annals of church history are littered with debris from the lives of people who had clear life missions and were intent on serving Christ faithfully, but who were so mission dominated that they forgot everything else. Most of us can think of examples—highly visible Christian leaders whose pursuit of a worthy mission caused them to push aside their families, deny the need for accountability, ignore their financial responsibilities, cross sexual or other boundaries, and shipwreck their lives, their ministries, and the dreams of their faithful followers.

Distracted by Self-Sufficiency

What lured Adam and Eve into disobedience to God was the devil's promise that they could be self-sufficient, filled with knowledge and wisdom; they would be exactly like God.[23] Centuries later, when Jesus was tempted in the wilderness, Satan used almost identical tactics, promising spectacular events and full control over "all the kingdoms of the world."[24] It is an old line that is still used, often as effectively as when it pulled down Eve and Adam. In its modern form it says, "You don't need God. You are quite sufficient and capable to handle it on your own." It steers us away from a critical truth: *self-sufficiency is one of the greatest enemies of a life well lived.*

We can go back to the beginning of this chapter, read about developing a life mission, answer the questions that are suggested, enthusiastically pursue our goals, and hardly ever give God a thought in the whole process. In his mercy, God sometimes even allows a measure of success. We glow in what we know and take pride in what we're accomplishing. We can even be doing what appears to be God's work, telling the world about Christ, helping hurting people, building big churches or organizations, ministering to the needy, attracting crowds and acclaim, but doing this all in our own strength and with human wisdom. A mission that is built on our own energy without supernatural power and direction is a mission built on sand, ultimately destined to collapse.

A life that is genuinely well lived is a life that is dependent on Christ. As we will see next, it is also a life lived in partnership with other believers who help one another move away from self-sufficient and breathless lifestyles so they can plan and serve together.

TAKING A STEP TOWARD
Understanding Your Life's Mission

As you reflect on this chapter, take some time to answer these questions. You may want to do that in a journal, with a

friend, or in a group. Allow the questions to help you focus on how you will live a life that has purpose.

1. Who are some of the visionaries you know? Are you a visionary?
2. What is your mission in life? Have you been able to express that purpose in a mission statement? If you have not, use the next six questions to help you move ahead.
3. What do you do best? List five things in which you have demonstrated competence over the years. How do those five things line up with the spiritual gifts God has given you? Whose input will you seek in trying to answer this question?
4. What have you done consistently and well? Whose input will you seek in trying to answer this question?
5. What do you care about deeply? What drives you? What are you willing to die for? Whose input will you seek in trying to answer this question?
6. What is your style? How does this style help you fulfill your mission?
7. What are your "toe" values? Whose input will you seek in trying to answer this question?
8. If you have not already done it, write a mission statement that not only describes your life's purpose but also will direct it. Ask your spouse or a few friends to help you hone the statement.
9. What are the greatest obstacles to your pursuing this mission? What can you do to overcome those obstacles?
10. Using the list on page 132 as a starting point, make a list of questions that will help you make major decisions.

CHAPTER 8

Teamwork
Sharing and
Growing Together

THE STUDENTS at Westminster College must have been surprised when President Peggy Stock began her speech to the graduating class. She didn't talk about the topics they expected—their dreams or their destinies—but chose instead to talk about geese.

"Yes, you heard me correctly," the college president began. "As you go forth from Westminster College, I would like you to remember some simple facts about geese, as you wing your way through life. One, geese fly in a V-formation because they have a 71 percent greater flying range together than they do when flying alone." As each bird flaps its wings, this creates an uplift for the geese that fly behind.

"Two," the speaker continued, "whenever a goose flies out of formation, it soon feels the added drag and quickly tries to get back into position. Three, when the lead goose gets tired, it rotates further back in the formation, and another goose takes the lead." Finally, if a goose becomes sick or wounded and can't keep up with the flock, two other geese also leave the formation and stay with the wounded goose until it either revives or dies.[1]

My wife and I live near a pond where geese land frequently. I have watched them often. They are stately looking birds, but they can be vicious, noisy, and filthy. The college president's commencement talk gave me a new perspective on birds that I had grown to dislike. I came to appreciate the instinctive, God-given inclination of geese to fly together and move in formation toward their goals.

In some parts of the world—Asia is a good example—people almost always move toward their goals by working together in partnerships. Employees join companies and stay for life. Family togetherness and loyalty are precious commodities. People know about sharing a common sense of purpose and realize that their lives will be better if they are interconnected as part of a team. Inspired by this example, perhaps, forward-looking business leaders around the world have begun stressing "strategic alliances" and urging cooperation, instead of competition, between employees and companies.[2]

This type of thinking has not been emphasized in English-speaking North America. We prefer the can-do, frontier spirit that praises individualism. A fascinating book titled *The Stuff Americans Are Made Of* demonstrates that "from the Pilgrims to the Pioneers, from the American Revolution to the Industrial Revolution, seven forces have fueled the American experience" and still drive us as we move through the information age.[3] These forces are

- an insistence on independent, individual choice;
- the love of pursuing impossible dreams;
- an obsession with big and more;
- an impatience with the restraints of time, including annoyance when time is wasted;
- a willingness to accept mistakes and try again;
- a love of improvising; and
- a fixation on things that are new and innovative.[4]

Look closely at this list. The "seven cultural forces that define Americans" all imply the superiority of individuality. Teamwork or partnerships are rarely mentioned, and the authors even imply that teams can interfere with our individualistic lifestyles. If you talk to employees about teamwork, the book suggests, you will find that they are preoccupied with two self-centered questions: What's in it for me? and What will I have to give up in order to participate?[5] We Americans don't think much about the example of geese that fly in formation; we know more about the aggressive nature, squawking, and annoying droppings of individual birds.

The students who heard about geese at that college commencement also heard a second speaker, who warned about a "frightening disconnectedness" infecting so much of life today. She argued for "political *connected*ness" in place of the destructive political *correct*ness that infects so many colleges and universities. When we are disconnected from our history, from our communities, and from other cultures, we become prisoners of our own narrow worlds, the graduating students were told. If you don't know what came before, "You can never know what will come next. . . . You're frozen in 'me,' and most often in 'now,' when it should be 'we'" moving and looking ahead together.[6]

MOVING FROM ME

We all have times when we feel disconnected from others and frozen in the "me" thinking that still dominates our culture. We try to solve our problems alone, reach goals on our own, and even serve Christ with an individualistic mindset. Eventually most of us come to realize that we work better and find most fulfillment when we are in contact and cooperating with others. God told Adam that it was not good to be alone, so God created Eve and gave her to Adam.[7] In the centuries that followed, many individuals were described in the Bible, but almost all are portrayed in the context of their families, cultures, or involvements with other people.

Think of biblical leaders, for example. Moses spent many years in the desert, but when he was picked to be a leader, Aaron and others came alongside to give assistance in guiding the nation and holding up their leader's arms. Nehemiah was charged with building a wall around Jerusalem, but he found a team of wall builders, and they worked together. Paul was given a unique mission to bring Christ to the Gentiles, but he never tried to do this alone. His letters are filled with references to Barnabas, Timothy, Titus, and others who were his partners in spreading the Good News.

Nobody illustrated this with greater clarity than Jesus. All of the Gospels include the account of how he chose his disciples at the beginning of his ministry. We see this, for example, in Mark 1, where Jesus walks along the seaside and encourages some men to leave their nets and follow him.[8] They became his constant companions and co-workers. They were the people whom he mentored, taught, encouraged, and trained to carry on his work. As his ministry unfolded, he got frustrated at times with the disciples' lack of understanding, but Jesus never even implied that his Father's kingdom would be built without them, by individuals working alone. When Jesus talked with the disciples before his death, he gave them instructions for continuing his work together after he was gone. When he prayed in the Garden of Gethsemane, he asked the Father to bond the disciples together so that they would become one, just as Jesus and his Father were one.[9] When he said his last words before ascending into heaven, he promised that they, as a team, would receive power and would be his witnesses throughout the world.[10] They were to be the people who would begin the task of building the church and changing the world. They must have understood this to be a joint venture because almost immediately the believers banded together to worship, pray, share things together, and start spreading the Good News.[11]

One of this country's best-known experts on leadership is a writer named Warren Bennis. In a book that he co-authored, Bennis wrote about our persisting tendency to assume that great accomplishments are the work of great men and women working individually.[12] People strive to distinguish themselves as individuals, he suggested, but the greatest achievements in this modern world come not from great leaders doing things alone, but from "Great Groups." Often these groups are motivated and inspired by a leader, but together the group members do what none of them could do alone. To illustrate this conclusion, the book describes a number of successful projects—like developing the personal computer or getting a new president elected.

These efforts succeeded because people worked together. For most of us, the goals are much smaller than building a computer system. We're involved in building families, churches, businesses, or Little League teams. Whatever our goals, however, surely this conclusion is true: *We cannot expect to have lives that are well lived and free from persisting pressure if we are lone rangers who try to make things happen on our own.* God has given us individual gifts and strengths, but these are to be used in partnerships with others who have similar goals and commitments.[13]

ALLIANCES AND PARTNERSHIPS

At one time I was grounded firmly in the individualistic way of thinking. I got through college "on my own." My church stressed private devotions and an individual commitment to Christ, but we heard little about the church as a body or the community of believers. In my psychological training, group counseling was acknowledged, but the emphasis was on helping individuals deal with their personal insecurities, inner conflicts, impulse control, self-interests, and what we called internal dynamics. The individuals who paraded through our counseling offices often had problems rooted in their families, interpersonal relationships, and cultural backgrounds, but we had learned counseling theories and methods that focused on our clients' private worlds. We gave little attention to how these struggling people were influencing or being influenced by their communities, work settings, or churches.

Rugged individualism still may be a cherished American value, part of the stuff we are made of, but increasingly we are coming to value partnerships, team efforts, and working together. We see this in the field of counseling, where counselors and clients spend more energy understanding the impact of cultures and working with their communities. We see similar trends in churches. Ego-driven pastors still dominate some pulpits, but many of the small churches and almost all of the seeker-sensitive and megachurches that grab media attention tend to be led by pastors who thrive on building teams and sharing leadership. Books about leadership emphasize that good leaders, like good coaches, must build teams that work together, drawing on the team members' different abilities, bringing out the best in each person, and aligning everybody together to reach common goals.[14]

Several years ago I was involved in the challenge of starting a new church. I had been in a church that had grown so large that despite multiple services there was no room for any more people in the sanctuary or cars in the parking lot. Everybody agreed that we should find a couple of hundred volunteers and send them off to start a new congregation. Julie and I joined the volunteers. The group formed committees to discuss the theology of the new church, the place where we would worship, the children's ministry and youth program, the church constitution, the type of music we would have, the way leadership would be organized. Every one of the volunteers joined at least one committee, and we all worked together. When we were ready to launch out on our own, we had a big send-off celebration in a local high school. Everybody was there—the entire congregation of the sending church and all of the new church volunteers. We worshiped together, and then our group was sent off to start our new venture. It was an example of a partnership of ordinary people working together to establish a new church that still exists, thrives, and has continuing good rapport with the church from which we were launched.

Insurance executive Jack Callahan, who headed the second-largest personal property and casualty insurer in the country, believes that "teams are the most powerful tool we have for creating change."[15]

Words like these about partnerships, team building, networking, and pulling together can be inspiring. We all might agree that work can be more fulfilling and less burdensome when we share responsibilities. You may even accept the conclusion that people with well-lived lives are most likely to be in partnerships with others. Earlier we mentioned the team of nuns who work in Mother Teresa's centers in India, and most of us are aware of evangelistic teams like those who worked for so many years with Billy Graham.

LIVING AND GROWING IN PARTNERSHIPS

When people trust each other and are motivated to work together, teamwork can be invigorating and teams can accomplish a lot. It is harder when there are tensions that threaten to weaken partnerships, when people need to be brought together to work in harmony, or when trust needs to be built. James DePriest encountered such a situation when he moved to Oregon. A tall, imposing figure with a resonating voice, DePriest had conducted orchestras all over the world, but the symphony that he inherited was different. At best, it could have been described as a provincial ensemble, with underpaid musicians who all needed outside jobs. Every year they played a limited number of concerts in a crumbling facility. DePriest arrived in town with a vision for a top-quality symphony, and he began sharing his dream almost immediately with anybody who would listen. He also got active, combining his idealism with down-to-earth reality.

The new maestro lobbied the city and state for a new facility. He took his musicians to parks, county fairs, colleges, and even shopping centers to touch people with the music and to break down artificial barriers of snobbery about classical compositions. He showed that he believed in his players, encouraged them to become the best they could be, and inspired them with his vision for great music. He led them with his example and his baton, but he reminded them that every instrument and every talent was needed. Before long, a hundred egos were pulling in the same direction, and soon the group's performances were notably deeper and richer. Today the Oregon Symphony rehearses and performs in a new concert hall, musician salaries have more than doubled, and the symphony is the pride of Oregonians and broadly acclaimed beyond the state.[16]

DePriest has described how he stimulates the musicians to work together and how the orchestra maintains partnerships with supporting corporations and music lovers who come to the concerts. Underlying all of these efforts is a conductor who keeps remembering, refining, and communicating his mental vision of what can be accomplished. This goal is shared with everybody involved, and people are encouraged to think of *"our* vision" for *"our* orchestra." Independent, distinct voices are heard, not silenced, but individuals are encouraged to pool their unique talents into a collective whole intent on reaching a common goal. The leader labors to create an environment that makes the vision become a reality.[17]

Much of this sounds similar to what the Bible calls the body of Christ. This is a picture of the church as a body or group of Christians, where all believers are important and each has a part to play in building God's kingdom.[18] Some people in the body are chosen to be leaders, just as James DePriest was chosen to lead the Oregon Symphony. More of us are given talents to be used faithfully and blended together into the team. We are responsible for developing our abilities and trusting God to show us where and how he expects us to fit with his divine purposes. Ideally, individual gifts and abilities are encouraged, not squelched, but the diversity blends together to become a unity. When we share similar visions and determine to work together, partnerships emerge, and we see not one, but numerous well-lived lives.

THE HEART OF EFFECTIVE PARTNERSHIPS

Similar goals and shared values are good starting points for team building, but the core ingredient of effective partnerships is *trust*. This has been called the glue that holds relationships together. Without trust, no vision ever becomes a reality, and partnerships never work smoothly. "In fact," writes one leading business consultant, "without trust nothing works very well."[19]

There is harmony when the team members trust their leader, when the leader trusts his or her players, when the people in a business, church, or group trust one another—as James DePriest and his musicians trust each other. Sincere, heartfelt trust cannot be demanded; trust is earned as a result of a person's behavior over time. Such genuine trust takes a long time to build, and it can be lost quickly in a moment of thoughtlessness.

If you trust another human being, or if another human being trusts you, several underlying traits are always present.

You see them in the people you trust. You make them a part of your own life when you want people to have trust in you.

1. Predictability builds trust. The first of these traits is predictability. If your behavior or values are inconsistent, erratic, confusing, or indecisive, then others cannot predict what you might say or do. As a result, other people don't feel safe enough to work together and to be vulnerable. Trust grows only when there is consistency and predictability.

2. Dependability builds trust. Closely connected to predictability is dependability, which involves doing what you say you will do. When Jesus was talking about oaths, he used a phrase that summarizes the basis of dependability: "Simply let your 'Yes' be 'Yes,' and your 'No' [be] 'No.'"[20] This entails taking your commitments seriously and not treating your promises lightly. Problems are certain to arise when a team member says he or she will do one thing and then does another or does not follow through.

I have seen this repeatedly in my work as a magazine editor, trying to keep deadlines. We need to have our authors, editors, advertisers, designers, printers, and everybody else working together. When a person promises to have something to us by a certain date and then fails to follow through or communicates that the original promise cannot be kept, then quality and efficiency go down, costs of production go up, and, if this happens repeatedly, morale eventually slides. In contrast, when there is a climate of mutual honesty and reliability, the level of trust goes up and so does the morale.

3. Faith builds trust. Faith is not strictly a religious word. If others have faith in you, they believe that you will be responsible to fulfill your commitments. They believe that your words will match your actions, that they can trust you to keep confidences, and that they can depend on you to do the right thing. We trust in God because we have the faith that he will keep his promises consistently, do what he has said he will do, and do what is right.

4. Truth builds trust. We cannot trust people unless we know they are truthful, keep their promises, and show that they are consistently honest. People will not trust you if they have any reason to think that you are being manipulative, secretive, disrespectful, or deceptive—saying something to one person and giving a different message to another. None of us can trust a person who distorts facts, talks behind our backs, gossips, or isn't up-front in telling the truth. Human chameleons are not trustworthy.

5. Integrity builds trust. When people show a desire to do what is right, other people learn to trust them. People of integrity are people whose actions are predictable. They are people who get respect and who often show respect to others because it is the right thing to do.

6. Competence builds trust. When I ride on an airplane, I trust the captain to get us to our destination because I am convinced of the captain's competence. In one of his insightful books about leadership, businessman Max DePree writes that trust is maintained over time only when others see competence in the person they trust.[21]

7. Caring builds trust. Trust must be characterized by caring or benevolence. This means that others can feel secure that they will not be unfairly treated, embarrassed, harmed, or caught off guard by something you say or do. Others will not trust you if they detect that you don't really care about them.

8. Authenticity builds trust. I would be reluctant to trust a person who appeared to be phony, whose words and behavior did not match, who didn't seem real. People don't trust us so much because of what we say; they trust us because of what they see as they watch us over time.

My wife and I have a mutual trust that enables us to have lives that are well lived. After three decades of marriage, we can predict what the other will do in a variety of situations. We can depend on what we hear the other say, knowing that we will do what we say we will do. As I have traveled over the years, often by myself and sometimes in lonely situations, Julie knows that I have kept my promise to be faithful. On occasions when I have been tempted to unfaithfulness, I have told her about this later. As a result, she has learned to trust my honesty and credibility. I, in turn, can trust her to pray for me because she has done it for years. In addition, we have a common faith in God and can freely confide in each other. We both know that we will not secretly spread rumors or unkind remarks about the other. Because of these commitments and behaviors, we have become a team built on trust.

Trust is "the lubricant for individual and organizational change," according to leadership experts James Kouzes and Barry Posner.[22] People cannot take risks unless they feel safe, unthreatened, and able to trust. Only then do they feel self-confident and secure enough in their relationships to explore new opportunities, take on fresh challenges, and join with others in taking risks and moving forward together.

ROADBLOCKS THAT HINDER PARTNERSHIPS

I live in an area where people joke about the fact that we have only two seasons of the year: winter and road construction. Maybe you live in a similar community. As soon as the snow melts, the road construction begins with inevitable delays, inconvenience, and barricades.

Life is often the same. We start moving toward our goals, trying to fulfill a mission, but we find our progress hindered by roadblocks, many of which we didn't expect. Marital conflicts, unanticipated illness, interpersonal tensions, personal crises, or even the incessant demands of a busy life can all get in the way, sidetracking our dreams and diverting us from our goals. Especially frustrating are two barricades that interfere with our willingness and ability to form necessary partnerships.

The first of these obstacles to teamwork comes from within ourselves. It is the almost universal tendency to compete and compare ourselves with others. Sometimes we make comparisons and conclude that we are superior. More often we decide that we are inferior and less capable or desirable than others. In either case, we are reluctant to align ourselves with others or to work together in partnerships.

The second obstacle to teamwork comes from outside ourselves. It comes when we are rejected or disrespected. This can lead to anger or to withdrawal, both of which hinder partnerships.

Making Comparisons

When the summer Olympics were held in Atlanta, Matt Ghaffari was determined to win the gold. The 286-pound, superheavyweight American wrestler had spent years preparing for this event. Twenty times before, he had wrestled with Aleksandr Karelin, the world champion from Russia. Twenty times before, Matt Ghaffari had lost. The final Olympic match found the two wrestlers facing each other again. They were so evenly matched that the event was forced into over-time. Ghaffari lost.

On the winners' stand the contrast between the two was glaring and open for all to see. The Russian stood erect with the gold medal around his neck, listening to his national anthem. To his right, a little lower was Ghaffari, his head hung low, tears streaming down his face and dropping to the second-place medal that hung from his neck.

"I'm not quitting until I win a gold medal, until I beat Karelin," the second-best wrestler in the world vowed later. His self-castigation reminded some observers of ninety-one-year-old Abel Kiviat, who competed in the 1,500-meter track event as part of the 1912 Olympics and lost the gold medal by one-tenth of a second. Now, seven decades later, the silver medalist told the *Los Angeles Times* that he still wakes up in the night and wonders, "What the heck happened to me? It's like a nightmare."[23]

Competition is supposed to motivate us and push us to greater achievements, but something is wrong when we equate being second with being a loser. One of Nike's advertisements at the Atlanta Olympics declared: "You don't win silver, you lose gold." When interviewing a silver medalist, one television reporter's first question was, "How does it feel to be a failure?"

This winning-is-everything attitude is not limited to sports. It begins with children in the home, is reinforced through the school years, and transfers to the adult world, so that it becomes a destructive force in the lives of many people. Competition and the making of comparisons can destroy teamwork, increase pressure, and shoot down our efforts to have well-lived lives.

I have made mental comparisons for much of my life. Most of us do, until we reach the point of seeing how this can destroy productivity and create constant inner feelings of self-condemnation and self-doubt. It is easy to ruminate on our lives and especially on our careers, convincing ourselves that others are more capable, more successful, and better off financially. We assume—sometimes in error—that others "have it together," and then we struggle because we do not.

A surprisingly large number of psychological studies have investigated the impact of making such comparisons.[24] Some researchers have found that self-esteem and self-evaluations can go up when we make comparisons and find that we are better than we thought. No one is likely to feel very secure or fulfilled, however, if life becomes a constant effort to make comparisons in an attempt to boost self-esteem by proving one's superiority to others. It has been argued that comparisons motivate some people to try harder and improve themselves, but how many of these people become like Olympian Matt Ghaffari, who keeps driving himself harder but feels more and more like a failure? How many are like Abel Kiviat, who has spent his life in self-condemnation because he failed to win a gold medal and live up to his self-imposed standards of superiority and competence? More often than not, comparisons are ego-deflating, leaving us frustrated and often miserable.

If you make frequent comparisons with others, it may help to realize that you are not alone in this mental self-abuse. Comparisons start with the insecurities that we all feel or are made to feel because of our failures or the words of people who criticize. Eventually we respond to these insecurities in one of two ways—sometimes both. In our minds we decide we are better than the competition and swell up with internal, self-centered pride. Or we agree that we really are less capable or successful than others. Then we slide into self-pity, adopting a poor-me attitude that believes we deserve better than this. All of this can be draining and depressing. It can pull us into self-centered and self-destructive ruminations that are pointless, displeasing to God, and probably coming from the father of lies himself.[25] God is interested in our obedience, faithfulness, and good stewardship, not in how we compare to somebody who *appears* to have more or to be more successful.

To have a life that is well lived, we must resist making comparisons, refocus on our life goals and God-given missions, then move ahead, working in partnerships instead of competing and comparing ourselves with what other people might be doing. None of this is easy, especially in a society where we make incessant comparisons and have admiration for people who keep trying harder to overtake "number one." Sometimes we need the aid of a counselor or friend who can help us deal with the insecurities and threats that trap us in comparison thinking in the first place and prevent us from being either happy or productive.

Jesus dealt with this directly when he encountered competition and comparison thinking in the disciples. Remember James and John, the two brothers who came to Jesus asking to sit on his right and left when he established his kingdom? We can only guess why the other ten disciples were indignant when they heard about this request, but we do know how Jesus responded. In stating that God-given greatness comes to those who are servants, he said nothing about competing and making comparisons. His comments suggested that people who are willing to serve have less concern about competing or making comparisons. When we have a servant

mentality, we are freer to work with others in building teams
and moving forward together.

Dealing with Rejection

Corey Barenbrugge was only nine years old when he entered
a competition at the DuPage County fair. Contestants were
invited to construct small wooden figures and enter them in a
"miniatures contest." Corey worked enthusiastically to build
a little desk, closet, and medicine cabinet. "I tried to make
them good," he said after entering his work. Even though he
was near the bottom of his age category, he had prepared his
entry carefully and hoped that he might win a ribbon.

When the fair opened, Corey hurried to the science building to see if his entry had won. There, for all to see, was
Corey's work. Alongside was a card bearing his name and
these words: *Poor quality. No ribbon awarded.* The boy hurried from the building, found his mother, but said he didn't
want to talk about his entry.

When Corey's mother discovered the problem and saw
how humiliated her son had felt, she called the fair and
asked that the little exhibit bearing her son's name be taken
down. The fair officials refused. It was a "good learning
experience" for him, they said. It was an example to show
that "you can't enter any old thing and expect a ribbon."
When a newspaper reporter took up the case, the fair officials changed their minds. The judges admitted that they had
not realized that Corey was only nine years old, and when the
reporter kept asking questions, he discovered that Corey was
the only one to submit an entry in his age category. He was
the only kid in the county who even bothered to try.

The newspaper writer, syndicated columnist Bob Greene,

acknowledged that this was not an earth-shattering event of great significance. But he put Corey's picture in the paper and called him the fair's "grand champion" because he undertook something difficult and was willing to try. In a world that seems to endorse indifference and apathy, it is hard to make a young person eager and enthusiastic, Greene wrote. "When a child does work up that eagerness—it is so wrong to carelessly extinguish it. So thoughtless to make him feel like a fool."[26] I read the story and wondered if the boy would ever try again.

Not far from the community where Corey lives, the corporate offices of a large, national retailer sit in a setting of beauty surrounded by parklands and flower gardens. Not long ago, at some place in those offices, the company executives made a decision to cut fifty thousand people from the nationwide payrolls in an effort to stem a growing financial slide. Like corporations all over the land, the employer needed to downsize to keep solvent and avoid bankruptcy.

For all of the dismissed employees this was a devastating time in their lives and careers. Some used the experience to jump-start new careers. Others entered a traumatic time of fear, lost dreams, and insecurity with which they still struggle, several years after the layoffs. When many of these former employees were interviewed, researchers found a common thread in their thinking. They had all become a little less trusting, less loyal, less willing to get involved emotionally with subsequent employers. Some of the dismissed men and women had been dedicated employees of the company for twenty or more years. They understand that jobs are always being created and lost in the ebb and flow of the economy. Most of them understand the company's decision to downsize. But their confidence and self-esteem have been devastated. Most are reluctant to form bonds with another company or to build new partnerships with co-workers. They are afraid of being hurt again in the future as they have been hurt in the past.[27]

These downsized workers have something in common with Corey Barenbrugge. They all have experienced the pain of rejection. When we make commitments, including commitments to work together with others, we can work in tandem toward common goals if we feel accepted and respected. When we are rejected or when we are shown no respect, however, we are reluctant to commit to other relationships, especially if the disrespect and rejection has occurred more than once.

RUNNING TOGETHER

Building and working with teams is difficult for people who feel insecure because they compare themselves to others and for people who have been rejected and find themselves afraid to make new commitments. Without support, encouragement, and a sense of community from others, we become more self-sufficient, insensitive, and disconnected. We are more inclined to feel overwhelmed by pressures and less likely to have well-lived lives that are secure and anchored in community.

The most fulfilled lives are not those characterized by independence, self-sufficiency, greed, or the drive for success. We are happier and more fulfilled when we determine to encourage others and show respect, to build trusting relationships, and to avoid competition that hurts others while it builds inflated pride in ourselves.

Almost ten years ago I was invited to give the opening speech at a large conference of Christian counselors. When I was putting the finishing touches on my talk, somebody told me a story that I used to conclude my presentation. Periodically I still encounter people who were in the audience at the conference. They don't remember anything else that I said, but they still think about the story.

Apparently a large group of mentally handicapped children was attending a picnic at which there were games and races. In one of these races, the kids were lined up at the starting line, ready to run when the whistle blew. At the signal, they all took off and dashed down the track, running enthusiastically toward the finish line.

Then one of the kids fell and began to cry. The other racers heard the sound and rushed back to help their fallen friend. When the tears were wiped and the race was ready to resume, it was decided that the kids would line up where they were and not return to the starting place. To keep everybody in line, the children held hands and waited for the whistle. When it sounded, they took off again, but they forgot to let go of one another. Holding hands, they ran together and crossed the finish line at the same time.[28]

These children all won because they cared for one another and found it more valuable to move forward together than to drive to beat each other to the finish line. Running together in teamwork and helping one another finish strong is at the core of lives that are well lived.

TAKING A STEP TOWARD
Working Together

As you reflect on this chapter, take some time to answer these questions. You may want to do that in a journal, with a

friend, or in a group. Allow the questions to help you focus on how you will work in partnership with others.

1. Describe two or three groups that have succeeded only because the people in the groups have been willing to work together. What qualities do those groups have in common?
2. Reflect on your own life to detect areas in which your sense of individualism has hindered your growth. What can you do to change that?
3. Do you agree or disagree with the premise that teamwork is better than individualism? Give reasons for your answer.
4. In what specific area of your life could you move toward teamwork? What could you gain by moving toward teamwork and partnership in that area? What will other people gain if you involve them in this area?
5. Of the several components of trust (predictability, dependability, faith, truth, integrity, competence, caring, and authenticity), which needs the most development in your life? What can you do to begin the process?
6. What roadblocks do you face in building effective partnerships? Which is the greater threat for you, making comparisons or facing rejection?

CHAPTER 9

Adaptability
Dealing with
Continuing Change

WHEN THE SPEAKER stepped to the microphone, he looked at the crowd of reporters squeezed into the room and joked that he should have rented the local sports stadium for his hastily called news conference. Cardinal Joseph Bernardin, the sixty-eight-year-old leader of Roman Catholics in the Midwest, was about to announce that cancer had spread from his pancreas to his liver, that his condition was terminal, and that he would die within a year according to his doctors.

"While I know that, humanly speaking, I will have to deal with difficult moments, I can say in all sincerity that I am at peace," the religious leader told the crowded assembly. "I consider this as God's special gift to me at this moment in my life." Bernardin described his plans to continue working as long as he could, and he suggested that his most important life contribution might be the way in which he would handle

the last months of his life.[1] "For so many years I've tried to
help people learn how to live in a fruitful, productive, and
satisfying way," the Cardinal said. "Now, perhaps, I can
teach them how to die."[2]

Far away from Chicago, several years before Cardinal
Bernardin began coping with cancer, a young businesswoman faced a different type of change. Without the hope
and peace that sustained the Catholic leader, Amna Kunovac
had watched her friends shot down in the street by snipers,
knew the experience of being shelled on the way to find
bread in the market, and lived for almost four years without
electricity or water. Like the other residents of war-torn
Sarajevo, she often wondered when the end might come and
whether she or her devastated city would have any future.

While people all around gave up in despair, Amna continued to study the art, drawing, and clothing design that had
been her fascination since the time when her father, a textile
manufacturer, had brought swatches of cloth to their home.
When she moved into her twenties, Kunovac started a fashion business known as FMS (Fashions Made in Sarajevo).
Initially funded with seed money from Germany, the little
company seeks to create beauty in the midst of bombed-out
buildings, streets torn apart by explosions, and discouraged
neighbors who live in the midst of destruction. Some of the
FMS clothing was displayed recently in the Louvre of Paris
after Kunovac won a contest for young designers, but her
struggling business is always on the verge of collapse
because of the hardships and ongoing changes in Bosnia.[3]

Bernardin and Kunovac were vastly different in age, life
circumstances, religious outlook, and place of residence, but
they both faced the challenge of working in the midst of

change. It has been said that the only certainty in this world is change, but unlike changes that happened a decade or two ago, today's change comes on us much faster. People have always been jolted by the crises of life, including the jarring news that one's health has deteriorated and that life is coming to an unexpected end. Throughout history, people have suffered and adjusted to the changes wrought by war and other forms of mass destruction. We are not the first generation to grapple with layoffs, work pressures, the difficulty of maintaining balance in our overstretched lives, or the tensions that get in the way of teamwork. But we live in an information age that bombards us with more stimulation than any previous generation could have imagined. We are rocked by challenges to our cherished values, pushed to adjust to technology that advances almost daily, confronted with sweeping transformations in the way we view religion and "do church." We often feel helpless in the face of revolutionary economic, social, political, and workforce changes. Cardinal Bernardin and Amna Kunovac adapted and coped better than most.

How can the rest of us adapt, cope, and bounce back in the midst of sometimes life-shattering change? Imagine that you are climbing a hill and that you decide to pause, partway up, to see where you have come and to look at where you are going. In a somewhat similar way, we can pause as we make our way through the pages of this book. Our goal has been to find ways to rise above the strangulating demands that rush into our lives and pull us down into a valley of hyperactivity. We want to ascend to a higher, less chaotic place where we can be at peace in the midst of change and have lives that are well lived.

In the early pages of this book, we thought about our breathless lifestyles and then began to consider ten traits of a life
that is well lived. First, we saw how the divine commandment
to love God with our hearts, souls, and minds can bring a
calming effect that enables us to face crises, even death, with
the peace that Cardinal Bernardin experienced. In chapter 4
we looked at the importance of reaching out to others despite
our busyness. Me-centered people miss the joy and rejuvenation that comes from caring and are more inclined to be overwhelmed by their pressures. Chapter 5 drew our attention to
character, values, and integrity as core features of lives that
are at peace and well lived in the midst of energy-draining
demands for productivity. In chapter 6 we looked at balance.
Our focus was on accountability, boundaries, and the need to
maintain margins that can cushion us from the storms of life.
Chapter 7 emphasized purposeful living and helped us consider how to get focus and vision in our own lives so we can
make informed decisions in times of tension. The chapter
before this one discussed serving and growing together. We
have more fulfilling, useful, and well-lived lives when we build
partnerships with others and stop trying to cope alone.

Now we continue our upward journey toward a well-lived
life by looking in more detail at change and its impact.
Change is a reality that puts many of us under stress and
robs us of fulfilling lives.

TWO SIDES OF CHANGE

Like a coin, change has two sides. On one side is the
change that comes into our lives from outside; external
change is usually unbidden and sometimes unexpected.
Often this invasive change is disruptive. It can deflate our

dreams, steal away our hope, push us to alter our plans, and demand that we adapt to its resented restrictions. When we are called to adjust to this external kind of change, often we feel out of control. And we resist.

The flip side of this invasive change is the change that we initiate and sometimes even impose on others. When we are the initiators of change rather than the recipients of change, we still face resistance, often from others but sometimes even within ourselves. Church leaders, elected officials, even parents who propose change often encounter criticism and refusal to budge, even in people who know that the change could be advantageous. When others resist change that we initiate, we are tempted to give up ourselves and leave things the way they are. We all know that maintaining the status quo is more comfortable and far less disruptive than adapting to change or instigating something different.

The impact of these two types of change is a theme that appears often in the business and leadership books that continue to roll from the presses.[4] Frequently, these books give up-to-date insight into cultural trends and reach conclusions that can apply far beyond the business readers for whom the authors write. Men and women who lead companies have to cope with change that comes uninvited from the outside. They also must initiate change if they are to remain profitable and on the cutting edge of their businesses. Their experiences in the corporate world can teach all of us some lessons about adapting and thriving in the midst of change.

BUILT TO LAST IN TIMES OF CHANGE

Several years ago, two management consultants began an in-depth study of what they called "visionary companies."

According to researchers James Collins and Jerry Porras, some companies endure and are successful for long time periods, display remarkable resiliency in the face of constant change, and continue to thrive when their competitors begin to buckle under the stress. These visionary companies are "premier institutions—the crown jewels—in their industries, widely admired by their peers and having a long track record of making a significant impact on the world around."[5] Sometimes, but not always, these companies are founded or headed by visionary leaders. When the leaders retire or die, however, the companies keep prospering over long periods of time, even "through multiple product life cycles and multiple generations of active leaders."[6] These long-surviving companies bounce back and continue to thrive even in the midst of disruptive change.

How do they do this? What keeps them alive and growing in the midst of change? More important for us, how can their experiences apply to people who want to thrive and have lives that are well lived despite the hurricane forces that swirl all around? There are several answers.

Building for the Future
Companies and people who grow through change have a visionary perspective. They think ahead and don't get so distracted by ongoing demands that they forget where they are headed. At the press conference announcing Cardinal Bernardin's terminal illness, he stated that death could be seen as an enemy or as a friend. When we view death as an enemy to be feared, we slide into denial, he told the assembled reporters. As a believer, however, he saw death as a friend who would usher him into a better life. When we view death

as a prelude to something better, we face it honestly and continue to serve as best we can until the journey of life is ended.

Sam Walton, the founder of Wal-Mart, had a similar, forward-looking perspective. He assumed that he would not live until the year 2000. Nevertheless, shortly before his death in 1992, Walton set ambitious company goals for each year until the end of the century. "You can't just keep doing what works one time, because everything around you is always changing," Walton pointed out. "To succeed you have to stay out in front of change."[7] With this in mind, he thought often about the future and had a deep confidence in what his company would achieve after he died and others assumed leadership.

We handle change best when we maintain a long-range perspective that always keeps the future in view.[8]

Preserving the Core
We also handle change effectively when we know and stand firm in our core values. "If an organization is to meet the challenges of a changing world, *it must be prepared to change everything about itself except [its basic] beliefs,*" said the founder of IBM in words that could apply with equal validity to individuals.[9] When the giant computer company began to wander from its founder's core beliefs, it began to lose its stature and impact.

Collins and Porras repeat this idea all throughout their book. They write, "over time, cultural norms must change; strategy must change; product lines must change; goals must change; competencies must change; administrative policies must change; organization structure must change; reward systems must change. Ultimately, the *only* thing a company should *not* change over time is its core ideology."[10]

I have tried to communicate a similar message throughout this book. Stresses will come into our lives. Increasing demands and sweeping tides of information will pull us in different directions. On occasion, we will feel overwhelmed by tornadolike, potentially destructive winds of change. At such times, however, trustworthy stability is not found in a time-management program or a neatly ordered computer calendar, helpful though these may be. We cope and adapt most effectively when we know our rock-bottom values, stick with them, and refuse to budge on our commitments to love God, show compassion for others, maintain integrity, develop our spiritual gifts, and stand firmly anchored in biblically based beliefs. That's preserving the core of our values.

Stimulating Progress

Although the long-lasting visionary companies that Collins and Porras describe have clearly articulated core values, they are not stuck in routines or focused on the past. On the contrary, these companies hold firmly to their basic values and sense of purpose, but then they stimulate progress with all the creativity and enthusiasm that they can muster. In times of stress and unexpected change, it never occurs to people in highly visionary companies that they can't "beat the odds, achieve great things, and become something truly extraordinary."[11] They are always moving ahead.

To keep going forward, we must never allow ourselves to become complacent and satisfied. The people who work in successful companies keep looking for ways to improve, make progress, and do things better than they have been done in the past. They assume that "good enough never is." When stresses or unexpected changes jolt their company, the employees bounce back, encourage one another, and look for ways to make the company stronger.

Collins and Porras write that the best companies are willing to make bold commitments to "'Big Hairy Audacious Goals' (BHAGs). Like climbing a very high mountain or going to the moon, a BHAG may be daunting and perhaps risky," but it stimulates excitement and a sense of adventure. It is so challenging that it grabs people, "gets their juices flowing, and creates immense forward momentum."[12]

These BHAGs are not irresponsible goals, pursued without forethought or planning. They are creative, motivating, compelling, outside of one's comfort zone, but always consistent with the company's core values. These goals are so bold and exciting that they continue to stimulate progress even after the organization's leaders or the originators of the goals are long gone.

Bringing These High-Flying Ideas Down to Earth
I am realistic enough to know that BHAGs are attractive to high-energy, risk-taking, enthusiastic people but probably not very motivating to those who are more laid back. Most of us go through life trying to survive, hoping to get control of our schedules, and wanting to find some sense of fulfillment without having to worry about long-lasting corporations or "big, hairy, audacious goals." But we have taken several paragraphs to summarize the conclusions of the Collins and Porras book because they can apply to all of us.

Like the companies described, we all live with change, and we sometimes stimulate change in others. We calm the

167

demands and build better lives when we keep a future perspective, preserve our core values, and keep looking for ways to improve and grow.

When I first heard about Carla Gorrell, I could see a woman whose life demonstrated these principles, even before Jim Collins and Jerry Porras began their research.[13] Gorrell studied pastoral counseling and theology, but she failed to get even a single job offer after three years of contacting churches. Described as a woman who "turns obstacles, mishaps, and rejections into learning opportunities," Gorrell is a resilient person who sees adversity as a challenge rather than as a threat. When no jobs appeared, she started a not-for-profit company that she named Food & Friends. A divorced mother with three children, Gorrell would have preferred the security of steady employment. She had never run anything before, knew nothing about business, didn't know how to raise funds, and had no experience in delivering food. But she saw a need to have meals delivered to the growing numbers of HIV or AIDS patients in her neighborhood of Washington, D.C., so she created Food & Friends. Operating initially from the church where she was a member, the enterprising woman determined to create a caring cadre of volunteers who would deliver love, support, and much-needed food to sick people.

The company faced innumerable challenges and unanticipated change from the beginning. Gorrell encountered repeated rejection from organizations and people who might have been expected to help. She started applying for grants and donations but was turned down repeatedly (unlike today, when Food & Friends operates on a $2 million budget that comes almost totally from grant and donation money). When she formed a board of directors, she soon learned that two of the board members wanted her job and were determined to force her out. When snowstorms threatened to interfere with the deliveries or when volunteers failed to appear, Gorrell would respond with characteristic optimism and flexibility. Slowly, the organization grew to employ 20 people, to involve more than 800 volunteers, and to deliver more than 100,000 meals a year. When Gorrell and her board concluded together that there was need for a new leader who had better administrative and fund-raising skills, the founder of Food & Friends again faced the challenge of vocational change.

It is unlikely that Carla Gorrell ever expected to be held up as a model of leadership. One writer described her as a leader who has a special ability to rise above changing circumstances, to "be comfortable with the unknown, curious about it, and most important, willing to grow and adapt, based on what she learns. It is these qualities that prepare a leader [or anyone else] for the pressures of a rapidly changing world."[14] Like the visionary companies that we described earlier, Gorrell had a clear mission and direction for where she wanted to go and what she hoped to accomplish with her organization. She built on core values—values that the company still preserves—such as compassion, dependability, and a commitment to help people. Building from this core, she stimulated progress by trying whatever she could in order to get funds and to further the mission, learning from her failures and successes, and moving ahead when it might have been easier to give up.

Resisting Change

Everybody knows that the deluge of change that floods our lives can make our days more pressured and our lifestyles more hectic. It is not surprising, then, that we resist

169

change—even when we know in our minds that the changes might lift some pressures and ultimately be good. I went through this when I got my first computer and forced myself to shift from writing the old-fashioned way—with a pencil—to using a word processor instead. At first I resisted the change. Then I adapted. Now I'm glad I did.

Resistance to change is so common in counseling that "client resistance" has become a standard topic in every counseling textbook. Churches have resisted change since the time of the apostles. In businesses, governments, and academic institutions, some of the people who talk most enthusiastically about progress, moving forward, and making things better are the same people who dig in their heels and hold the line against making changes in their own lives and departments. Talking about change is always easier than making it happen.

We resist change and prefer the status quo for a variety of reasons. At the center of these suggestions is the issue of fear. Change can be threatening. We may not like the present situation, but if we dare to change, it is possible that we will lose something familiar and gain something that we won't want. It also is possible that change will make demands that we prefer to avoid.

I know a man who struggles with the decision to become a Christian. He is unsatisfied with his life at present and knows that he should make the commitment to Christ. But he is afraid of how this decision might change his lifestyle and his circle of friends. For him, making the change to becoming a believer is too risky.

Threat, fear of the unknown, and fear of failure are among the most common reasons for resisting change, but there are others.

1. The demands. Sometimes we resist making changes because it requires effort, adjustments, and time, all of which are in short supply.

2. Lethargy. We may keep things the way they are because we believe that the way we are doing things now has always worked, so why change? This might be called the "if it ain't broke, don't fix it" mentality that lets us cling to our old ways of doing things, no matter how outdated or inefficient those ways are.

3. Groupthink. This style of thinking becomes an obstacle to change. It maintains that since nobody else is changing and since everybody else seems content with the way things are, it makes no sense to change.

4. Procrastination. Sometimes we convince ourselves that the time for change is not ripe. Felix in the New Testament is an example. He was stirred and afraid when confronted with the sinfulness and inconsistencies in his life, but he abruptly ended his discussions with Paul and put off any decision about Christ until some later time that would be more convenient.[15]

5. Lack of confidence. Some changes can upset our self-confidence and self-esteem. We resist, then, because we're not sure we have the abilities, attitudes, or skills to meet the new challenges. Taking a familiar path is much safer in the short-term than venturing onto a road that is less traveled and not well mapped.

6. Status quo. Moving to new paths also can upset our traditions. As a result, we resist change because of a commitment to self-preservation and self-perpetuation. We convince ourselves and one another that if we change, we could become too liberal, too faddish, too irrelevant, too removed from "everything that has made this country great." The list of excuses for staying where we are is almost endless.

7. Pessimism. On occasion we become convinced that change won't really make any difference, so we decide not to bother. This kind of thinking surfaces before political elections. Perhaps with a touch of cynicism, we conclude that things haven't changed much in the past, so why should we bother to vote for one more politician promising change in the future?

8. Limited knowledge. A genuine lack of knowledge also gets in the way. We may want to tackle a new job or do creative things with our computers, but we don't know how to proceed.

9. Beliefs. Our values and attitudes also can get in the way of change. If we have a microwave mentality that values speed in getting things done, we have little interest in change that might slow us down. Many among us have myopic beliefs, concluding that the way *we* do things is the right way, so why should we change? Others like to keep their focus on the present, so they resist changes that promise long-term benefits but might involve some sacrifice or inconvenience right now. Why pass up the chocolate cake, change our eating habits, and go on a lengthy diet when the weight loss might not be visible for months?

This list of resistances could continue.[16] It could be illustrated with stories of people who use each of these ways of thinking to stay where they are and not change. These are people who have not, maybe cannot, and probably will not adapt to change. Like all of us, they continue to be inundated by change, but they resist. This, in turn, adds more pressure to their overcharged lives because they have to expend extra energy fighting off the changes.

We move forward more confidently when we carefully evaluate the changes that come into our lives and courageously throw off resistance when it keeps us stuck. Then we can accept the changes that are both consistent with our core values and able to stimulate the progress that will let us move ahead.

TAKING CHARGE OF CHANGE

When I finished my education in the mid sixties and entered the workforce, jobs were plentiful. Everybody assumed that by working hard, we could be fulfilled in our lives, move forward in our careers, do well financially, and expect to have bright futures, especially if we had ambition, marketable skills, and a good education. None of us paid a lot of attention to the hippies protesting in the streets. They didn't speak for us. We didn't worry much about job security, and if we thought about change, we assumed that in the future things would only get better. Some people talked about a time when there would be a four-day work week, and we worried a little about how we would spend all of the free time that the new labor-saving devices would provide. We were too young to think about retirement, but we knew in the back of our minds that social security and our pension plans always would be there to take care of us when we finished our careers. We assumed that our generation would retire in better health and at a younger age than our grandparents were when they left the workforce.

Things haven't turned out that way.

We never expected big government debt, deficit financing,

173

or the mismanagement of pension funds that now threatens to slash our incomes in later life. We didn't anticipate global competition that would highlight our weaknesses, new technologies that would make our skills obsolete, and massive downsizing that would strip away our job security. When I entered the workforce, nobody thought that future companies would avoid paying insurance and health-care benefits by hiring mostly part-time employees. We would never have predicted that our advanced degrees would make us over-qualified, that the jobs we hoped to get would go to people who had less training but were willing to accept smaller salaries. In those days we didn't know about the information age, about the dramatic changes in values that would permeate the society, or about huge specialty stores that would put little mom-and-pop businesses out of operation.

I'm not among those who long for the elusive "good old days" that probably were in reality a lot different from the fantasies that we carry in our memories. We live in exciting times, times that are different from anything that we expected and unlike anything in history before. If we are to maintain lives that are well lived, however, we cannot watch the rising and swirling waters of change and hope that by determining to stand firm, we will avoid being drowned.

What, then, do we do? How, then, shall we live?

We Remember the Source of Our Stability
The Bible reminds us that God is an anchor that holds us firm, a solid rock on which we can build, a safe haven to give us shelter in the midst of life's storms.[17] These are more than clichés that have been dropped into hymns over the centu-

ries. They are reminders that we cannot and we dare not try to deal with change and pressures on our own.

This conclusion seems to be seeping through the culture. Look at popular magazines. Tune in to talk shows. Listen to lyrics of popular music. Skim the shelves of bookstores, or look at the themes in many contemporary films. It is clear that people are searching. Many are looking for answers, for security, for spiritual guidance that our hedonistic, technological, change-driven society cannot provide. Sooner or later, the spirituality searchers will recognize that we don't find stability by cutting ourselves adrift from the almighty God and tying our lives to elusive guides and anchors within.[18] In an era of change, it is God who gives stability and provides a true moral compass to keep our lives on course and unswayed by the demands of life.

We Commit to Community
We need one another for support, encouragement, practical help, and the mutual planning that enables us to take practical steps for dealing with change. This is a recurring theme throughout these pages.

The Japanese sometimes talk about *kaizen,* a word that means "continuous improvement."[19] In the Asian culture that means growing and improving together. Teams of workers plan their work, develop new projects, evaluate progress, think creatively about the future, and develop strategies for coping with change—together, in community. We North Americans are more inclined to do things on our own. Without support or encouragement from others, however, it is harder to deal with change. All of us need other people with whom we can talk, laugh, handle life's surprises, and grow together. We need some local *kaizen* set within a context of community.

We Develop Change Hardiness

It is easy to be concerned about change or to feel over-whelmed by it. Taking action to do something about it is more difficult. I thought of this recently when a college news-paper described an alumnus whose consulting firm helps people develop "career hardiness." By learning new skills and attitudes, employees are able to remain flexible and shift direction if one career path ends. These are career hardy people.

Why couldn't we learn to develop a "change hardiness" that lets us remain flexible and stay strong whenever we encounter change? We keep our core beliefs, of course, but with resilient attitudes and continual improvement (*kaizen* style) in what we know and can do, we will find change less threatening or immobilizing.

How do we build change hardiness?

1. Learn to be flexible; plan ahead. Planning ahead is easier for some people than for others. It involves keeping contact with a network of co-workers, neighbors, fellow believers, and others who can give us help and assistance in times of stress or unusual change. It means thinking about possible scenarios in your life—like a terminal ill-ness, a forced layoff, or a serious loss. It involves giving thought to how you might prepare now so that coping will be easier later. Think about taking out insurance policies, keeping healthy, getting regular checkups, refining your mission. You may want to look at your work skills, consider taking courses to help you improve, and ponder alternative

lines of work or skills that you might develop now in case
your present job ends or your career collapses.

2. Be aware of your tendencies to resist. Resistance to
change is not always bad, providing we don't become rigid,
unteachable, and unwilling to grow. When you do choose to
resist, look at why and how you resist. If you are being
swayed by groupthink, for example, you may want to talk to
somebody outside the group and be sure that your resistance
is not being swayed by others. If you resist because you are
too busy to make any changes, ask if that is a good enough
reason to keep the status quo.

3. Keep the right mind-set. Shortly after I began taking
trips overseas, I developed a little motto that I carry in my
mind: *If you can't be flexible, stay home.* So often I have
watched disgruntled travelers loudly complaining to airline
employees, often about things that nobody can control—like
bad weather. Whenever I get stuck in an airport, I remind
myself of my motto and then try to do the hard part of waiting
calmly. Getting upset at the changes usually accomplishes
nothing.

In times of change and pressure, remind yourself that God
is in control, that our value as persons does not depend on
our being successful, that we don't have to be perfect parents
or perfect employees, that a little humility makes life a lot
less stressful, that God loves us unconditionally, and that he
is strong enough to give us help.

DID JESUS CHANGE?

Assuming that Jesus is our model of a well-lived life,
how did he deal with change? In at least two significant ways
he was different from those of us who live in these modern

times. First, he lived in a much simpler, nontechnological culture in which life was slower and change was much more gradual. Second, unlike us, he had knowledge of what was coming in the future. Before it happened, he knew that Judas would betray him, Peter would deny him, and the disciples would desert him. We don't have that advantage. Even so, Jesus lived in the midst of change. He created change, he coped with change in his own life, and he helped others anticipate and adapt to change.

Consider, first, how he created change. His teachings were so revolutionary that they shook the comfortable complacency of the religious leaders, radically altered the lifestyles of his disciples, and powerfully impacted people like Zaccheus and many of those who were healed.[20] Long before there were authors writing about businesses that last, Jesus stuck with his core values but then stimulated progress with what must have seemed like some "big, hairy, audacious goals." He challenged people to move away from the long entrenched traditions of their hypocritical leaders and to live lives that were consistent with the Scriptures. His sermon on the mount was one of many such proclamations that introduced new ways of thinking, brought amazement to his listeners, and so angered his smug religious critics that they began plotting his arrest. Today, followers of Christ are different from what they might have been because they have encountered Jesus and have been changed both now and for eternity.

In addition to creating change, Jesus also faced and handled change. Consider again the leprous man who aroused Jesus' compassion and was healed. Instead of keeping quiet about his newfound health, the man went out and began telling everybody about the good news. As a result, Jesus apparently couldn't enter public places without being overwhelmed by crowds, so he had to make a change in his ministry and stay in more out-of-the-way places.[21] Even there, the crowds came looking for him, maybe creating more pressure. Despite this, there is no evidence in Scripture that Jesus resisted or resented the apparent interruptions of unexpected requests for help. When he was going with Jairus to the bedside of Jairus's dying daughter, they were interrupted by a woman with a lifelong illness, but Jesus dealt calmly with the woman's need and then went on to Jairus's home. When he was walking along a roadway and spotted Zaccheus in a tree, Jesus stopped in the midst of his walk, told the man to come down, and went off to pay a life-changing visit to his house. Day after day Jesus dealt with the changing circumstances that came into his life.

Near the end of that life, Jesus turned much of his attention to helping his disciples and others anticipate and adapt to the major changes that were ahead. He told them that he was leaving, that he would die, and that he would come again. He assured them that they would not be left alone and that he was going to prepare a place for them. He prepared them for the work that they would do after he was gone, warned them that there would be opposition, and gave them encouragement.

Jesus was an initiator of change, a source of encouragement in the midst of change, and a teacher who prepared his followers to anticipate and cope with coming change. From his quiet Middle Eastern society he taught us—as the next chapter shows and as Cardinal Bernardin demonstrated—

that we will deal best with the changes of life when we learn to order our private mental worlds.

TAKING A STEP TOWARD
Becoming Adaptable

As you reflect on this chapter, take some time to answer these questions. You may want to do that in a journal, with a friend, or in a group. Allow the questions to help you focus on how you will learn to deal with continuing change.

1. How do you respond to change at this stage in your life?
2. Are you more likely to resist change or initiate change?
3. If you resist change, what most often fuels your resistance? How does your resistance affect the people around you?
4. If you initiate change, what most often compels you to change? How does your initiating change affect the people around you?
5. In your experience, what are the key ingredients to positive change?
6. What can you do to develop change hardiness?

Soul Care
Nurturing
Your Inner World

HENRYK GÓRECKI has been called one of
this century's most important living composers.[1] His classical works have outsold pop music for the first time in the
history of rock 'n' roll. He is revered by music critics,
known by British punksters, and embraced enthusiastically
by a music world that saw his Symphony No. 3 top *Bill-
board* magazine's hit list for two years.

Despite all of this acclaim, the composer lives quietly,
with his wife of four decades, near his hometown city of
Katowice in the south of Poland. Residing only a few miles
from Auschwitz, Górecki and his family survived the Nazi
atrocities but then faced the hardships of Communism. In the
1960s, as provost of Poland's premier music academy, he
fought ideological battles with the Communist party and
struggled to break their grip on the nation's arts. When he
wrote *Miserere*, a musical work commemorating a violent

police action against Solidarity protesters, the work was banned in Poland by General Wojciech Jaruzelski.

Now, Jaruzelski is gone, but Górecki and his musical works are growing in popularity and acclaim. When he meets the media hounds who push for interviews, however, the composer is very clear about the source of his strength and musical creativity. "Faith for me is everything," he says without hesitation. "If I did not have that support, I could not have passed the obstacles in my life."[2]

Unlike most musical idols of our day, Górecki doesn't like talking about himself. Musicologists might describe his works as evidence of inherent musical greatness, but the composer would rather give the accolades to his Creator and Redeemer. This commitment is reflected in the music. It draws from a variety of sources, including Polish folk songs, but the composer often chooses texts from the Psalms or Catholic liturgy. His once-banned *Miserere* has only seven words of text, "Lord our God, have mercy on us."

Górecki is a *"rare God-tinged individual who labors quietly, against discouraging odds, patiently honing his gift in relative anonymity."*[3] Please read those italicized words again. Can you think of a better description of a life that is well lived, a life that has been like an island of stability in a part of the world undergoing significant political, economic, and moral change? The composer with the unsought and unanticipated fame has moved calmly through life, productive, fulfilled, and untainted by the acclaim. Clearly something about the man's inner nature keeps him from crumbling under life changes and challenges or from being swept along by cheering fans.

NEGLECTING OUR PRIVATE WORLDS

Far from Henryk Górecki's Poland, a pastor in Oklahoma struggled with his busy life—running a church, being a husband, trying to be a good father to his four children, writing books, ministering to needy people, struggling to pay bills when there was not enough money. Eventually the pace took its toll. There was no theological heresy, misuse of power, financial improprieties, or sexual immorality for the tabloids to splash into their headlines. Instead, according to the pastor, "I lost touch with the center of my being. My soul just disappeared beneath the weight of college degrees, sacks of groceries, piles of bills, and the burden of too many worries and not enough hours in the day for extended prayer, personal reflection, and solace."[4] Sadly, in the midst of his busyness, pastor Robert Wise didn't even notice that his inner life had shriveled from neglect.

Regardless of our age, occupation, or lifestyle, we all have private thoughts that fill our minds, stir our emotions, motivate our actions, shape our self-concepts, influence our relationships, and have an impact on the way we live. Psychologists sometimes refer to these private thoughts as "self-talk," the inner conversations that we carry on in our minds, with ourselves, most of the time.

Whatever words we use—private thoughts, self-talk, inner conversations, personal reflections, or some other terms—they all point to a private world within. It is a world in our brains, a world that can't be observed by a CAT scan or dissected surgically. It is a world that can be cultivated and nourished, but a world that more often is neglected, ignored, and allowed to be overgrown with harmful values and distorted perspectives. Sometimes this secret world is filled with self-deceptive ideas, sexually explicit fantasies, or self-berating conclusions that nobody else can see. When we keep our inner worlds hidden securely from the prying eyes of others, there is no one to warn of the inaccuracies or dangers in this mental weed patch of self-destructive ideas. By keeping our thoughts rigidly private, we surround our minds with a Berlin Wall that keeps out anybody who might challenge the evidences of mental neglect or hold us accountable for nourishing and cultivating our inner worlds.

When Robert Wise was swept along in a hectic schedule of busyness and "nervous activism," he failed to see that he was surrounded by many others whose inner terrains were empty, like his own. These people were contemporary examples of what T. S. Elliot called hollow men. Pastor Wise saw this wasteland most clearly in the movies that he frequently attended. "Antiheroes had become new heroes; degenerate people with degrading values gained cinema star status. Gangsters, psychotics, and the promiscuous were Hollywood's fascination. The music industry bestowed on us rappers, Madonna, Mick Jagger, and a host of rock stars (many of whom jettisoned themselves into eternity with drugs) for our adulation. Something was seriously amiss."[5]

Jesus knew something was amiss when he walked the earth and encountered the distorted inner worlds of his day. Mincing no words, he accused some religious leaders of being full of greed, self-indulgence, hypocrisy, and wickedness.[6] Herod, the local political leader, surrounded himself with the prestige and outward trappings of his office, but Jesus knew that on the inside, in his inner world, Herod was a fox—sly, scheming, insecure, and morally weak.[7]

Two millennia have passed since the time of Christ, but human nature has not changed. We enter the twenty-first century pushed by more changes and demands than any generation has seen before, but still our inner worlds are filled with distorted perspectives, decadent values, and self-imposed demands that undermine our efforts to build well-lived lives.

The religious talk of many sermons often makes little contact with people whose inner lives have withered or been twisted by distorted thinking. The interventions of professional therapists may fail as well to touch the inner emptiness of people in desperate need of help. Even the carefully developed time-management programs can falter because they don't connect with the inner worlds of the people who struggle to control their schedules and comply with the time-management packages.

FOUR INTERNAL FORCES

Following a busy summer filled with travel, people, and pressures, Julie and I reached the end of an action-packed conference in Singapore and flew with some friends to a seaside town in Thailand. Our friends had invited us to travel as their guests, and we all had a wonderful few days together. During that minivacation, the book that you are reading now was stirring in my mind. I was wondering if I should, or could, write it. This must have come into our conversation more than once, because our traveling companions kept telling us about a still relevant little publication that appeared in 1941. When we left Asia to return home, they gave us a copy as a parting gift.

The book's author was a Quaker educator with a heart of compassion and a mind sharpened by advanced studies in theology and philosophy. But Thomas Kelly never lived with his head in the clouds. Our lives have grown too complex and overcrowded, he wrote:

> Even the necessary obligations that we feel we must meet grow overnight, like Jack's beanstalk, and before we know it we are bowed down with burdens, crushed under committees, strained, breathless, and hurried, panting through a never-ending program of appointments. We are too busy to be good wives to our husbands, good homemakers, good companions of our children, good friends to our friends, and with no time at all to be friends of the friendless. . . . And in frantic fidelity we try to meet at least the necessary minimum of calls upon us. But we're weary and breathless. . . .
>
> We are giving a false explanation of the complexity of our lives. We blame it upon the complex environment. Our complex living, we say, is due to the complex world we live in, with its radios and autos, which give us more stimulation per square hour than used to be given per square day to our grandmothers.
>
> We Western people are apt to think our great problems are external, environmental. We are not skilled in the inner life, where the real roots of our problem lie. For I would suggest that the true explanation of the complexity of our program is an inner one, not an outer one.[8]

Kelly lived at a time when people were made weary and breathless by stimulation coming from radios and autos. He

never could have imagined the enormously more complex
world that we inhabit. Living in this world, it seems that most
of us have inner lives that are dominated by one or more of at
least four perspectives.

Driven

Some people are *driven*. They tear through life, feeling
pushed to get things done, determined to make the best use
of every minute, controlled by the tyranny of the urgent. In
their minds they know that their lives are too busy, that balance is essential, that their bodies can be pushed only so far
before they collapse. Even so, they keep going as if they are
invulnerable and indestructible, charged with more to do
than any normal human could handle. Their friends rarely
challenge this way of life. Instead, we applaud their energy,
admire their creativity, and reinforce their lifestyles. This
encourages them to run faster. In time they become like the
cars on a roller coaster, moving at breakneck speed and with
such momentum and excitement that they wouldn't know how
to stop even if they tried.

Distracted

Other people have inner worlds that appear to be *distracted*.
These people are no less busy than their neighbors who are
driven, but the inner life of distraction has no direction. It is
true that chemical imbalances, the basis of Attention Deficit
Disorder, can thwart the ability of some people to focus their
efforts and attention. But with or without biological abnor-
malities, easily distracted people spend their days feeling
scattered, unproductive, and frustrated. Life for them is filled
with obligations, demands, and unfinished projects. Talk to

them about ordering their private worlds, and they might agree, but they don't get very far in organizing their lives before they are pulled in yet another direction.

Drifting

Very different are people who are *drifting*. They might be committed Christians, dedicated employees, people who love their families and work to provide for them. If we could catch a glimpse of their private thoughts, however, we would find that their inner worlds are mostly empty, their thinking superficial, their knowledge of God limited, and their spiritual lives virtually nonexistent. Often these people have few goals and no real purpose in life. They drift along, sometimes swept by the trends and shifting values that pour from their television sets. Maybe they are like the people that Jesus described, who build their houses on sand, without any firm foundation, putting themselves in danger of being blown away by the storms of life.

Dogmatic

Sometimes people who neglect their inner lives become *dogmatic*. They make up their minds about issues and refuse to budge. Bias, prejudice, and intolerance have caused incredible harm and misery in this world, often coming from people whose inner worlds are constricted, rigid, and so firmly set in a mental cement that change is almost impossible.

I am uncomfortable looking at this list. I have some strongly held beliefs and firm values, but I never want to be dogmatic, insensitive, and unwilling to listen to others with whom I disagree. My friends probably would never call me a drifter. I fit a little more closely with those who are distracted. But mostly, my inner world has been driven. I can understand some of the reasons for this, but whatever the causes, it is clear that those of us who are driven on the inside have difficulty resisting pressures from the outside. We embrace new opportunities, activities, and projects enthusiastically. We immediately see their potential, and they keep our lives moving and exciting. They also keep our lives pressured and breathless.

THE INNER WORLD OF THE SOUL

Many of our private thoughts are shielded securely from others because we are afraid that our inner reflections might show a side of us that almost nobody knows or would understand. It is a side that includes thoughts about possibilities, failures, dreams, fears, insecurities, desires, sexual preferences, beliefs, regrets, and opinions. "We fear that if anyone eavesdrops on our private thoughts, we will be exposed as shallow, sleazy, ignorant, evil, or immature. Or we worry that people will think us arrogant, egotistical, selfish, or sentimental."[9] We try not to think about the biblical statement that someday the Lord himself will "bring to light what is hidden in darkness and will expose the motives of men's hearts."[10] It is hard to accept the idea that God sees my inner world, has perceived "my thoughts from afar," and someday will expose this to any who might listen in.[11]

The private inner world that we have been discussing seems very similar to what the Bible means by the word *soul*. Unlike modern scientific writers, people in biblical times did not worry about giving concise, technical definitions of words like *heart, mind,* and *soul.* Sometimes the Greek word for *soul* is translated "life"; at other times the word refers to the inner self or personality.[12] When God created Adam, he became a living soul—a personality distinct from all animals. In Luke 1:46 Mary sang about her soul [inner self] magnifying the Lord, and Jesus once indicated that his soul was sorrowful.[13]

"The soul is something within every one of us—a self—that is unique, God-created, and eternal," according to Gordon MacDonald, who writes often about our inner worlds.[14] The soul is an "inner space" intended to be a dwelling place for God, although it has been polluted by sin. When we get caught in nets of hedonism, materialism, rationalism, or bustling hyperactivity, the soul is neglected and we live as if we are soulless. It is then that one becomes "a strangely hollow person, almost an automated kind of human being who spends most of life simply responding to events and circumstances, to glands, instincts, and passions or ambitions beyond explanation."[15]

Christians have been talking about the soul for centuries, but something unexpected has happened within the past couple of decades. The soul has become a popular topic. If you walk into the religion section of any secular bookstore, you will find dozens of books about the soul, books with titles like *Care of the Soul, Soul Mates, The Soul's Code, Handbook for the Soul,* or *Soul Searching.* Even *Time* magazine has dealt with the soul, calling it "a place where spirit and body interact."[16] If you look carefully at these secular writings, however, you will discover that Jesus Christ is missing. People who write popular books about spirituality and soul care use many of the same words that Christians use, but the meaning is different. This can lead to a lot of confusion.[17]

Writing from his strong Christian perspective, Gordon MacDonald refers to the soul as "the deeper part of all of us that others cannot see. It is the quiet place where people are most apt to connect with God."[18] Undoubtedly, many contemporary New Age people could agree with such a statement, but they would have a different view of God. Christians know God as a supernatural being of infinite majesty, holiness, compassion, and mercy—Lord of the universe, Creator of all things, Redeemer, giver of abundant and eternal life. The god of contemporary writers is more like a force, slowly enveloping people who look within themselves for enlightenment and who want a sense of oneness with the universe. These individuals would agree with the theme of this chapter: we cannot get free of driven, distracted, drifting, or dogmatic lifestyles until we make changes in our inner lives. They would not agree with the assertion that such inner change, such *soul care*, comes only when we submit to the sovereign God who has revealed himself in the Bible and who alone can transform us within.

INNER SOUL CARE

The work of Jesus was all about transforming lives. He challenged his listeners to repent, to believe, and to change their behavior.[19] When he was presented with a woman caught in the act of adultery, he forgave her and instructed her to leave her life of sin.[20] He was gentle and forgiving with people who admitted their sin, but some of his strongest criticisms were directed at the ostentatious teachers of the law, who paraded their piety but were spiritually dead on the inside. He called them "whitewashed tombs, which look beautiful on the outside but on the inside are full of dead men's bones and everything unclean." These were people "who appeared to be righteous but on the inside were filled with hypocrisy and wickedness."[21] They were people who needed inner transformation.

It is logical to assume that when these powerful people were publicly criticized, they would try hard to find in Jesus' life some hypocrisy that they could use to launch a counterattack. Instead they found a man whose outward life was consistently beyond reproach or criticism. Jesus showed and taught how this could be possible. "It is the thought-life that defiles you," he said. "For from within, out of a person's heart, come evil thoughts, sexual immorality, theft, murder, adultery, greed, wickedness, deceit, eagerness for lustful pleasure, envy, slander, pride, and foolishness. All these vile things come from within; they are what defile you and make you unacceptable to God."[22]

For a life to be well lived on the outside, there must be purity on the inside. This is purity that comes only as we strive to keep our minds free from Hollywood impurity, cultural perversity, Internet pornography, and polluted mental fantasies. It is purity that comes only to those who determine, with God's help, to keep their minds focused on things that are true, noble, right, pure, lovely, admirable, excellent, and praiseworthy.[23] It is purity that comes best when we pull away from the pressures of our busy lives, meditate on Scripture, and, like Jesus, find the time to spend with the Father in prayer.[24]

Jesus did not let the pressures of his life interfere with his time alone with the Father. He must have been aware of the limited time allotted to him, but he was never hurried or rushed. He wasn't driven, distracted, or drifting; and despite his firm beliefs, he could never have been called dogmatic and rigid. Because he took care of his inner world, he was free from hypocrisy. Everybody could see that his life was well lived.

INNER CARE AND IMPOSSIBLE ACTIVITIES

Brother Andrew knows about transformed lives. He must be a remarkable man, but he probably would deny this. He never went to high school or college but got his training at a missionary school, where he spent much of his time crippled with back pain. He describes himself as a "dumb Dutchman, the son of a blacksmith" who now works "for a Jewish carpenter. In other words, I'm just an ordinary guy who has tried to listen for God's calling in my life and then obey."[25] In 1955, when Communism held Eastern Europe in its grip, Brother Andrew slipped behind the Iron Curtain with Bibles for Christians who lived under the constant danger of arrest, imprisonment, or death because of their faith. Soon the man who would come to be known as "God's Smuggler" was risking his own life in a very dangerous, one-man mission to bring the Scriptures to people who needed encouragement and copies of God's Word.[26] Today his activities continue in other countries where Bibles are forbidden. He has visited house churches in Muslim countries, organized the smuggling of over one million Bibles into China, and even proclaimed his Christian faith and given Bibles to guerrillas in Latin America.

More than forty years ago, when Brother Andrew was a student in Scotland, he read *My Utmost for His Highest,* a book by Oswald Chambers, whose widow was living at that time in the south of England. Andrew wrote to Mrs. Chambers, expressed appreciation for her husband's book, and received a warm reply inviting him to visit at some time. Christmas was coming, and the young student had no money to go home to Holland, so he asked Mrs. Chambers if he could spend the holidays with her family.

Back at the college in January, the principal asked Andrew

where he had been during the previous two weeks. When the young man answered that he had stayed with the Oswald Chambers family, he got an astonished reply. "You can't do that!" the principal exclaimed. "You do not just go and visit the family of a great spiritual man such as Oswald Chambers."

"Maybe not," Andrew answered with a smile. "But I just did it."[27]

Brother Andrew has been doing "impossible" things all his life. He feels a kinship with the ordinary Bible people who went to impossible places and did remarkable things because they decided to obey God, even when other people said "You can't do that!"[28]

I have never met Brother Andrew, but his books give the impression of a man whose life is full and busy but whose inner world is serene and confident, without being driven, distracted, drifting, or dogmatic. So many of us rush about, working hard, building careers, doing things for God, pulled by countless obligations that tug us in different directions. Then we run into people whose lives are full, even busy, but who exude a cheerful disposition that seems unpressured, unflustered, untangled in the worries of this life. These are not people in denial, individuals out of contact with reality, or super-saints who spend hours in meditation. They are people like the man Brother Andrew seems to be—individuals who radiate a quiet inner peace and power, even in the midst of their active lives. The rest of us look on with admiration but tell ourselves "I can't do that!"

ORDERING OUR INNER WORLDS

When I read Thomas Kelly's book on the plane bringing us back from Singapore, I was fascinated with his suggestion that each of us has a "committee of selves." I spent enough years as a professor to know that colleges, universities, and seminaries are filled with committees that consume huge amounts of time, engage in endless talk, and take forever to make decisions. I know a number of slow-moving churches, businesses, and professional organizations that work in the same way. It was disconcerting to read that I might have a committee inside of me.

"Each of us tends to be, not a single self, but a whole committee of selves," writes Kelly. "There is the civic self, the parental self, the financial self, the religious self, the society self, the professional self, the literary self." Probably all of us could add other "selves" to the list. "And each of our selves is in turn a rank individualist, not cooperative but shouting out its vote loudly for itself. . . . It is as if we have a chairman of our committee of the many selves within us who does not integrate the many into one."[29] Instead, the self that clamors for attention gets heard, and the others are disgruntled and still clamoring. This is an interesting and disturbing picture of the life that many of us live. We feel divided by the competing selves or demands on the inside and pulled in different directions by pressures on the outside.

But life does not have to be that way. We can be transformed into people with less clamor and more serene centers to our lives. The transformation doesn't come suddenly, like a revolution that disrupts our schedules and topples our stability. The change does not come by adding more religion, rules, or requirements to our already busy and complex schedules. On rare occasions, God may work in special ways to change lives abruptly—as he changed Saul of Tarsus. More often the transformation is a slow and steady pilgrim-

195

age that moves us toward greater inner serenity, abiding peace, and continual communion with God so that we grow into people who are more and more like Christ.

As we grow internally, we don't ignore the demands of our daily schedules, push aside exciting opportunities, or throw away the goals and dreams that add purpose to our lives. But as we nurture and keep aware of the inner world that is guided by the Holy Spirit, we begin to sense a growing serenity and stability deep within. Slowly we begin to sense a personal peace at the core of our lives despite the hectic demands coming from our everyday worlds.[30] Instead of being dogmatic, drifting, distracted, or driven by an inner committee of selves and a host of outer demands, the soul undergoing transformation is marked by devotion and discipline.

Devotion

If people looked at your life, what would they conclude about your devotion? Would they assume that you are devoted to work, television, sports, religious activity, music, making money, building your career? What would they see if they could look past your outward behavior and into your inner world? Would they see a drive for success, fame, or wealth?

Some spiritual giants suggest that there may be different levels of the inner life. Much of our thinking is superficial and useful self-talk concerned with our feelings, evaluations, and decisions about events in our daily lives. But there also can be a deeper level, an inner sanctuary of the soul, a place where we commune with God in adoration, worship, prayer, and listening. "It is at this deep level that the real business of life is determined," writes Thomas Kelly.[31] The "religious person is forever bringing all affairs of the first level down into the Light, holding them all there in the Presence, reseeing them and the whole of the world of people and things in a new and overturning way. . . . Facts remain facts when brought into the Presence [of God] in the deeper level, but their value, their significance, is wholly realigned."[32] It is at this center of life that we can sing with the psalmist, "Praise the Lord, O my soul; all my inmost being, praise his holy name."[33] It is here that we can pray, "Search me, O God, and know my heart; test me and know my anxious thoughts. See if there is any offensive way in me, and lead me in the way everlasting."[34] It is at this deepest level that we stop trying to tell God what to do and become listeners who, like Mary, can say without hesitation, "I am the Lord's servant," ready to obey.[35]

A life well lived is a life devoted to knowing God as he has revealed himself in Scripture. It is a life that seeks to bring every decision and every thought captive to Christ.[36] It is at this core of life that we determine to be honest with God, genuinely sorry for our sins and failures, sensitive to his leading, willing to obey completely. Here is soul care at its deepest level—a level that most people in our rush-about world know nothing about, a level that New Age searchers look for but never find.

Discipline

When Robert Wise lost touch with this deepest level and noticed that his inner life had withered from neglect, he went for spiritual refreshment and soul care to a Benedictine monastery. Most of us can't do that. To be honest, I don't want to do that, helpful as it might be. Certainly, our spiritual lives would deepen and our lifestyles would be far less hectic if we could set aside long periods every day for prayer, Bible reading, and meditation at the deepest levels. In doing this, however, a lot of us would lose our jobs, our incomes, and our families. I see no evidence in Scripture to suggest that God expects all of us to stop our lives and withdraw into days or months of solitude and reflection. But God does want us to be disciplined.

Most adults understand the value of discipline. Every athlete or musician knows the importance of consistent, sometimes tedious practice if one is to play well. We teach our children the value of discipline and know that we must discipline ourselves if we are to get control of our time, weight, careers, schedules, spending practices, or harmful habits. The spiritual disciplines that have captured our attention during the past few years are practices that can make us more Christlike, more in contact with God at the deep levels of the soul, and more at peace inside.[37] These disciplines include prayer, knowing Scripture, solitude, worship, serving, stewardship, and evangelism. They are spiritual exercises, commanded in the Bible (not optional for believers), intended to help us grow and mature spiritually.[38] God expects us to permanently and consistently bring devotional exercises into our lives for the promotion of godliness. To find this inner peace and godliness, we must squeeze some time into our frenzied lives to be still and to acknowledge that he is God.

How can busy people do this? Start realistically. Adding ten minutes to your daily schedule for prayer and Bible reading is realistic for everybody; suddenly adding an hour is a setup for failure. In developing the disciplines, be creative. Almost every day I go for a walk early in the morning. This is a quiet time and a wonderful opportunity to talk with God and to let my mind dwell on praise and worship. Bible reading, reflection, and other disciplines come at other times, but I can worship while I walk.

Former Dallas Cowboys coach Tom Landry once described his job as making men do what they don't want to do in order to achieve what they've always wanted to be. Spiritual disciplines are similar. They are exercises that we don't naturally want to do—especially when we are busy with so many other things. But they are exercises that enable us to be like Christ at the core of our being—just as we have always wanted to be.[39]

Exercises like this serve a purpose. When there is discipline without direction, we easily get discouraged and feel defeated. We are more willing to commit to discipline when we realize that such a commitment leads to closer communion with God, greater inner purity, and a more consistently well-lived life. The growth that will come from spiritual discipline will be slow and often imperceptible. But to avoid giving up, remember where you are going—to a deeper level of commitment, Christlikeness, and inner peace that is beyond understanding.[40] Remember, too, that like dieting, the spiritual disciplines are less likely to fail if you are involved with others who have similar goals, convictions, and commitments. "No one can journey alone—much less grow—in the pursuit of spirituality."[41] We need others for mutual submission, accountability, support, and encouragement as we discipline ourselves to grow in godliness.

A FRESH REMINDER FROM AN OLD HYMN

As I have grown older, I have become more and more convinced that worship in the company of other believers is an important part of my inner spiritual growth. Just as I make room for personal times of solitary listening and spending time with God, I must not neglect time for corporate praise and teaching. For many years I attended churches where we sang very old hymns, whose words I can sing today from memory. While the church I attend now sings contemporary Scripture songs rather than hymns, I still appreciate many of those old hymns. They contain some rich lyrics that sometimes pop into my mind. Probably you are familiar with this one:

> *Trust and obey,*
> *For there's no other way*
> *To be happy in Jesus,*
> *But to trust and obey.*

The simple words of this hymn can be a clear guide for effective soul care and for nurturing the inner world. To trust and obey is the God-given way to deal more peacefully with demanding daily pressures of living, to fill the emptiness of our inner worlds, and to have lives that are well lived.

TAKING A STEP TOWARD
Becoming Christlike

As you reflect on this chapter, take some time to answer these questions. You may want to do that in a journal, with a friend, or in a group. Allow the questions to help you focus on how you will nurture your soul.

1. What are the greatest obstacles to the care of your soul?
2. In what ways are you driven or distracted or drifting or dogmatic? What can you do to counter that?
3. What "selves" are struggling inside you?
4. What will you do to increase your devotion?
5. In what areas does your inner world need discipline? What steps will you take to bring discipline to that area?
6. How does your time of worship with other believers affect your life and contribute to building your inner world? What changes can you make to ensure that your worship and interaction with other believers is even better? How will you do this, and when will you start?

CHAPTER 11

Growth
Sharpening Your Mind
and Moving Forward

EVERYBODY had heard about them. They were known as the two best and fastest lumberjacks in the West. They could cut down more trees and clear through more brush in a day than any of the other workers.

One day somebody suggested having a contest between the two men, and a week or so later a small crowd gathered for the big showdown. The lumberjacks started promptly at sunrise and worked the whole day. One man labored with incredible enthusiasm and energy, pushing himself to the limit without stopping until quitting time. The other man worked with equal diligence, but at various times during the day he stopped and sat for a while on one of the fallen tree trunks.

When the trees were counted at the end of the day, the man who had worked without stopping was declared the loser. "I don't understand that," he said. "I worked the hardest. I kept going. I never stopped. Why didn't I cut down the most trees?"

"That's an easy question to answer," replied the winner. "Whenever I stopped, I sharpened my saw."

The story sounds more fictional than real. I said so when a friend shared it with me during an especially hectic time in my life, but I got the point.

Stephen Covey made a similar point in one of his best-selling books.[1] Highly effective people consistently take time to "sharpen the saw" of their lives by stretching their minds and investing in themselves. The only instrument you have for making a difference, being effective, dealing with life, and making a contribution is *you*.

Maybe you resist this idea, as I did at first. To make a difference, don't we need other people who can work alongside us? Aren't opportunities important? Aren't we supposed to be like clay in the divine potter's hand, willing to let God work through us to touch others? Doesn't education have some bearing on the contributions we make in life? Of course the answer to these questions is yes. But if we don't take care of ourselves—resting our bodies, sharpening our minds, being with people, cultivating our spirituality—we dry up mentally, become sluggish physically, cool down spiritually, and drain away the energy and fresh perspectives that give zest to living. In time, our efficiency declines, others pass us by, opportunities become fewer, and past experiences or a good education cease to make much difference.

Not far from the place where I am writing these words, a sad-looking houseplant sits on a counter where I have been trying to work some resuscitation. It was healthy once, but I got busy and forgot to fertilize and water it. When plants are neglected, they wither and eventually die. A few feet away, outside the house, is a magnificent splash of color. The tiny impatiens plants that I set out in the spring have flourished and now overflow the flowerbeds with a profusion of pink, red, white, coral, and rose-colored blossoms. Every day I have watered these plants—sometimes twice on days when the sun was hot. I have encouraged their growth with fertilizer and watched them flourish. Anybody who passes the house can see this from the street. In a few weeks the frost will end this show, but for now the plants are thriving.

You know where I am going with these examples. Take the time and extend the effort to renew yourself, and you can expect to flourish. If a storm or two come along, you will be robust enough to survive and grow stronger. If you dismiss the need to care for yourself, your impact will be dulled, your resiliency weakened.

Growth is slow. We can't see it while it happens, and initially we don't notice if it stops through lack of nourishment. When we are busy being productive, driven, and distracted by all the pressures or possibilities of life, we can forget about the need to care for ourselves. Often we don't even notice the neglect until our bodies collapse, our relationships disintegrate, our souls wither, or our minds become dull and flabby. Unsharpened saws, untended plants, and uncultivated lives have this in common—eventually they lose their effectiveness and potential to make an impact. Without a commitment to growth and self-improvement, we can never hope to get control of our breathless lifestyles or have lives that are well lived.

STARTING WITH THE MIND

In Gordon MacDonald's classic book about ordering your private world, he wrote about busy pastors who struggle with

feelings of failure and ineffectiveness. In talking with these
pastors, MacDonald often asks the question, What are you
reading lately? Most often, the answer is nothing. People who
don't read get out of shape intellectually, start depending on
the thoughts and opinions of others, and become "mentally
empty people who have stopped growing and are spending
their lives in the pursuit of little more than amusement."[2]

Journaling

Reading is one way to sharpen yourself mentally, but there
are others. For many years I have kept a journal. It isn't anything fancy. I use an inexpensive loose-leaf notebook. When
I travel, I take a few blank sheets with me, jot down my
reflections, and slip the pages into the notebook after I return
from the trip. I don't force myself to write every day, but usually once or twice a week I record reflections on what has
been happening, describe conversations that I have had, jot
down my reactions to a sermon, or work through my struggles
on paper. For me, writing is a form of therapy. Thinking with
a pen and paper reinforces my values, clarifies my direction,
and keeps me from jumping in response to every pressure,
demand, or opportunity that comes into my life. I rarely look
back over what I have written, but the process of writing
keeps me sharp.

Learning from Living

I have a good friend who studied for several years in the
United States and recently returned to his home country.
When we talked by phone a few days after the move, he
described the adjustment difficulties that he and his family
were having, and we reflected on the ways in which his life

had changed so significantly. Another friend lost his mother without much warning and is having to reorganize his life. These men are learning from their experiences and growing while they struggle with the changes.

"As long as you live, keep learning how to live," Seneca said, centuries ago. Sometimes when I drive to work, I keep the radio off and reflect on where my life has been going and how I should make changes. I think about what I've accomplished during the previous day or two and ask myself what could be done better. Sometimes I conclude that "I have done those things that I ought not to have done, and left undone the things that I ought to have done."[3] I ponder ways to use my time better, to reach my goals, to resist temptation, or to grow spiritually. I think about things in my life that I don't like, and I plan ways to change. I reflect on my relationships and try to reach conclusions about how I can build quality time with others into my schedule.

This is not unhealthy introspection. It is ongoing self-reflection and self-renewal that keeps me growing and prevents me from getting into a rut. I read once that Socrates thought most of us approached life backward. We give most attention to the least important things and the least attention to things that are most important.[4] Self-reflection and learning from the way I am living helps me to put the most important things first.

GROWING SHARPER THROUGH INTERACTION

On a recent Valentine's Day a friend of mine held a party for his single friends, many of whom can feel left out on a day devoted to lovers. "We had a wonderful time," my friend related enthusiastically a few days after the event.

"When I have a party, we have lots of food and plenty of conversation. I like to ask my Christian friends to come, and I invite non-Christians as well. We don't play games or watch videos. We sit around and talk." Apparently the conversation at the recent party was stimulating and enjoyable to everybody who was present.

Idle chatter about nothing does little to stimulate our minds. Equally useless is gossip about others or excessively detailed, one-sided conversations about somebody's relatives, vacations, work problems, or physical ailments. But when people get together to talk about issues that are mutually interesting, everybody can grow. My friend likes to read, and so do many of his friends, so the conversation at his parties—and whenever he meets somebody for lunch—can be mind sharpening. Just as iron sharpens iron, so one person can sharpen another whenever there is mutual interaction.[5]

THE ART OF MENTORING

For many generations, as people got older they shared their knowledge, wisdom, and insights with family members and younger acquaintances. The passing on of skills, talent, and folklore from one generation to another was the basis for survival. Mothers taught their daughters and fathers taught their sons about life, work, and maturing. Scholars often taught students like Mentor (a character in Homer's *Odyssey*), who gave us the word *mentoring* and who gave himself to educating the young Telemachus. Knights taught novice soldiers how to fight, and spiritual mentors like the apostle Paul taught younger men like Timothy about living and growing as disciples and committed followers of Christ.

Much of this faded as society got more complex and our

lives became more hectic, but recently mentoring has returned to popularity. It is mentioned so often in business books and management theory that some see it as a fad that will fade.[6] For many years, however, medical interns, articled law students, apprentice tradespeople, and graduate students writing dissertations all have experienced mentoring. Recently, the Christian community has been flooded with books and articles about mentoring; some of these writings turn mentoring into a formal and highly structured process.[7]

More often, mentoring is seen not as an organized program but as an ongoing relationship, sometimes formal but more commonly informal, between a person with skills, knowledge, experience, or maturity and another person who is usually younger, often with similar interests or in a similar vocation, and has a willingness to learn. Probably each mentor and each protégé define mentoring a little differently, and it is likely that every mentoring relationship is unique and in some ways different from all others.

Often the mentor is a model, an encourager, an informal teacher, and a spiritual coach. Sometimes mentors and their protégés are in the same family or same workplace. While mentors and protégés usually are people who meet together in a one-to-one relationship, there are variations. In marriage mentoring, for example, more experienced married couples mentor newlyweds as they begin their marriages. In the changing world of business, "Having just one guide along the career path now seems as quaint as a lifetime job," so career builders look for multiple mentors who tutor them at different times and through different phases of their careers.[8]

Because of the diversity of approaches, definitions, goals, and misunderstandings, I sometimes avoid using the term *mentoring,* but undoubtedly that is what I do whenever I meet with younger Christians and younger professionals. It has been a part of my life for years. Because I tend to be informal, our meetings—most often over breakfast—are informal and unstructured.

Person A (I want to keep names anonymous to respect privacy) is a seminary student, studying theology and counseling, feeling his way into the profession we share. But he is struggling with the recent death of his father. His dad was this young man's mentor, and he sees me as an older man with whom he can share his heart and some of his grief. I am not his counselor or a substitute father. Both he and I view my role as being like an older brother who is giving a younger man encouragement and unhurried opportunities to talk about his values, his career, his marriage, his disappointments, and the recent unexpected changes in his life.

Person B lives hundreds of miles from me, but we talk often on the phone and look for every opportunity to get together. When he finished graduate school, he was surprised and disappointed to discover that neither his former professors nor his present work associates had much interest in helping him become a competent Christian psychologist. I volunteered, and we have built a close relationship. We pray for each other regularly, read the same Bible passages every day, share our experiences as psychologists, sometimes speak at conferences together, and often check with each other before we make any important career choices or accept new opportunities. I do whatever I can to encourage Mr. B. in his career, his life, his marriage, and especially his spiritual growth. Sometimes I challenge his values, and he has no hesitation to question mine. We have a brotherly relationship between two men, separated in age by almost three decades, but sharpening each other consistently, as iron sharpens iron.

Person C is not a psychologist, isn't much interested in my field, and made it clear from the beginning that he isn't looking for another father. (He has a great dad—as does person B). Person C holds a significant pastoral position at a local church, and in our meetings we often discuss ministry, personal career struggles, marriage, and sometimes our personal lives. Neither of us thinks of our relationship as mentoring. We both prefer the word *journeying*. Each of us is on a journey through life. Because I'm older, I've been on the road longer, have had more experiences, and am more aware of some dangers, stumbling blocks, and dead ends. We don't journey together intimately or every day. We meet about once a month for a couple of hours over breakfast, grow together, and then go off on our separate journeys and our busy lives without much contact until we meet again.

Sometimes mentoring relationships continue for a long time; others are shorter. Occasionally an older person will be threatened by the energy and successes of the protégé, but when these insecurities are acknowledged, they can be learning experiences that need not hinder the relationship. Sometimes mentoring relationships are like the one Paul had with Barnabas. They were good friends and traveled together for a while. Then they separated following a difference of opinion and went off in different directions before coming together again a few years later.

The various mentoring books give endless directions about how to find a mentor, be a mentor, build a mentoring relationship, avoid unhealthy emotional dependencies, and terminate the relationship. These guidelines can be helpful, especially if you are getting started. But you may want to ask God to show you somebody to mentor and somebody to mentor you. In time your prayer will be answered.

Then you will have a relationship (or relationships) that can challenge your style of living, force you to pause at least for brief periods, and help you to focus on a life well lived. Few things can be better antidotes to breathless lifestyles than good mentoring relationships.

WHAT DID JESUS DO?

I wonder what it must have been like for Mary and Joseph to be the parents of Jesus. The Bible gives only one glimpse of those days when Jesus was growing up. He was twelve years old when he traveled with a group to Jerusalem for the Feast of the Passover. After the celebration was over, the group started the journey back home without realizing that they had left Jesus behind. His parents found him, three days later, "in the temple courts, sitting among the teachers, listening to them and asking them questions."[9] The Bible adds that everyone who heard Jesus was amazed at his understanding and his answers.

There is no biblical basis for the view that Jesus continued to sharpen his mind like this when he grew up, but it seems likely that a person who was this interested in learning at age twelve would continue to stretch his mind when he became an adult. Of course, because Jesus was God, he was all-knowing. He did not have the need to learn that we do. Nevertheless, the sharpness with which he debated his critics suggests that he kept his mind honed and free from mental lethargy.

Today we might assume that reading is the best way to sharpen the mind, but as we have seen, we can keep it sharp by debate, interaction with other people, and keeping aware of cultural and political influences. Jesus probably did all of these. He didn't hesitate to interact with others, including his critics. He was well acquainted with his society. He knew, for example, about Herod, about greed and immorality in his culture, and about illegal buying and selling in the temple.

Mark 1 shows us two other ways in which Jesus kept sharp. First, Jesus taught. Every teacher knows that one of the best ways to learn and to keep a sharp mind is to teach others. Most teachers would agree, as well, that the more capable and challenging the students, the more a person will learn and grow from the teaching experience. Jesus taught often and in ways that amazed his audiences.[10] At times, his teaching was interrupted by articulate antagonists with razor-sharp minds and fierce determination to trap him. He answered so convincingly that, after a time, nobody dared ask any more questions.[11]

Second, as we have seen, Jesus spent time with his Father in prayer.[12] Prayer has been described as "one of the principal ways of enlarging our awareness of God and of the universe."[13] Jesus prayed often and taught his disciples to pray. Writers Glandion Carney and William Long suggest that it was prayer that "gave Jesus his powerful sense of awareness and insight into people and the world. . . . The practice of prayer gave Jesus an intuitive grasp of the truths of life as well as the political and religious realities around him."[14] Prayer let him know God better and understand God's ways. As a result, he had a better understanding of the world and culture in which he lived.

These examples from the life of Jesus suggest that there are different ways to keep growing and moving forward. I'm a reader, and so is any person who has read thus far in this book. It is logical for many of us to assume that if reading is not the only way to sharpen our minds, then it certainly must be the best way. The life of Jesus suggests otherwise. He showed that we also can stay mentally alert by keeping close contact with God, with other thinking people, and with the society in which we live.

Why then do so many people get mentally lazy? Why do we fail to evaluate the movies or television programs that impact us, the advertisements that manipulate us, or the words of persuasive speakers that move us? Sometimes the answer lies in our frantic lifestyles, which keep everybody running incessantly and leave us with little time, inclination, or energy to sharpen our minds or rejuvenate our bodies. Some of us are like that lumberjack who rushed from sunrise to sunset, working enthusiastically, without stopping to sharpen his saw.

The life of Jesus may suggest another reason for our mental lethargy. Unlike many of us, he had a healthy perspective of both success and simplicity.

GROWING TOWARD SUCCESS

Tom Morris must be an interesting professor. Describing himself as a "Southern Baptist–born-and-bred professor of philosophy at a great Catholic university," he wrote a book giving his principles for success, inserted a host of quotations from long-dead philosophers, and described some of his lively lectures in the classrooms at Notre Dame.[15] The shelves in my office hold a number of success books, most of them written by possibility-thinking, career-oriented, motivational speakers writing for status-driven career builders. Morris, in contrast, doesn't assume that wealth, power, fame, and status necessarily indicate success. "The happiest people in the world are people who love what they are doing, regardless of whether wealth, fame, power, and elevated social status ever come their way," he writes. "The most fulfilled people are individuals who delight in their work, whatever it might be, and strive to do it well. . . . They are people who relish the challenge to pursue excellence in their activities."[16] With this perspective, Morris gives a seven-part framework for achieving success built on excellence.

1. Conception. We need a clear conception of what we want to accomplish. A steady purpose and a sharp set of goals can stabilize life and protect us from the frantic pace that pressures, confuses, and pushes us in a variety of directions.

2. Confidence. We need confidence that we can and will reach our goals. Christians might not be able to put confidence in themselves, but we can be confident in God's provision, compassion, and direction. That's guaranteed!

3. Concentration. We must have concentration on where we are going. Morris gives a P-L-A-N for success. First, we **P**repare for the journey by deciding how we will act. Then we **L**aunch out in action, motivated by the fact that there tend to be two kinds of people in this world: those who watch things happen and those who make things happen.[17] Next, we **A**djust as we go, expecting the unexpected and being flexible enough to make changes along the way. Then, in all of this, we **N**etwork with people who are knowledgeable and able to help as we go. That's the PLAN.

4. Consistency. We need consistency as we move toward success. This implies a determination to stick with our values and move toward our goals. In an article that he titled "Standing Firm, Moving Forward," Billy Graham wrote that the twin enemies of vision are complacency and discouragement.[18] Complacency makes us lazy and self-satisfied. Discouragement paralyzes us and makes us afraid to move ahead. Instead we need to trust God, courageously make adjustments when necessary, and move forward.

5. Commitment. We need an emotional commitment to the importance of what we are doing and to the people with whom we are doing it.[19] Think again of Mother Teresa. Her work moved forward because she moved with a team of people who showed commitment to each other and to their goals, even when they faced resistance and discouragement.

6. Character. We need high-quality character to guide us and keep us on course. Newspapers and the pages of *People* magazine are filled with stories about "beautiful people" who have fame, acclaim, and possessions. Behind the glitter, however, these lives are often empty, insecure, ego-driven, and lonely. Here are people with all the trappings of success accompanied by an inner void that reflects a lack of clear values and moral character. In contrast to some of these celebrities, people of good character can stay on course in their lives because they aren't much concerned about making impressions or being swayed by incessant demands from others. Throughout history, the greatest human beings are those characterized by humility. Jesus humbled himself and took on the role of a servant.[20] His humility and servant attitude were at the core of his greatness and his character.

7. Capacity. We need a capacity to enjoy the journey of

life. A life well lived is not a life of misery, sober determination, incessant reactions to ever-present pressures, or withdrawal into our work. We need to enjoy the beauties of
nature, the laughter of friendships, the joy of enthusiastic
corporate worship, the refreshment that comes from relaxation, and the fun and periodic silliness that is a part of play.
God gave us taste buds to appreciate good food, senses to
enjoy music and beauty, and the ability to enjoy soaring sex.
We don't fall for the ultimate emptiness of selfish hedonism,
but we want to have self-controlled lives and to experience
joy on the journey as God intended.

Living as God intended was a prime motivation for Jesus.
He came to accomplish a task, and undoubtedly he wanted to
succeed. But he wasn't distracted by the drive for success
that sidetracks so many of us. By spending time with people
and by pulling away for periods alone with the Father, he
kept his life in perspective and his mind sharp.

THE SIMPLE LIFE

I enjoy reading books about success, managing time,
mentoring younger colleagues, overcoming stress, and building careers. Most often, the writers of these books assume
that their readers want prestige, positions, power, and possessions. Why be successful if there are no perks at the end,
if there is no fulfillment, or if we don't find security when we
reach the top? The success books on my shelves focus on
self-promotion, career management, and getting control of
one's destiny.[21] Words like *servanthood, submission,* or *simplicity* rarely appear; they don't fit very well into the action-
packed mentality of our contemporary lives.

In contrast, Jesus never sought a self-centered, success-oriented, status-driven lifestyle. He joyfully lived a life of simplicity and service. He was the son of the King, entitled to live in palaces, but he had no home of his own, made himself nothing, took on the very nature of a servant, and humbled himself to live a life of obedience and suffering.[22] He lived without fanfare or concern about being noticed, and he taught that servanthood is the essence of greatness.[23]

Jesus taught that we don't become great by getting prestige and power. The truly great person is the self-sacrificing individual who is willing to give his or her life in service to others.[24] I'm not the only person who struggles to apply these ideas to my own life. I could admire Mother Teresa's simple, serving lifestyle, but I wonder if we will be buried by the competition and doomed to career failure if we live by these unsettling principles in modern America.

While grappling with these issues in my own life, I have watched my Generation-X children and their friends apply these principles with greater ease than I seem to possess. In preparing for her wedding, one of my daughters determined to maintain simplicity and resist a status-driven show. She concluded that an expensive dress, which would be worn for only a few hours, was an extravagant waste of money when a simpler dress that could be worn later would make more sense. She and her future husband wanted their wedding to honor Christ and involve their immediate family and closest friends, so they trimmed the total guest list to less than twenty people and didn't bother with expensive flowers and tuxedos. After the wedding, they purchased a small house and began with a manageable mortgage, in part, because they didn't want to be struggling to make big monthly payments, like those their parents make.

Jesus lived and taught in a society much simpler and less affluent than ours, but he spoke more about money than about any other single social issue. He strongly emphasized the dangers of clinging to our possessions, accumulating riches, and striving for material things.[25] Years earlier, the psalmist had warned that if riches increase, we should not set our hearts on them.[26] Later, the Epistles condemned greed, blamed violence on a lust for possessions, warned believers to trust in God rather than in their wealth, and urged us to share generously with others.[27] These instructions are hard to apply and at odds with the mentality of our society. They make us uncomfortable. Nevertheless, simplicity and servanthood are at the core of well-lived lives and of crucial importance if we are to be free of breathless lifestyles.

"Contemporary culture is plagued by the passion to possess," wrote Richard Foster in his book *Freedom of Simplicity*.[28] "The complexity of rushing to achieve and accumulate more and more frequently threatens to overwhelm us; it seems there is no escape from the rat race. Christian simplicity frees us from this modern mania. It brings sanity to our compulsive extravagance, and peace to our frantic spirit."[29]

How do we live simple lives of service but still function effectively in our fast-paced jobs, homes, and communities? As a start, consider integrating the following three principles into your life. This will not be easy and might take more time to accomplish than you would like, but these guidelines are proven. They have worked for others, they're beginning to work for me, and they can work for you, especially if you share them with one or two friends and agree to work on them together.

1. Pray for changed attitudes. Ask God to free you from the love of possessions, the need to be noticed, the overemphasis on success, the drive for power, the incessant comparisons of yourself and your career with others. Simplicity and service begin with changed inner attitudes. Changed behavior follows. For most of us the changes will not come quickly; without divine help they are not likely to come at all. Paul wrote about this from what might have been a damp and dingy prison cell. He was free of anxiety and a man at peace who had learned to be content "whether living in plenty or in want."[30]

2. Curb your urge to accumulate. Buy what is useful, not what brings status. Resist the temptation to charge (leave your credit cards at home), and remember that clever advertisers are masters at manipulating people—like you and me—to "buy now, pay later" for gadgets and other possessions that nobody really needs. Recognize that we can enjoy things in this life without owning them. You can appreciate nature without owning a park, music without owning the most expensive stereo system, friends without having a big house. I have learned, as well, that one can enjoy a beautiful and meaningful wedding without taking a second mortgage on the house to pay the costs.

3. Develop a giving, caring mind-set. I know of one sure-fire way to be free from self-centeredness and the love of money: Develop a habit of giving things away. This includes your money, your possessions, and your time. I write about this better than I practice it, and apparently I am not alone.

Richard Foster has described a time in life, "in the frantic final throes" of writing his doctoral dissertation, when a friend called, stated that he was without a car, and asked if he could have a ride to complete a number of errands. "Trapped, I consented, cursing my luck," Foster wrote later. "As I ran out the door, I grabbed Bonhoeffer's *Life Together*, thinking that I might have opportunity to read it." At every stop, Foster stayed in the car, inwardly fuming and fretting at the loss of precious time. Finally, at the last stop, the frustrated chauffeur encountered these words in the Bonhoeffer book: "Nobody is too good for the meanest service. One who worries about the loss of time that such petty, outward acts of helpfulness entail is usually taking the importance of his own career too seriously."[31]

The issues that we have discussed in this chapter—stimulating your mind, setting some guidelines in your approach to success, stripping away your excess accumulations, and serving others—can all be ways to slow the pace and find more meaning in a life well lived. None of this implies that we should go to extremes. Of course we don't give away our houses and force our families to go homeless so we can be free of possessions. God is not pleased with acts of simplicity or service that tear us away from family responsibilities or rob our employers of the time and effort that they have the right to expect. Surely he isn't honored when we let others steal our time or when we respond to every call for service and fail to distinguish the voice of God from the manipulation of others. In his wisdom, God allows some people to have riches, success, and status, but if they come, he expects us to hold these lightly, acknowledge their divine source, and be free to use these gifts for his glory.

MOVING FORWARD

Do you ever give any thought to what you will be like if you live into old age? If I survive into my eighties or nineties, it would be nice to have a healthy body, but I sure hope I have an alert, inquiring, growing mind. If I ever stop growing mentally, I'll dry up and risk sliding into the outdated, rigid, and stereotyped thinking that I want to avoid as long as I can.

After I'm gone, nobody will care about the books I've written, the classes I've taught, the speeches I have given, or the occasional awards that I might have received. I want only to leave lives that have been touched in some way by mine and nudged in the direction of being less hectic and more Christlike as a result. What does it matter if people recognize my name or wonder if I had any kind of an impact? In the light of eternity maybe it doesn't matter who made a difference; what matters more is that people were pointed toward Jesus, into excellence, competence, trustworthiness, service to others, obedience, and greater Christlikeness.

Call it mentoring, journeying, or just "hanging out together." The life well lived is a life that honors Christ by knowing him better and pouring into others—serving, helping, giving, invigorating, encouraging, equipping, challenging, stimulating growth. No legacy is greater or of greater importance.

TAKING A STEP TOWARD
Growth

As you reflect on this chapter, take some time to answer these questions. You may want to do that in a journal, with a friend, or in a group. Allow the questions to help you focus on how you will sharpen your mind.

1. In what ways are you thriving? In what ways are you wilting?
2. What are you reading lately? How does this sharpen your mind?
3. Who has been an effective mentor for you? What makes that person effective?
4. If you do not have a mentor, how can you work toward finding one?
5. If you are in a position to mentor other people, what qualities of your life would you like to pass on to them?
6. If your life is successful, what will it look like when you get to the end? Is this what you really want?
7. Which of the seven components in the Tom Morris list is most important for you to develop more fully if you are to be successful? How will you begin to develop the component you selected?
8. How can you simplify your life in ways that would help you have a well-lived life?

CHAPTER 12

Hope
Living in the Present,
Aware of the Future

A FEW DAYS AGO I went to a funeral. The family had asked me to speak at the memorial service, so I flew to another part of the country, went directly from the plane to express my condolences, and joined an old friend in leading the mourners the next morning. It was a sad occasion with lots of tears, flowers, and expressions of love. But it also was a time of joy. Most of the family members are believers, convinced of the reality of the Resurrection and confident that they will be together with their departed loved one, with each other, and with Christ at some future time. So we gathered on a hillside on that cool morning, surrounded by trees resplendent in the bright yellows and glorious reds of autumn, knowing that we were saying good-bye to one who was absent from the body but already present with the Lord.

Back home, preparing to write this chapter, I came across an article written by a Manhattan therapist and social worker. "I have no conception of what happens when we die, nor do I have any faith in life after death," the article began.

> I believe this lifetime is it; no heartwarming reunions in some puffy-clouded heaven, no karmic roulette followed by rounds of rebirth. I suspect that who and what we are simply ends, our hopes, dreams, memories, pains and frailties draining from us as consciousness dims and finally switches off. In clinical situations, I have to tread carefully around my own metaphysical skepticism when clients who are grappling with life-threatening illness talk about an afterlife. I let them know I think it's wonderful that they have their faith and try to guard them from my own suspicion that death is an empty abyss.[1]

The contrast between this therapist and the family members at the funeral I attended could not be greater. The family grieved with hope and anticipation of the future. The therapist, who works with dying and grieving people, is a sad and modern version of people described in the Bible many centuries ago—those whose only hope is for this life. They are to be "pitied more than all men."[2]

FIVE LIVES

According to popular legend, cats are supposed to have nine lives. It's a belief tied to the assumed ability of these agile animals to escape from close encounters with death, to land on their feet, and to keep on living even when humans might have expected them to die. I don't know much about cats, but I do know about people, and it seems to me that we human beings have five "lives." We don't give them equal attention, but we live them simultaneously. They influence much of what we do, they help us handle pressure, and they have a bearing on whether or not our lives are well lived. Each of us is influenced by a life in the past, a life in the present, a life within, a life ahead, and a life beyond.

Life in the Past

Everybody knows that experiences from the past influence how we live, work, think, cope with stress, and get along with others in the present. All of us have perceptions of the world (sometimes we call these worldviews) and ideas about ourselves (self-concepts) that are shaped by prior experiences and that shape the way we live every day. Freud wrote about the impact of the past, as have more recent writers in the recovery movement with their emphasis on dysfunctional families and adult children of abusive parents. Most of us can think of past events, fears, losses, embarrassments, expectations, or comments that influenced our lives permanently and did damage.

But events from the past can also be positive. You won't find books about this, but many people are adult children of *functional* families. These were families characterized by love, support, clear values, consistent Christian living, and models provided by relatives and neighbors whose lives were well lived. We can be shaped in positive ways by our communities, ethnic identities, religious affiliations, cultural backgrounds, and family traditions. Also influential are involvements with other cultures and our contacts with people whose backgrounds are different from our own.

If you tend to be relaxed or if you are caught in a hectic lifestyle, ask yourself if your background has something to do

227

with your present way of living. Better still, ask somebody who knows you and your past well. Without sliding into poor-me thinking, I can see events in my background, expectations that came from my parents, persisting fears, and ingrained attitudes that shape some of the ways in which I live my life today. The work of therapists and counselors often focuses on helping us appreciate positive influences from the past and get unhooked from leftover attitudes and painful memories that are detrimental to us as adults.

By yourself, or with the help of a friend or counselor, try to deal with past issues that affect you in the present. When you understand and sometimes unhook from past influences, you can be freed to move away from a breathless lifestyle and toward a life that is better lived.

Life in the Present

All of us know people who live in the past, people who have a constant need to bask in previous accomplishments or to complain about past hurts. In contrast, other people seem to live in the future, dreaming incessantly about better days that will come after graduation, after marriage, after a promotion, after the kids leave home, or after retirement.

While some people overemphasize the past and others are fixated on the future, another group has a narrow preoccupation with the present. I once spent a lot of time with a young man who hated the family that had raised him and tried to ignore that they existed. He had no plans for the future, no goals and, saddest of all, seemingly no awareness that his present decisions and actions could have future consequences. Intellectually he knew that writing bad checks and using illegal drugs would lead him back to prison, but he lived for the pleasures of the present. His life was guided by an ancient, feel-good philosophy that says "let us eat and drink, for tomorrow we die."[3]

This way of thinking is common, even among people who would never dream of breaking the law. Watch the advertisements on television, look at the letters in your mailbox, or leaf through almost any magazine, and you see the message repeated: "You deserve a break today." "You can have it all." "Somebody has to win the lottery; it might as well be you." "You have been preapproved to buy now and pay later—with easy installments."

This attitude has even penetrated the church. "As we race toward the close of the twentieth century, most of the emphasis in Christianity is on becoming happier here, healed here, more blessed here, and more fulfilled here," we read in a book by Joseph Stowell. "Worship must excite our spirits, sermons must entertain and enthrall our minds, music must penetrate and propel us. And our counseling must make us feel better about ourselves and strengthen our human bond of friendship and family." The church, then, becomes a self-serving entertainment or therapeutic center, where believers are encouraged to meet their present needs, without much emphasis on serving and sacrificing with the future in view.[4]

Within arm's length of the computer where I am writing these words, there is a pile of bills that have come within the past week and need to be paid before the end of the month. They are a reminder that we all have to live, meet our obligations, and deal with pressures in the present. Sometimes when these pressures and demands mount, we run off to life-management or successful-living seminars that promise to help us keep everything in balance. But we don't need seminars or books to remind us that balanced lives are aware of the past without dwelling there, are sensitive and responsive to the demands of the present without getting tyrannized by the urgent, and keep looking to the future without unrealistic dreaming or overemphasizing things that are ahead.

Life Within

Often I ask myself a question that maybe you ask as well: Why is my life so busy and my to-do list so long when other people seem to live at a more leisurely pace? I can rush around, scrambling to get things done, when others seem to have lots of time for hanging out with their friends or staring at a television screen.

Events from our pasts and pressures from the present can give some insight into how we live. More often, it seems, our lifestyles are molded by the private inner thoughts that we considered in an earlier chapter. Think about the expectations and the demands you put on yourself. Unlike much of the world's population, we live in an affluent, materialistic, hedonistic society in which our minds are fueled with ongoing thoughts about the things we can get, the successes we can attain, the pleasures we can experience, and the satisfactions to which we are entitled. Often we set high expectations for ourselves, push to reach impossible goals, and then are frustrated, disillusioned, and deeply disappointed if our dreams do not become reality.

I have reached some conclusions that account for much of my busyness. These are inner thoughts or beliefs that probably are very common.

First, I believe that *God accepts me because of who he is.* The Bible is clear that our own efforts do not earn God's

favor, but because of his great mercy and willingness to forgive, he accepts people who put their confidence in him.[5] I
am accepted by God, unconditionally, because of his grace.[6]

Second, *my friends, my family, and especially my wife
accept me because of who I am.* I don't have to do anything,
accomplish any goals, or write any books to earn the
approval of those who are closest to me. They accept me and
love me, despite my faults and failures, because of who I am,
what I am like, and what I am becoming.

Third, *I accept myself because of what I do.* I know God
accepts me completely, forgives me freely, and loves me
regardless of my activities. I know that my wife and closest
friends accept me without strings attached. But I have trouble
accepting myself in this way. To be successful and worthwhile
in my own eyes, I have to get things done, to be productive. As
a boy in church I learned that there is "only one life that will
soon be past" and that "only what's done for Christ will last."
My teachers taught me not to waste time, and I picked up that
my father—whose approval I craved—wanted me to be successful. Over the years this achievement mentality lodged in
my mind and shaped my thinking. It's not logical or even
valid, but it is there, along with another idea that is especially
devastating.

Fourth, *nothing that I do is good enough to meet my self-
imposed standards.* I don't know where this originated, but it
ties into my commitment to quality, my desire for excellence,
my determination to be doing more, and my striving to be
doing things better than I have done in the past.

Those of us who think like this tend to keep driving ourselves. We like time-management programs because they help
us squeeze more into our days so we can push further and get

more done. For some people these activities are attempts to please God or to meet the expectations of somebody whose approval we desperately want. Very often, however, we are trying to boost our self-image by proving to ourselves that we can achieve. We are seeking to prove, at least to ourselves, that we are not the failures that some person in the past assumed or predicted we would be. Down deep we long to overcome our insecurities with accomplishments, but the insecurities are so entrenched that nothing we do or achieve ever satisfies.

If you are constantly under pressure, pushing yourself to do more and more but never satisfied with your efforts, ask yourself what thoughts in your inner world are driving you onward. You might find help by discussing this with a friend or counselor. Then practice positive self-talk and remind yourself of these healthier perspectives.

None of this is meant to deny that the drive to get things done sometimes is squarely rooted in external reality. If you are a parent of young children, ever scrambling to keep up, you are normal and are driven by the harsh realities of parenthood. Relax. In time things will settle down. If your employer expects you to keep pushing and performing, you have a good reason to feel driven. But sooner or later, you must decide whether you want to stay under these outside pressures or whether you should find ways to downscale or find less demanding employment elsewhere.

Life Ahead

I like reading about the future, planning for the future, and thinking about challenges that might be coming in the future. Books with titles like *Thinking in the Future Tense, With an Eye to the Future, Managing for the Future,* or *Competing for the Future* grab my attention and stimulate my creativity, even though I realize that only God knows with certainty what lies ahead.[7] When Bill Clinton and Bob Dole were campaigning for the presidency, they challenged each other about who had the best and boldest vision for the future. Mr. Clinton's cause was helped by a preelection book that he wrote, lauding his own accomplishments, but also including insightful ideas that go beyond politics or political parties.

"We must make a choice," the president wrote in words that can apply to us all. "Shall we live by our fears and define ourselves by what we are against, or shall we live by our hopes and define ourselves by what we are working for, by our vision of a better future? This is the choice that each of us—every individual, every family, every community, every generation—must make every day."[8] A few pages later, the book acknowledged that people react differently to the "bewildering, intense, sometimes overpowering change" that we all face.[9] Some people try to avoid the future, cling to the past, and hold out for as long as they can. Others embrace the future and move ahead, guided by their values, stimulated by their creativity, working in partnership with others, and confident in the realization that our all-knowing, all-powerful God guides as we go.

I thought about some of this recently when I was invited to address a group of African church leaders on the topic of hope. Living in the midst of political uncertainty and economic hardship, these brothers and sisters were giving many of their limited resources to nearby nations engulfed in suffering, injustice, hunger, violence, and despair. My talk to the group could have only one focus. Our hope is not in political leaders, emerging technology, creative innovations, more international conferences, or a willingness to take risks—important as some of these may be. It is only when we put our confidence in God that we have hope for the future, strength for the journey, and the courage to move ahead.[10] The idea was stated concisely on a sign outside a church. It read: *Fear Not the Future: God Is Already There.*

What we think about the future will influence how we live in the present. If you ignore the future, give no thought to your retirement, or overlook the later consequences of your present actions, then you will live to meet your needs now. You will be motivated to "get all the gusto you can get" at present and give little consideration to how present planning and sacrifice can make things better later. In contrast, if you keep the future in mind, your present activities are more likely to be those that have long-term implications. This awareness of the future while you live in the present will be healthy if you keep your life in balance. It will be unhealthy if you drive yourself to store up treasures for use on earth at some later time but give little thought to anything else, including life after death.[11]

Life Beyond

The fifth life that can influence our lifestyles often gets ignored. It is life beyond this world, life that is still to come, life in eternity. It is a life that breaks into our thinking to grab our attention when we watch a loved one die, when we go to a funeral, or when we hear an occasional sermon about heaven. It is a life that has strong implications about the way we live now, on earth.

According to Joseph Stowell, the more we think about the world to come, the more our earthly lives become trans-

formed and our priorities are readjusted.[12] People, possessions, careers, time, pain, and pleasures all have a different
meaning when we look at them from the perspective of
heaven. C. S. Lewis reached a similar conclusion in a statement that has made its way into many books: "A continual
looking forward to the eternal world is not (as some modern
people think) a form of escapism or wishful thinking, but one
of the things a Christian is meant to do. It does not mean that
we are to leave the present world as it is. *If you read history,
you will find that Christians who did most for the present
world were just those who thought most about the next.*"[13]

DREAMS ON EARTH

Thinking about the next world is not a priority for most
of us. We're more consumed with the ever-present challenge
of surviving and succeeding in the world where we live now.

This must have been on the minds of the Chicago area
people who left their jobs for a day recently and poured into
a crowded seminar. They came by the thousands—nearly
twenty thousand to be exact. Many had paid as much as $225
for the privilege of sitting in a huge auditorium, eagerly
anticipating words of wisdom from some of the most popular
motivational experts, success gurus, and influential people
in the country. Bill Cosby was one of the speakers; so were
Larry King and Barbara Bush. They joined a roster that has
included Gerald Ford, Colin Powell, Margaret Thatcher,
Johnny Cash, and a host of others who reportedly pick up
a sixty-thousand-dollar check for their thirty-minute talks.

These famous speakers and their expectant listeners are
part of a movement that has existed for decades but currently
is soaring in popularity. It has been called a "merger of suc-

cess and religion, capitalism and spirituality, as red-white-and-blue as the Mall of America."[14] It is known as the motivational industry, fueled by hope, dreams, spiritual hunger, a drive for achievement, and promises of success. It convinces people they are not as successful as they can be, that greater success is possible, that there are leaders to show them the way, and that endless books, tapes, day planners, and other materials are available to give better direction to their busy lives. One after another the speakers offer their secrets for getting ahead. They talk quickly, move about the stage enthusiastically, and proclaim catchy, hope-filled messages built, for example, on the two P's (Passion and Purpose), the three C's (Courage, Character, and Conviction), the three E's (Enthusiasm, Excitement, and Energy), and the ten steps to top performance. Enthusiastically, they tell inspiring stories, describe how they overcame their failures, laugh with the audience, and demonstrate their phenomenal abilities to hawk their motivational books and tapes. Orchestrated by motivational speaker Peter Lowe—a dedicated Christian with missionary parents, a degree in theology, and a willingness to talk about his faith without embarrassment or apology—the local seminar was only one of many that have reached more than 650,000 eager participants at last count.

"It's like a religion," one man told a reporter as he left the seminar.[15] "I looked at Peter Lowe and thought, *Boy, have you ever tapped into a great market. We're all so busy, when he says you should go to church, it sounds new.*"

"I went because I needed a chance to step back," another participant exclaimed, admitting as he left the auditorium that he had purchased several thousand dollars' worth of motivational tapes for the staff in his office. The speakers all had a "belief in God and in themselves," according to this man. "If they didn't have it, they developed it." And they implied that all who listened could go forth and do likewise.[16]

Seminars for Christians often proclaim something similar. These seminars may not be as large or feature such prominent speakers or sell as many books and tapes, but every week, Christian seminar leaders crisscross the country, filling churches and giving advice to people who are searching for guidelines and stability in their busy lives. Often speakers proclaim messages that are close to those given at Peter Lowe's extravaganzas. They promise that we can have success if we follow the examples of others who have reached the top. They promise that we can have better careers and relationships if we work hard and follow the speakers' advice. They promise that we can have spiritual ecstasy now, in this present world, if we apply the principles that are taught in the seminar.

Is this wrong? The messages of these seminars are not immoral or illegal, but they also do not appear to be biblical. Surely there are many people, maybe millions, who have been helped by seminars to have better lives and marriages. But there is a fine line between motivating audiences and manipulating them, between providing products for sale and pushing people to buy what they can't afford, between giving guidelines for success and generating unrealistic expectations in people who will never reach the top or resolve their persisting problems. If they are not guided by scrupulous integrity and accountability, even Christian seminar speakers and book writers—including the author of this book—can proclaim principles that have little factual basis and make promises that we can't realistically fulfill. Almost all of the hope-generating seminars, speeches, books, and tapes, both Christian and secular, focus on ourselves and our own efforts, emphasize this present world, and assume (without saying so) that life on this earth can be great and better than it is. There is little talk about suffering, serving, or sacrificing our dreams so we can be faithful to Christ. And there is rarely any mention of heaven.

People who attend the seminars or read the books are given hope, but it is a hope in lesser things. These are not bad or sinful things. They are merely earthly things like the prominence, riches, and stability that don't extend beyond this life. Too often these lesser hopes become driving forces that leave us breathless, disappointed, and unfulfilled, "persuaded that what is heavenly is no earthly good and what is earthly is irrelevant to heaven."[17]

A DIFFERENT PERSPECTIVE

Jesus had an entirely different perspective. Like the rest of us, he was influenced by those five lives. He was shaped by the past, well aware of the ancient prophecies that told of his coming and of the historical role of John the Baptist in preparing the way for Jesus' arrival.[18] He lived in the present, helping people with their struggles and dealing with pressures in his own life.[19] As we saw earlier, he was well aware of his life within, spending time in prayer and in solitude, demonstrating that when we take care of life on the inside, it shows on the outside. Certainly Jesus looked ahead. One of the richest parts of the Gospels gives a detailed description of his last hours before the Crucifixion, his instructions to the disciples, and his promises for their futures after he was gone.[20]

Throughout Jesus' life, however, one of the most commonly recurring themes was the message of hope for a life beyond the present. "Do not let your hearts be troubled," he told the discouraged disciples. "Do not be afraid," he urged them as he told them about the coming of the Holy Spirit, who would be a comforter and a guide.[21] He announced that he would be going to be with the Father, to prepare a place for his followers, and eventually to return to take us to be with him forever.[22] Jesus saw his time on earth as a brief sojourn, a prelude to the eternity that we will spend with him after life on earth is over. Especially as he approached the end of his life, Jesus thought about life in the world to come. For him, the reality of heaven in the future was like a beacon that guided his life and enabled him to find hope that, in turn, he could give to others.

DESTINED FOR HEAVEN

One of my younger friends recently described the members of his Generation X as people who are "into spirituality but not into church." Many who attend motivational seminars are into success but not into sacrifice. Many who go to church every week are into singing but not much into service, into hearing inspirational sermons but not into doing things to change their lives. And many of us who are into religion, including the Christian religion, are not much into heaven.

We believe in the existence of heaven, of course. We are sure that there is an afterlife in a place that is far better than the world in which we now live. But we don't have details about what heaven is like, so we view it with uncertainty. We know that people who are faithful followers of Jesus Christ will spend eternity with him, but we are fuzzy about when and how we will get there, so we feel out of control and reluctant to give heaven too much thought. We know that old people, fundamentalist preachers, and long-dead theologians have talked about heaven, but people who are dynamic, up-to-date, and "with it" rarely discuss the subject, so we avoid it as well. We agree that heaven is important and may want it to be at the center of our thinking, but we are busy people and find that the ongoing demands of this world pull us back.[23] We put our energies and attention into meeting our earth-side needs, reaching our goals, and enjoying our present Christian experiences. And we leave heaven as a postscript to life, a divinely guaranteed insurance policy offering eternal benefits that come later but aren't of much importance now. In practice we are not far from that Manhattan therapist who writes that "most of the time I don't worry about what happens when we die. I try to stay focused on how to live life well and how to help my dying clients end their lives well."[24]

It is sobering to ponder Joseph Stowell's observation that *"a heaven dimly lit results in a life poorly lived."*[25] God once gave the apostle Paul a brief glimpse of heaven, and that glimpse changed Paul's life perspective, altered the way he viewed his earthly efforts, and showed him that life after this world was far better than anything we have here.[26] A few years later, the apostle John was exiled to a lonely, windswept island, where he had a hope-filled vision of heaven that no words could describe adequately.[27] Much more informed was Jesus, who knew about heaven because he had lived there. He eagerly anticipated his return to heaven, promised that he was going to prepare a place for his followers, and urged us to focus attention on his kingdom rather than worrying exclusively about the pressures of this life.[28]

For most busy people, thinking more about heaven will require a mental shift, a willingness to give greater attention to "things above," and a determination to be less consumed with the things that are on this earth.[29] This is not a call to be starry-eyed, with our heads in the clouds, our friends all in the church, and our focus so much on another place that we ignore the needs, suffering, sin, and misplaced values in this world, where we are called to be salt and light.

To be heavenly minded means that

- we will think differently about the meaning of success, knowing that what we achieve or fail to accomplish in this world may have no importance or bearing on the next.
- we will have different priorities in life, realizing that knowing God, doing his will, and serving him faithfully are ultimately what matters in this life and in the life to come.
- we will put a different value on our possessions or honors, knowing that a life well lived does not consist of the things we possess or knock ourselves out trying to attain.[30]
- we will differ in the way we interpret world events, many of which can be devastating and life altering but all of which ultimately are under the wise and mighty hand of God.
- we will approach death differently. Philip Yancey describes the experience of his wife, who worked with the elderly in one of the poorest communities of the country. Many of these people had a bedrock belief in heaven, maintained good humor and a triumphant spirit even though they had good reasons to be bitter and despairing. In contrast, the people who had no hope for heaven became increasingly fearful and anxious as the end approached. They complained about their lives, their fami-

lies, and their deteriorating health. Their thinking was limited to the painful realities of this earth; they had no reason to be hopeful about a life that would be better.[31]

- we will have unique views about people. They are the only part of this earthly life that will last for eternity. People are loved by God, who wants us to show care, compassion, and sensitivity to others.

Do It Anyway

I don't know if the sisters at the Shishu Bhavan children's home in Calcutta have their minds on heaven, but they don't seem to be much concerned about success, acclaim, possessions, or the other topics that dominate the lively sessions in American motivational seminars. "We are street people, and our work is in the streets," writes Sister Charmaine Jose, who runs the center that cares for three hundred sick or malnourished children and that sometimes takes in their poor, unmarried mothers.[32] "We pray as we walk, going out to visit families, to be with a dying child, or to bring medicine to those in need." They go to the villages where there are no medical facilities. They have a school for street children who are abused and in prostitution but who often have no food, support, or medicine until they are "collected," fed, dressed, taught, and enabled to complete their education.

On the wall of the home hangs a sign that challenges the nuns in Calcutta, but the sign could be a model for any of us who want to live in the present with an awareness of the future. The words on this sign summarize much of what it means to have a life well lived, a life freed of hectic hyperactivity, a life that impacts this present world but keeps an awareness of the world to come. The sign reads:

ANYWAY

People are unreasonable, illogical, and self-centered;
LOVE THEM ANYWAY.
If you do good, people will accuse you
of selfish, ulterior motives;
DO GOOD ANYWAY.
If you are successful, you win false friends
and true enemies;
SUCCEED ANYWAY.
The good you do will be forgotten tomorrow;
DO GOOD ANYWAY.
Honesty and frankness make you vulnerable;
BE HONEST AND FRANK ANYWAY.
What you spent years building
may be destroyed overnight;
BUILD ANYWAY.
People really need help but may attack you
if you help them;
HELP PEOPLE ANYWAY.
Give the world the best you have,
and you'll get kicked in the teeth;
GIVE THE WORLD THE BEST YOU'VE GOT ANYWAY.[33]

TAKING A STEP TOWARD
Hope

As you reflect on this chapter, take some time to answer
these questions. You may want to do that in a journal, with a
friend, or in a group. Allow the questions to help you focus
on how you will think about the past, present, and future.

1. When you think about your "five lives" (past, present, within, ahead, and beyond), which life needs most to be brought into balance?
2. How has your past life had a positive influence on you? How can your past prepare you to have a well-lived life in the future?
3. If you find you are too preoccupied with life in the present, what can you do to stem that preoccupation? Whom will you enlist to help you do that?
4. What inner thoughts are a threat to your having a well-lived life? What can you do to lessen the impact of those thoughts?
5. How do you view the life beyond? How does your view of heaven affect your life on earth?
6. How can you become more heavenly minded?

PART THREE
Breathing Easy

CHAPTER 13

Managing Life and Leaving a Legacy

ALFRED NOBEL, following the death of his brother, turned to the obituary section of the morning paper and made a startling discovery. An editor had made a mistake, assumed that Alfred—and not his brother—had died, and printed an obituary describing Alfred as the inventor of dynamite.

Nobel realized that if he had died that day, he would have left a legacy associated with death and destruction. Unlike his brother, Alfred Nobel still had time to change. Encouraged by his friends and drawing on some of his considerable wealth, he established a prize to honor those who would make the world a better place. Today, few people know (or care) who invented dynamite, but everybody has heard of the Nobel peace prize, named after a man who looked ahead, beyond his scientific accomplishments, and into the future.

John Sculley changed the future of his life while standing atop a thirty-story building in New York City. He was forty-two years old at the time, president of Pepsi-Cola, a man who had risen through the ranks and up the ladder of success faster than anybody else in the company. His picture had been on the cover of *Newsweek,* and he was used to being acclaimed in business journals. But Steve Jobs, creative genius and founder of Apple Computer, wanted John Sculley to leave Pepsi and take Apple to a higher level. The recruitment effort had not worked until Jobs asked a life-changing question: "John, do you want to spend the rest of your life selling sugared water, or do you want a chance to change the world?" A short time later, Sculley shocked the business world by resigning from his prestigious position at Pepsi and becoming CEO at Apple.

Bill Hybels was a student when he changed the direction of his life. When he started college, Hybels had his future planned: he intended to get his degree, then return to Michigan to work in his father's successful produce business. But the student took a class from Dr. Gilbert Bilezikian, a college professor who dreamed of a church where people would find acceptance, love, challenge, and an authentic new community experience built on a commitment to Christ. Periodically the professor would ask his students a disturbing question, "What are you going to do with your life that will last forever?"

The question changed the direction of young Bill Hybels' life. Years later, as pastor of one of the country's largest churches, Hybels wrote about the hollowness of the American Dream with its emphasis on driven lifestyles, its bankrupt belief that "more is better," and its willingness to sacrifice everything on the altar of things. Individuals and cultures that encourage self-indulgence will, in the end, self-destruct, Hybels states.[1]

The Bible helps us counter this empty American Dream with truth.

Be the salt of the earth, Jesus tells us. Be lights to the world. Stay clear of the applause of man. Do good deeds constantly. . . . Turn the world's order of greed, selfishness, and hate on its head. . . . Make people, not things, our priority. For me, these are some of the most powerful commands in the Bible. I have periodically awakened in the middle of the night, drenched in a cold sweat, at the horror of wasting the life God has given me in a series of trivial pursuits. I have only one chance to live, and I want to make it count.[2]

FARM TIME

Stephen Covey, Roger Merrill, and Rebecca Merrill in their classic book about life management describe what they call the Law of the Farm. To get a good crop at the end of the growing season, the farmer doesn't ignore planting in the spring, rest during the summer, and then cram everything into the fall—ripping up the soil, throwing in the seeds, watering, and cultivating all within a few days—expecting a bountiful harvest before the winter frosts arrive. Growth of a crop takes time. That's the Law of the Farm. It's a law that applies as well to the growth of a life well lived.

We all know about students who coast through a semester and then drive themselves mercilessly trying to get everything done before the deadlines and final exams. This works sometimes. Quick fixes occasionally bring short-term success and sometimes get crammers through college. But in the long run, the Law of the Farm governs life. Cramming does not work to build solid and lasting character, integrity, values, relationships, marriages, careers, spiritual and emotional maturity—or balanced, well-lived lives. Growth in life takes effort, determination, and persistence. Most of all, the universal Law of the Farm involves time.

Probably you remember the frustrated mother described in the opening chapter of this book. She yanked the microwave oven from the wall, threw it into the garbage pail, and determined to slow the pace of her life. I wonder if she has succeeded. Since the time of her self-described "explosion," a *Wall Street Journal*/NBC News poll found that 59 percent of those questioned described their lives as too busy, 40 percent said they would choose more time over money if they had a choice, and almost one in five (19 percent) reported a time crunch that causes serious personal stress.[3] To cope with time crunches like these, a physician named Stephan Rechtschaffen has proposed a solution less abrupt than tossing out a microwave oven. He believes that we can create more time and enjoy more of life if we try *time shifting*.

TIME SHIFTING

The principle is simple. We can't add more hours to the day, of course, and we can cram only so much activity into our overbooked days. Even so, we are bombarded with messages telling us to go faster, do more, produce more, and stop wasting time. Rechtschaffen's perspective on all of this changed when he went to India for further medical training, met a Hindu mystic named Shri Bhagwan, got involved with a Zen monk named Thich Nhat Hanh, and came home to lead seminars drawing on Buddhist meditation practices.

Time shifting involves deliberately focusing our attention

on the present. Rechtschaffen tells people to quit worrying so much about the past or the future. "Working on a tight deadline or attending a rock concert can be invigorating. But it's what you do in between those quickened times that makes the difference in your health."[4] The doctor tells people to make it a practice to stop at different times during the day to notice their breathing, relax their muscles, focus on the sounds and colors around them, and pay attention to what they are experiencing in the present moment.

Stress-reducing exercises like this do slow down our lives and reduce the feelings of pressure. But do they really "give you back all the time you need to accomplish what you want," as the jacket on Rechtschaffen's book promises? Does this subjective focus on the present let us "take back the control of our lives by changing the way we think about time" and allow us to be "less stressed-out and better able to enjoy the best things in life"?[5]

And does this effort to change the way we look at time prepare us for eternity, enable us to build well-lived lives, lead us to serve Christ better, care for others more compassionately, find purpose in our earthly journeys, work with others in community, sharpen our minds, or make a difference in this world? Time shifting seems like another gimmick to slow us down, focus on ourselves, and withdraw into mental emptiness that does little to leave the world a better place in which lives are changed and Christ is honored.

Alfred Nobel shifted the focus of his time in a different way when he read an obituary and redirected his life as an older man. John Sculley was in the prime of his life, barely into his forties, when he made a career shift. Bill Hybels was a young college student when he determined to refocus his life. Each of these shifts, made at different times in life, permitted these people to influence the world in ways that they might not have done otherwise.

What about us? We know that time pressures will persist and probably increase as long as we live in this fast-paced era and culture. We know that no person can do everything, know everything, or control every demand. Downshifting is a nice idea that isn't practical for many of us. Time shifting is a New Age, mystical strategy that can help us relax but that doesn't do much to reduce the demands on our lives or enable us to make an impact for Christ. Time-management seminars and programs, as we have stated repeatedly, can reorder our lives but sometimes leave us breathless and organized, instead of simply breathless.

Time pressures and demands are not going to disappear from our lives. They are part of contemporary living. This book has argued that we cope best when we make it a habit to back away from our busy activities on occasion and to ponder what it means for each of us to have a life well lived. Maybe we also need to consider the legacies that we will leave behind when our life journeys are over.

WRITING AN OBITUARY AND LEAVING A LEGACY

Have you ever taken a few minutes to write your own obituary? What would people read if you died tomorrow and your obituary was published a day or two later? What would you like them to read, assuming you could shift the focus of your life and, like Alfred Nobel, live a little longer?

A friend recently described his reaction when a college professor assigned the obituary-writing exercise in class. "I wrote a glowing picture of myself at the end of life," my friend said. "Then I realized how far my life was from the words that I had written." This led to some changes, less dramatic perhaps, but certainly as life changing as the obituary that Alfred Nobel read, the question that John Sculley answered, and the challenge that Bill Hybels heard from Dr. Bilezikian.

In the midst of the activities in your life, ask yourself what kind of a legacy you will leave. What kind of legacy would you like to leave? How can you change your life, your values, your relationships, your time allocations, and your career to get from where you are to where you want to be? In a practical way, how can you have a life that is well lived?

Christopher Parkening made a shift to a life well lived. When he was eleven years old, he learned to play the guitar. Although he liked popular music, he didn't follow in the footsteps of Jerry Garcia or Eric Clapton. Instead, he took the advice of a relative, began to study the classical guitar, and was hailed as a prodigy while he was still in his teens. When Parkening was nineteen, he released his first recordings, to outstanding popular and critical acclaim. Soon he was off on a career of incessant worldwide touring that left him burned out by the time he reached age thirty.

Then he quit.

He disappeared to a ranch in Montana, put aside his guitar, and spent his days fly-fishing. During that sabbatical time, however, he heard a moving and convicting sermon that led him to give his life to Christ. Later, when he was reading the Bible, he saw these words: "Whether you eat or drink or whatever you do, do it all for the glory of God."[6] Parkening was inspired to pick up the career that he had laid aside three years earlier. "When you can sincerely and with your whole heart play an instrument for the purpose of glorifying God, it gives you a joy and peace that you won't know when you're doing it for yourself and for the money," he stated in a *Christianity Today* article.[7]

Parkening has recorded hymns and spirituals, but he also plays classical works and performs numerous secular concerts every year. The *Washington Post* has hailed him as "the leading guitar virtuoso of our day," and his recordings have been called "brilliant," "eloquent," and "flawless." A warm, approachable, and humble man, he seeks to be like Johann Sebastian Bach, who often wrote *Soli Deo Gloria*—"To God alone be the glory"—on his musical compositions. "Success seeks to please men," the guitarist believes, "but excellence seeks to please God."[8]

Christopher Parkening appears to have learned a lesson that many Christians never discover, even though the Bible states it clearly: "Whatever you do, whether in word or deed, do it all in the name of the Lord Jesus, giving thanks to God the Father through him."[9] A life well lived is not a compartmentalized life, with work, family, relaxation, and religion neatly pigeonholed into different times of the week. A life lived with maximum fulfillment, impact, and joy is a life that seeks to honor and please God in whatever we do. To do everything "in the name of the Lord Jesus" is to make up your mind to please God in your work, chores, relaxation, worship, thinking, lovemaking, money management, family relationships, contacts with your friends and neighbors, and every other aspect of life. God expects *Soli Deo Gloria*—"To God alone be the glory"—to permeate every part of our lives.

A Personal Postscript

Not long ago I received a letter from England congratulating me on having been selected as an "International Man of the Year," one of "only a few illustrious individuals whose achievements and leadership stand out in the international community." Before throwing the form letter into the wastebasket, I looked to see what the people who mailed this were selling. I did not have to look long. For only $155 I could get a personalized and hand-signed citation printed in two colors on fine parchment paper announcing my selection for this honor. For an extra $100 I could have my citation laminated on a wooden base ready for hanging on the wall. For another $210 I could get a silver gilt medal of honor with a clasp and ribbon so I could wear the medal or display it in its own beautiful presentation case. For a mere $425 I could get everything. I didn't bother.

I'm not opposed to honors, plaques of appreciation, personal trophies, or medals. When they aren't thinly veiled appeals for money or blatant ego-stroking efforts like the letter that came from England, awards can honor people for their accomplishments and give the presenters opportunity to express their appreciation. Ultimately, however, earthly trophies mean very little, and sometimes they are harmful, stroking the self-centered egos of their recipients and turning attention away from the only One who is worthy to receive glory and honor and praise.

Some time ago, I read a newspaper column written by business guru Tom Peters, who stated that the best and most successful human activities have less to do with making a living and more to do with leaving a legacy. That may be true, but as I approach the age where I can get senior citizen discounts and possibly should be thinking about these things, I've got other goals and interests.

I don't want my life to be breathless, but I intend to keep using the brain that God has given me, keep working enthusiastically with the energy that he has abundantly provided, keep developing and using the creativity that he has allowed me to have, and keep building a life that is well lived and active, as long as God allows me to do so. I don't care about citations, medals, or beautiful plaques. But I care very much about pouring myself into those younger men and women who are coming behind me, encouraging them as they build their careers, shape the future of the church, and learn how to please and serve Christ more effectively. I care a great deal about doing whatever I can to stimulate visionary thinking, life focus, creativity, integrity, and even a few Big Hairy Audacious Goals in the people I meet and in people like you, who read my books. And I care a lot about being a man who serves Christ, shows compassion, and never stops learning. Most of all, I care about living a well-lived life that pleases and brings honor to God.

Recently, Billy Graham was asked how he would like to be remembered. He paused for a moment then said, "That I was faithful to what God wanted me to do, that I maintained integrity in every area of my life, and that I lived what I preached."[10] Could there be a better, more admirable legacy?

I agree that the key to life is not in spending, saving, or managing time. It is more important to be investing time into causes that will have a lasting impact and into people whose lives can make a lasting difference. Ultimately, in this breathless age in which we live, the best thing you can leave behind is the example of a life well lived.

TAKING A STEP TOWARD
Managing Your Life

As you reflect on this chapter, take some time to answer these questions. You may want to do that in a journal, with a friend, or in a group. Allow the questions to help you focus on how you will be better able to leave a legacy.

1. Take the time to write your obituary, allowing the exercise to help you focus on what you would like your life to accomplish. (This exercise will help you define what a life well lived would look like in your life.)
2. What shift, if any, do you need to make in your life to make your obituary be a realistic one?
3. Whom will you enlist to help you in this process?
4. Take time to thank and praise God for all the good things he has given you. Give those things back to him, for his glory alone.

Chapter 1—Rushing: Getting Control of Our Time-Starved Lives

1. Michele Ritterman, "Stop the Clock," *The Family Therapy Networker* 19 (January/February 1995): 45–6.
2. John Marks, "Time Out," *U.S. News and World Report* (December 11, 1995): 85.
3. Richard Simon, "From the Editor," *The Family Therapy Networker* 19 (January/February 1995): 2.
4. I believe there is more substance to these conclusions than my personal bias. For insightful critiques of the impact of television and other media, see Neil Postman, *Amusing Ourselves to Death* (New York: Penguin Books, 1986); Michael Medved, *Hollywood vs. America: Popular Culture and the War on Traditional Values* (New York: HarperCollins/Zondervan, 1992); and S. Robert Lichter, Linda S. Lichter, and Stanley Rothman, *Prime Time: How TV Portrays American Culture* (Washington, D.C.: Regnery Publishing, 1994).
5. In addition to the books by St. James, "voluntary simplicity" books include Duane Elgin, *Toward a Way of Life That Is Outwardly Simple, Inwardly Rich* (New York: William Morrow, 1993); and Janet Luhrs, *Simple Living Guide* (New York: Broadway Books, 1997).
6. Philippians 2:3-4.
7. Philippians 2:6-7.
8. Matthew 20:26-27.
9. Amy Saltzman, *Downshifting: Reinventing Success on a Slower Track* (New York: HarperCollins, 1991).
10. Ibid., 66.
11. John Marks, "Time Out," *U.S. News and World Report* (December 11, 1995):86–9.
12. The seminar brochure was distributed by The Dun & Bradstreet Corporation Foundation, Business Education Services, P. O. Box 5100, New York, NY 10150-5100.
13. Stephen R. Covey, *The 7 Habits of Highly Effective People: Powerful Lessons in Personal Change* (New York: Simon & Schuster, 1989).
14. Stephen R. Covey, A. Roger Merrill, and Rebecca R. Merrill, *First Things First* (New York: Simon & Schuster, 1994).

Chapter 2—Defining Moments: Ten Traits of a Life Well Lived

1. Cited by Lucinda Vardey in *Mother Teresa: A Simple Path* (New York: Ballantine, 1995), xxii.
2. Stephen R. Covey, A. Roger Merrill, and Rebecca R. Merrill, *First Things First* (New York: Simon & Schuster, 1994), 11.
3. Ibid., 23.
4. Ibid., 76.
5. Traits are those long-lasting characteristics that make us unique and that others see in our actions, talk, attitudes, and mannerisms. Traits appear to be inborn tendencies, but we know that traits can change. People who are self-driven and pressured, for example, can forge new lifestyles and develop traits that let them live more productive, even-paced, well-lived lives. Changes like this rarely come easily. They often need the help of encouraging friends as well as guidance and power from the Holy Spirit.

Chapter 3—Spiritual Passion: Getting beyond the Religious Talk

1. Matthew 22:37-38.
2. The quotation is taken from M. Scott Peck, *Further along the Road Less Traveled* (New York: Simon & Schuster, 1993), 160, as quoted by Philip Yancey, *The Jesus I Never Knew* (Grand Rapids: Zondervan, 1995), 257.
3. Ibid., 265.
4. Darrell Bock, "My Un-American Faith: Why I Stopped 'Doing' All I Could for God," *Christianity Today* 40, no. 1 (8 January 1996): 21–3.
5. 1 Thessalonians 4:11-12.
6. Psalm 46.
7. Henri J. M. Nouwen, *Making All Things New: An Invitation to the Spiritual Life* (San Francisco: Harper & Row, 1981), 69.
8. Luke 10:38-42.
9. Rowland Croucher, ed., *Rivers in the Desert: Meditations and Prayers for Refreshment* (Sutherland, N.S.W., Australia: Albatross Books, 1991), 13.
10. From *Pensees* by Pascal, quoted without the original reference by Bob Buford, *Half Time: Changing Your Game Plan from Success to Significance* (Grand Rapids: Zondervan, 1994), 63.
11. Hugh McIntosh, "Solitude Provides an Emotional Tune-Up," *APA Monitor* 26 (March 1996): 1, 10. The following paragraphs are adapted from this article.
12. Ecclesiastes 1:2.
13. Ecclesiastes 2:4-10.
14. Ecclesiastes 5:17.
15. Ecclesiastes 5:15.
16. Ecclesiastes 5:7.
17. Wayne Schmidt, *Soul Management: Maximizing Your Spiritual Assets in a Bottom-Line World* (Grand Rapids: Zondervan, 1996), 106.
18. Mark 1:21-39.
19. John 14:15.
20. Stephen R. Covey, A. Roger Merrill, and Rebecca R. Merrill, *First Things First* (New York: Simon & Schuster, 1994), 73–4.

Chapter 4—Compassionate Caregiving: Reaching Out to Touch Someone

1. Mark 1:21-27.
2. Mark 1:29-31.
3. Mark 1:32-34.
4. Mark 1:37-38.
5. Mark 1:40-42.
6. Matthew 20:20-28.
7. The quotation from Barclay is taken from his *The Gospel of Matthew*, vol. 2, rev. ed. (Philadelphia: Westminster, 1975), 229; Jesus' statement about greatness and servanthood is found in Matthew 20:25-28.
8. Matthew 22:39; John 13:34-35.
9. Galatians 5:22-23.
10. Mary Pipher, *The Shelter of Each Other: Rebuilding Our Families* (New York: Grosset/Putnam, 1996), 93.
11. Mark 1:36-38.
12. Hal Lancaster, "Managing Your Time in Real-World Chaos Takes Real Planning," *The Wall Street Journal*, 19 August 1997.
13. Pipher, *The Shelter of Each Other*, 93.
14. William E. Diehl, *The Monday Connection: On Being an Authentic Christian in a Weekday World* (San Francisco: HarperCollins, 1991), 140–1.
15. From Bonhoeffer's 1938 book *Life Together*, quoted by Wendy Murray Zoba, "The Cost of Discipleship," *Christianity Today* 39 (April 3, 1995): 31. This account of Bonhoeffer's trip to the United States is adapted from the Zoba article.
16. James 1:27.
17. Ephesians 4:32; 1 Thessalonians 4:18; 5:11; Hebrews 3:13; 1 Peter 1:22; 2 Corinthians 1:3-4; Galatians 6:2; 1 John 3:18.
18. Galatians 5:22-23.
19. Galatians 6:10.
20. John 13:35.
21. Matthew 25:40.
22. Romans 12:6-8.
23. 1 John 4:7-8.
24. Diehl, *The Monday Connection*, 60, italics added.

25. Ralph Hamburger's story is included in Walter E. James with Christy Hawes Zatkin, *Tumbling Walls: A True Story of Ordinary People Bringing Reconciliation in Extraordinary Ways to an Alienated World* (La Jolla, Calif.: The Diaspora Foundation, 1990), 29. For information about this book, contact the Diaspora Foundation, Inc., 7504 Olivetas Avenue #C37, LaJolla, CA 92037. I mentioned Ralph's background in one of my previous books, Gary R. Collins, *The Biblical Basis of Christian Counseling for People Helpers* (Colorado Springs, Colo.: NavPress, 1993), 152–3.

Chapter 5—Character: Writing Your Own Book of Virtues

1. Bob Verdi, "The Mick Is Dead, and So Is His Era," *Chicago Tribune*, 14 August 1995.
2. Mike Dodd, "Mantle Dedicates Recovery to 'Giving Something Back,'" *USA Today*, 12 August 1995.
3. 1 Timothy 3:1-8; Titus 1:5-9.
4. Rick Love, "There's No Substitute for Character: The Neglected Key to Successful Church Planting," *Mission Today 96: An Annual Overview of the World of Missions* (1996): 116 (italics added).
5. Daniel Goleman, *Emotional Intelligence: Why It Can Matter More than IQ* (New York: Bantam Books, 1995), 285.
6. Mark 1:9-13.
7. Mark 1:16-20.
8. Mark 1:38, 45.
9. Luke 13:32.
10. Mark 12:24.
11. Endorsement from the dust jacket of William Bennett's *Book of Virtues: A Treasury of Great Moral Stories* (New York: Simon & Schuster, 1993).
12. Brooks Whitney, "What's the Story, Tori?" *Chicago Tribune*, 25 June 1996.
13. Reported by James M. Kouzes and Barry Z. Posner, *Credibility: How Leaders Gain and Lose It, Why People Demand It* (San Francisco: Jossey-Bass, 1993), 12.

14. Stephen L. Carter, *Integrity* (New York: HarperCollins, 1996), 7, 10–12.
15. Ibid., 12.
16. Ibid., 29.
17. Incidentally, I have heard more recently that Tomasz has risen back into the hit parade—without compromising his integrity.
18. Bill Hybels and Rob Wilkins, *Descending into Greatness* (Grand Rapids: Zondervan, 1993), 150.
19. The young seminarian in the story, John Bisagno, is now pastor of the First Baptist Church in Houston, Texas. The story came to my attention when it was told in a book by Steve Farrar, *Finishing Strong* (Sisters, Ore.: Multnomah, 1995), 5–6.
20. When Tomasz heard about my list, he asked to have his name included. I wrote him in as soon as I got home.
21. 2 Timothy 4:7.
22. 1 Corinthians 9:27.
23. 1 Timothy 4:7.
24. 1 Timothy 4:12.
25. 1 Timothy 4:12.
26. 1 Timothy 4:14.
27. See Romans 12:4-8; 1 Corinthians 12; Ephesians 4:7-13.
28. 1 Timothy 4:16.
29. The Bible quotation is from John 3:16. The Mantle statement was shared at Mickey Mantle's funeral by Bobby Richardson, the man who led Mantle to Christ.
30. Following Mickey Mantle's death, his wife (who heads the Mickey Mantle Foundation) and his sons wrote a book about their famous relative and about their struggles to live with his many problems. See Merlyn, Mickey Jr., David, and Danny Mantle (with Mickey Herskowitz) *A Hero All His Life* (New York: HarperCollins, 1996).

Chapter 6—Balance: Keeping Your Life Equilibrium

1. Robert L. Rose, "Running on Empty," *Wall Street Journal*, 26 February 1996. Reprinted in *Menninger Perspective* 27, no. 2 (1996): 19–21.

2. Wayne Schmidt, *Soul Management: Maximizing Your Spiritual Assets in a Bottom-Line World* (Grand Rapids: Zondervan, 1996), 151.

3. The information in this section is adapted from an obituary for Angel Wallenda, reported in the *Chicago Tribune*, 5 May 1996. Steve and Angel had one son (the last Wallenda), Steve II, who was nine at the time of his mother's death.

4. I am confident that God wants these attitudes because they are all commanded and/or approved by the words of Scripture.

5. Romans 8:5.

6. Philippians 4:8; Matthew 12:33-36; Proverbs 4:23.

7. John 4:7-27.

8. Matthew 23:23-28.

9. Mark 12:24.

10. 1 Corinthians 15:33.

11. Many of the ideas in this section of the chapter are adapted from Richard A. Swenson, *Margin: How to Create the Emotional, Physical, Financial, and Time Reserves You Need* (Colorado Springs, Colo.: NavPress, 1992). Swenson discusses overload in chapter 5, "The Pain of Overload." I highly recommend the book.

12. Ibid., 148.

13. Ibid., 103.

14. Ibid., 149.

15. Matthew 11:28-29. See also John 14:27.

Chapter 7—Purpose: Living a Focused Life

1. Bob Greene, "When Jordan Cried behind Closed Doors," *Chicago Tribune*, 14 May 1991.

2. Ibid.

3. Isaiah 61:1-2; Luke 4:16-21, 28.

4. Mark 1:38.

5. John 10:10; 3:16.

6. Galatians 2:7-9.

7. I am grateful to George Callendine for his continuing encouragement and friendship and for his hours of conversation in helping me clarify my mission. The five questions that I cite arose from our discussions and summarize some of what we considered. This is not a formal summary of our deliberations, and the discussion in this chapter does not convey the richness and depth of our interaction.

8. A good book for discerning spiritual gifts is Bruce Bugbee, *What You Do Best in the Body of Christ: Discover Your Spiritual Gifts, Personal Style, and God-Given Passion* (Grand Rapids: Zondervan, 1995).

9. James M. Kouzes and Barry Z. Posner, *Credibility: How Leaders Gain and Lose It, Why People Demand It* (San Francisco: Jossey-Bass, 1993), 232.

10. Rick Warren, *The Purpose Driven Church: Growth without Compromising Your Message and Mission* (Grand Rapids: Zondervan, 1995).

11. Ibid., 37.

12. Ibid., 355. This statement is attributed to Howard Hendricks.

13. Ibid., 357.

14. Peter Drucker, the management leader, suggests that two questions are important in helping people discover the roles for which they have been prepared. The first question is, What do you care deeply about? It deals with one's passion. The second question is, What have you achieved? It concerns one's competence. The two questions are cited by Bob Buford in his book *Half Time: Changing Your Game Plan from Success to Significance* (Grand Rapids: Zondervan, 1994), 125.

15. Stuart Briscoe, *Choices for a Lifetime: Determining the Values That Will Shape Your Future* (Wheaton, Ill.: Tyndale, 1995), 13.

16. Ibid.

17. The story of Joe Petricca, reported in the sports section of a newspaper, was part of a broader description of the football team at Palatine High School. Bob Sakamoto, "Quick Hits in Palatine Drill," *Chicago Tribune*, 19 August 1996.

18. Numbers 14:24.

19. In developing this plan, I am deeply grateful for the insights of my friend

the Rev. Edmund Chan of Covenant Evangelical Free Church in Singapore. When he learned later that I was writing this book, his encouragement and enthusiasm for the project was contagious and motivating.

20. The Greeks made a distinction between the most opportune time *(kairos)* and clock time *(chronos)*.

21. Matthew 25:21; Luke 12:42-44.

22. James 4:10.

23. Genesis 3:4-6.

24. Matthew 4:3-8.

Chapter 8—Teamwork: Sharing and Growing Together

1. The graduation speeches at Westminster College in Salt Lake City were presented on May 25, 1996, and reported by Georgie Anne Geyer, "Utah's Spirit: Too Bad They Can't Export It," *Chicago Tribune*, 31 May 1995.

2. One of the best books about business cooperation is written by three Australians: Cathy Howard, Murray Gillin, and John Bailey, *Strategic Alliances: Resource Sharing Strategies for Smart Companies* (Melbourne, Australia: Pitman Publishing, 1995). The concept of cooperation rather than competition is the theme of James F. Moore, *The Death of Competition* (New York: HarperBusiness, 1996).

3. Josh Hammond and James Morrison, *The Stuff Americans Are Made Of: The Seven Cultural Forces That Define Americans—A New Framework for Quality, Productivity and Profitability* (New York: Macmillan, 1996). The quotation is from the cover of the book.

4. Ibid., 5–6.

5. Their brief discussion on teams includes the two questions in the text and adds the observation that if you ask group members what they really want, they will "give you direction on where they want to go solo and why." Ibid., 251–3.

6. Geyer, "Utah's Spirit," was the second

Westminster College commencement speaker.

7. Genesis 2:18.

8. Mark 1:16-20.

9. John 17:11.

10. Acts 1:4-8.

11. See, for example, Acts 2:42-47.

12. Warren Bennis and Patricia Ward Biederman, *Organizing Genius: The Secrets of Creative Collaboration* (Reading, Mass.: Addison-Wesley, 1997).

13. There may be occasional exceptions to this. Sometimes individuals labor in isolation, like Jeremiah, who ministered without much encouragement from others, but in general the Scriptures emphasize people working together in partnerships.

14. Team building, for example, is a prominent theme promoted by John C. Maxwell, *Developing the Leaders around You: How to Help Others Reach Their Full Potential* (Nashville: Thomas Nelson, 1995). See also Calvin Miller, *The Empowered Leader: 10 Keys to Servant Leadership* (Nashville: Broadman & Holman, 1995).

15. From "Jack Callahan's Eighteen Success Imperatives," in Robert H. Rosen, *Leading People: Transforming Business from the Inside Out* (New York: Viking, 1996), 359.

16. Rosen, *Leading People*, 32–39.

17. Ibid., 37.

18. We have discussed this in a earlier chapter. See Romans 12 and 1 Corinthians 12.

19. Rosen, *Leading People*, 74.

20. Matthew 5:37. See also James 5:12.

21. Max DePree, *Leading without Power: Finding Hope in Serving Community* (San Francisco: Jossey-Bass, 1997), 132.

22. James M. Kouzes and Barry Z. Posner, *Credibility: How Leaders Gain and Lose It, Why People Demand It* (San Francisco: Jossey-Bass, 1993), 110.

23. As reported by Bob Secter, "Anguish of Second: One Step Short in the Race for

Gold," *Chicago Tribune*, 4 August 1996.

24. For a review of these studies see Rebecca L. Collins, "For Better or Worse: The Impact of Upward Social Comparisons on Self-Evaluations," *Psychological Bulletin* 119, no. 1 (1996): 51–69.

25. In John 8:44, Jesus described Satan as being a liar and the father of lies.

26. Bob Greene, "He's an 'Example,' All Right, and the Best Kind," *Chicago Tribune*, 4 August 1996.

27. The reactions of the laid-off workers is reported by Bob Secter, "Trust, Loyalty Went with the Jobs," *Chicago Tribune*, 15 March 1996. In recent years, of course, downsizing has become common in the United States—less so in other countries. Secter's article reported, for example, that between 1979 and 1996, the traditionally stable and well-paying Fortune 500 companies cut their combined workforce from 16.5 to 11.5 million people.

28. I have been unable to determine if the story describes an event that actually happened. From my perspective it sounds authentic.

Chapter 9—Adaptability: Dealing with Continuing Change

1. Sabrina L. Miller, "Dying of Cancer, Bernardin Is 'At Peace,'" *Chicago Tribune*, 31 August 1996.

2. Lori Sharn, "Without Despair, Cardinal Confronts Death," *USA Today*, 12 September 1996.

3. Kit R. Roane, "Siege Chic: Surviving amid the Ruins of Sarajevo Are Hope, Enterprise and—Yes!—Even Fashion," *Chicago Tribune*, 28 May 1996.

4. See, for example, James O'Toole, *Leading Change: Overcoming the Ideology of Comfort and the Tyranny of Custom* (San Francisco: Jossey-Bass, 1995). The subtitle of this book is of interest, reflecting a widely held view that comfort and custom are not good.

5. James C. Collins and Jerry I. Porras, *Built to Last: Successful Habits of Visionary Companies* (New York: HarperCollins, 1994), 1.

6. Ibid., 2.

7. Ibid., 81.

8. This futuristic perspective is discussed with more detail in chapter 12.

9. The words are those of Thomas J. Watson, Jr., reported by Collins and Porras, *Built to Last*, 81.

10. Ibid., 82.

11. Ibid., 84.

12. Ibid., 9.

13. Carla Gorrell's story is told by Robert H. Rosen with Paul B. Brown, *Leading People: Transforming Business from the Inside Out* (New York: Viking, 1996), 159–66.

14. Ibid., 166.

15. Acts 24:24-25.

16. See O'Toole, *Leading Change*, 159–64.

17. See, for example, Psalm 62.

18. I have written a book that summarizes the modern spirituality search, the tendency of many people to look for spiritual guides and anchors within themselves, and the Christian alternative. See Gary R. Collins, *The Soul Search: A Spiritual Journey to Authentic Intimacy with God* (Nashville: Thomas Nelson, 1998).

19. Masaaki Imai, *Kaizen: The Key to Japan's Competitive Success* (New York: McGraw-Hill, 1986).

20. Including the two men we have previously met in Mark 1, the demon-possessed man and the man with leprosy.

21. Mark 1:40-45.

Chapter 10—Soul Care: Nurturing Your Inner World

1. The composer's name is pronounced "Go-*ret*-ski." The material in this section is adapted from an article by Karen L. Mulder, "Move Over, Madonna," *Christianity Today* 39 (July 17, 1995): 66.

2. Ibid.

3. Ibid., italics added.

4. Robert L. Wise, *Quest for the Soul: Our Search for Deeper Meaning* (Nashville: Thomas Nelson, 1996), 3.

5. Ibid., 4.
6. Matthew 23:27-28.
7. Luke 13:32. At the trial of Jesus, Herod demonstrated his insecurity and lack of moral backbone by giving in so easily to the demands of the crowds.
8. Thomas R. Kelly, *A Testament of Devotion* (New York: Harper & Brothers, 1941), 69–71.
9. Gordon MacDonald, *When Men Think Private Thoughts: Exploring the Issues that Captivate the Minds of Men* (Nashville: Thomas Nelson, 1996), xix.
10. 1 Corinthians 4:5.
11. Psalm 139:2.
12. Mark 8:35-36 is an example of the Greek word for *soul* translated "life." Jesus stated, "For whoever wants to save his life [soul] will lose it, but whoever loses his life [soul] for me and for the gospel will save it." This discussion of the meaning of *soul* is adapted from *New Illustrated Bible Dictionary* (Nashville: Nelson, 1995), 1195–6.
13. Matthew 26:38.
14. Gordon MacDonald, *The Life God Blesses: Weathering the Storms of Life That Threaten the Soul* (Nashville: Thomas Nelson, 1994), xv.
15. Ibid., 17.
16. David Van Biema, "Of the Soul: Combining Medical Advice with Indian Metaphysics, Deepak Chopra Has Thrived, Telling Americans of a Place Where Spirit and Body Interact," *Time* 147 (June 24, 1996): 65.
17. I have written a book in an effort to clear up some of this confusion and distinguish contemporary New Age perspectives on the soul from the biblical perspective. See Gary R. Collins, *The Soul Search: A Spiritual Journey to Authentic Intimacy with God* (Nashville: Thomas Nelson, 1998).
18. MacDonald, *The Life God Blesses*, xii.
19. Mark 1:15.
20. John 8:11.
21. Matthew 23:27-28.
22. Mark 7:20-23, NLT.
23. Philippians 4:8.
24. Mark 1:35.
25. Brother Andrew with Verne Becker, *The Calling* (Nashville: Moorings, 1996), 4.
26. *God's Smuggler* is the title of Brother Andrew's book that describes his remarkable ministry. Published in 1967, the book has sold more than 10 million copies. Much of the royalty money has been used to print, purchase, and distribute more Bibles.
27. Ibid., 26.
28. Ibid.
29. Kelly, *Testament*, 71.
30. Immediately before the Crucifixion, Jesus promised a deep inner peace to his disciples. The events in their lives could leave them troubled or afraid, but they could rest secure in the peace that Christ gives within. See John 14:27.
31. Kelly, *Testament*, 13.
32. Ibid., 14.
33. Psalm 103:1.
34. Psalm 139:23-24.
35. Luke 1:38.
36. 2 Corinthians 10:5.
37. A pivotal book in this area has been Richard Foster's *Celebration of Discipline* (San Francisco: Harper & Row, 1978). See also Dallas Willard, *The Spirit of the Disciplines* (San Francisco: Harper & Row, 1989); Donald S. Whitney, *Spiritual Disciplines for the Christian Life* (Colorado Springs, Colo.: NavPress, 1991); and Siang-Yang Tan and Douglas H. Gregg, *Disciplines of the Holy Spirit: How to Connect to the Spirit's Power and Presence* (Grand Rapids: Zondervan, 1997).
38. 1 Timothy 4:7.
39. Whitney, *Spiritual Disciplines*, 18.
40. Philippians 4:6-7; John 14:27.
41. MacDonald, *The Life God Blesses*, 74.

Chapter 11—Growth: Sharpening Your Mind and Moving Forward

1. Stephen R. Covey, *The 7 Habits of Highly Effective People* (New York: Simon & Schuster, 1989).
2. Gordon MacDonald, *Ordering Your Private World* (Chicago: Moody, 1984), 101.

3. This is consistent with Romans 7:15.
4. From Plato's *Apology*. Reported by Tom Morris, *True Success: A New Philosophy of Excellence* (New York: Berkley Books, 1995), 18.
5. Proverbs 27:17.
6. "Acting as a Mentor," *Royal Bank Letter: Published by the Royal Bank of Canada* 76, no. 4 (July/August 1995): 2.
7. Mentoring books include Bob Biehl, *Mentoring: Confidence in Finding a Mentor and Becoming One* (Nashville: Broadman & Holman, 1996); Tim Elmore, *Mentoring: How to Invest Your Life in Others* (Indianapolis: Wesleyan Publishing House and Kingdom Publishing House, 1995); Ted W. Engstrom with Norman B. Rohrer, *The Fine Art of Mentoring: Passing On to Others What God Has Given to You* (Brentwood, Tenn.: Wolgemuth & Hyatt, 1989); Howard and William Hendricks, *As Iron Sharpens Iron: Building Character in a Mentoring Relationship* (Chicago: Moody, 1995); and P. Stanley and J. Clinton, *Connecting: The Mentoring Relationships You Need to Succeed in Life* (Colorado Springs, Colo.: NavPress, 1992). The Engstrom book is a good introduction. The Biehl book has a very good bibliography. The Hendricks book presents an approach that is more structured and education oriented than the others.
8. Mary Rowland, "Multiple Mentors," *USAir Magazine* 3 (October 1996): 20–2.
9. Luke 2:46.
10. Mark 1:22.
11. Matthew 22:46.
12. Mark 1:35.
13. Glandion Carney and William Long, *Yearning Minds and Burning Hearts: Rediscovering the Spirituality of Jesus* (Grand Rapids: Baker, 1997), 77.
14. Ibid., 80.
15. Tom Morris, *True Success: A New Philosophy of Excellence* (New York: Berkley Books, 1995), 87.
16. Ibid., 32.
17. Ibid., 125.
18. Billy Graham, "Standing Firm, Moving Forward," *Christianity Today* 40, no. 10 (September 16, 1996): 15.
19. Morris, *True Success*, 178.
20. Philippians 2:7-8.
21. Consider, for example, Noel M. Tichy and Stratford Sherman, *Control Your Destiny or Someone Else Will* (New York: HarperBusiness, 1994). The book includes a "handbook for revolutionaries" and describes how we can learn to master change by using the principles that CEO Jack Welch used to revolutionize General Electric.
22. Matthew 8:20; Philippians 2:6-8.
23. Matthew 20:25-28.
24. Ibid.
25. See, for example, Matthew 6:21; Luke 6:24, 30; 12:15, 33.
26. Psalm 62:10.
27. Ephesians 5:5; 1 Corinthians 5:11; James 4:1-2; 1 Timothy 6:17-19.
28. Richard J. Foster, *Freedom of Simplicity* (San Francisco: Harper & Row, 1981), 3.
29. Ibid.
30. Philippians 4:6-7, 12.
31. Foster tells this story in a chapter titled "The Discipline of Service," in Richard J. Foster, *Celebration of Discipline* (San Francisco: Harper & Row, 1978), 117–18. The quotation is from Dietrich Bonhoeffer, *Life Together* (New York: Harper & Row, 1952), 99.

Chapter 12—Hope: Living in the Present, Aware of the Future

1. Michael Shernoff, "The Last Journey," *The Family Therapy Networker* 20 (January/February 1996): 35.
2. 1 Corinthians 15:19.
3. Isaiah 22:13; 1 Corinthians 15:32.
4. Joseph M. Stowell, *Eternity: Reclaiming a Passion for What Endures* (Chicago: Moody, 1995), 58. In his book, Stowell notes that we live in three worlds: the world to come, the world around us, and the world within. This stimulated my thinking and led to the "five lives" perspective that I use in the present chapter.
5. Ephesians 2:8; Romans 3:22-24.

6. For a heavy but worthwhile discussion of how God's grace has saved us in the past and prepared us for the future, see John Piper, *Future Grace* (Sisters, Ore.: Multnomah, 1995).

7. Jennifer James, *Thinking in the Future Tense: Leadership Skills for a New Age* (New York: Simon & Schuster, 1996); Duane Elmer and Lois McKinney, eds., *With an Eye on the Future: Development and Mission in the 21st Century* (Monrovia, Calif.: MARC, 1996); Peter F. Drucker, *Managing for the Future* (New York: Truman Talley Books/Dutton, 1992); and Gary Hamel and C. K. Prahalad, *Competing for the Future* (Boston: Harvard Business School, 1994).

8. Bill Clinton, *Between Hope and History: Meeting America's Challenges for the 21st Century* (New York: Time Books/Random House, 1996), xiii.

9. Ibid., 15.

10. Psalm 31:24; 33:18. My talk on hope was given in Nairobi. For an insightful look at hope as it applies to Kenya, see Tim Stafford, "Finding Hope in Africa," *Christianity Today* 39, no. 8 (July 17, 1995): 22–7.

11. Matthew 6:19-20.

12. Stowell, *Eternity*, 96.

13. C. S. Lewis, *Mere Christianity* (New York: Macmillan, 1943), 118, italics added.

14. Cheryl Lavin, "Nothing Succeeds Like Success Seminars," *Chicago Tribune*, 16 October 1996. The following paragraphs, describing the success seminars, are adapted from the Lavin article.

15. Ibid.

16. Ibid.

17. Stowell, *Eternity*, 66, 60.

18. Mark 1:1-3. Jesus quoted the Scriptures, often as they related to himself. In an incident recorded in Luke 4:16-30, for example, he almost started a riot when he announced that the prophecy of Isaiah was fulfilled in him.

19. Mark 1:23-26, 29-31, 32-34, 38-42.

20. John 14–17. In Mark 1, the passage that has illustrated our descriptions of Jesus,

he announced that the kingdom of God was near, and he selected disciples promising to make them fishers of men, Mark 1:16-17.

21. John 14:25-27.

22. John 14:1-3.

23. Stowell, *Eternity*, 112.

24. Shernoff, "Last Journey," 36.

25. Stowell, *Eternity*, 113, italics added.

26. 2 Corinthians 12:2-4; 1 Corinthians 7:31; Philippians 1:23-24.

27. The New Testament book of Revelation is this description.

28. John 14:2-3; Matthew 6:33.

29. Colossians 3:2; Luke 12:31-40.

30. Luke 12:13-21.

31. Philip Yancey, *The Jesus I Never Knew* (Grand Rapids: Zondervan, 1995), 112.

32. *Mother Teresa, A Simple Path* (New York: Ballantine, 1995), 120–21.

33. Ibid.

Chapter 13—Managing Life and Leaving a Legacy

1. Bill Hybels and Rob Wilkins, *Descending into Greatness* (Grand Rapids: Zondervan, 1993), 180.

2. Ibid., 149–50.

3. Cited by Bob Condor, "Beating the Clock," *Chicago Tribune*, 28 August 1996.

4. Quoted by Condor, ibid.

5. From the dust jacket on the book by Stephan Rechtschaffen, *Time Shifting: Creating More Time to Enjoy Your Life* (New York: Doubleday, 1996).

6. 1 Corinthians 10:31.

7. Steve Rabey, "A Guitarist in God's Court: Christopher Parkening's Music Is Dedicated to the Glory of God Alone," *Christianity Today* 39 (December 11, 1995), 43.

8. Ibid.

9. Colossians 3:17.

10. Colin Greer, "'Change Will Come When Our Hearts Change,' An Interview with the Rev. Billy Graham," *Parade: The Sunday Newspaper Magazine* (October 20, 1996): 6.

INDEX

269

About the Author

GARY COLLINS studied in Canada, England, and the United States before earning his Ph.D. in clinical psychology from Purdue University. He was a student at a theological seminary for a year and worked as a professional psychologist before becoming a professor, first at Bethel College in Minnesota and later at Trinity Evangelical Divinity School in Illinois.

Dr. Collins has written about fifty books and has spoken at conferences in almost fifty countries. In addition to his writing and speaking, he continues to travel widely. He is past president of the fifteen-thousand-member American Association of Christian Counselors, executive editor of *Christian Counseling Today,* and chairman of an international committee that is forming the International Federation for Christian Counseling. He knows about breathless lifestyles from personal experience, and he is learning to turn his time-starved days into a life well lived.

Parents of two adult daughters, Gary Collins and his wife, Julie, live in a northern suburb of Chicago.